DEATH'S ECHOES

PENNY MICKELBURY

Bywater
BOOKS

Ann Arbor

Bywater Books

Copyright © 2018 Penny Mickelbury

Print ISBN: 978-1-61294-121-9

Bywater Books First Edition: February 2018

Printed in the United States of America on acid-free paper.

Cover designer: Ann McMan, TreeHouse Studio

Bywater Books
PO Box 3671
Ann Arbor MI 48106-3671
www.bywaterbooks.com

This book is dedicated to all of you who love Mimi and Gianna. They love you right back!

And to Peggy, as always.

CHAPTER ONE

Screams became shrieks became moans became muffled crying became, eventually, awful, deadly silence as five women lay on the sidewalk, broken, bleeding and dying. The folds of their robes spread out from around them, absorbing their blood. The hijabs, too, absorbed their blood but, as designed, left their faces open and visible for the horror, pain, and disbelief displayed on them to any and all who looked.

Rebel yells and shouts of "make America great again" alternated with the rapid fire of the AK-12 machine gun and the Makarov semi-automatic handgun, both Russian-made, that created the carnage on the sidewalk where a big pickup truck idled at the curb. The men in the pickup quieted when they saw the results of their work, saw that their objective had been accomplished.

From the minaret of the mosque half a block away, the call to prayer that reverberated from the sound system was the only remaining sound in the warm Friday evening air—the mosque that was the destination of both the dying women and the marauding men in the pickup truck.

It had begun and ended in a matter of several seconds. So momentous an occurrence in the lives of so many women and men began and ended in less time than a five-year-old would need to count to ten—two numbers that had even more meaning that Friday evening: Ten people were involved—five women and five men—but it had required much more time than mere

1

seconds for their lives to converge on a quiet, tree-lined street in the nation's capital on that May evening, to converge and to change dramatically and irrevocably.

The women, American-born Muslims, after much consideration and hours of discussion, had decided to wear the hijab and long skirts and walk to Friday evening service at their mosque. None of them regularly wore a hijab and one of them—the twenty-five-year-old daughter of one of the women—had never worn one. So why now? Because now everything had changed.

"We live in a country where we face discrimination not only because of our color and our gender, but now also because of our religion." And as a group the women, good friends for many years, agreed on their course of action for that Friday evening in late May. They shared their decision with their husbands and received support and encouragement. A few of the older men of the mosque still resented the presence of women but the younger men were more progressive and more inclusive in their reading and interpretation of the Quran. They agreed—the women and the men—that they would not allow their government to bully their religion into invisibility. Had the country ever had so distasteful and despicable a government? Of course there had been racist presidents and corrupt ones and warmongering ones. But had there ever been anything like the crude incompetence of this one? Even in the days of slavery? They didn't think so. But as they knew all too well, not everyone shared their opinion.

"We finally got somebody on our side! Somebody who believes America First is the right way to go! America for Americans!" Five of them, including the grandfather, three sons, and one grandson—the Holtons by name—had experienced unprecedented feelings of euphoria since the November election, though none of them had voted. Had ever voted—they didn't see the point. Now they did. They had wanted to drive to Washington for the inauguration but they hadn't planned properly, not realizing that it probably was an eleven- or twelve-hour drive from their home in western Indiana. But now was a good time, especially since it was warmer and they could sleep in the truck if necessary. They'd read that Muslims had a church near the Capitol and the White House, and they blared their Satan religion so loud the president could hear it! That needed to stop and they'd make sure it did.

The walk to the mosque was peaceful, a welcome respite to the end of the work week. Lost in their individual thoughts, the women had no sense of the danger coming their way. At least, four of them didn't. The fifth and youngest of their group also was a cop—a member of the Washington, D.C., Metropolitan Police Department—and her brain was processing an incongruous sound: the roar of a big engine moving much too fast toward them. She turned her head toward the sound, saw the big truck, hulking like an animal, and knew trouble was approaching fast.

"Get down!" She issued the command and pushed her mother down at the same time. The big truck was upon them so the cop fell on top of her mother to cover her. "Curl up into a ball!" she called out to the other women, but it was too late.

"America for Americans!" the men yelled as their weapons strafed the prone women, all of whom were hit multiple times. "We're making America great again!" The sixteen-year-old driver kept blowing the truck's horn as the bullets flew and the men continued to chant their slogans. Then, the shooting over, two of the men climbed out of the truck and walked over to the prostrate, bleeding, and dying women. They didn't notice that one of the women held her police-issued Sig Sauer. She quickly fired off four shots—two each to the heads of the two men who'd come to stand over the women and watch them die, but they both died first. Then the young cop emptied the clip into the pickup truck. She no longer was aiming because she no longer could see, but she could hear and she knew her bullets met their target. Stunned speechless, the three men remaining in the truck also were frozen and motionless for several long seconds, unable to move because their brains were not sending signals. The oldest, Mike Holton, recovered first, and in a weak voice ordered his youngest—and now only remaining—son to drive. But Sammy Holton didn't move. He couldn't. He'd just watched his big brother Mickey's head explode. Then his own head snapped forward. His father's voice now was as strong as the slap delivered to the back of Sammy's head. "Drive, boy! Drive!" And the big pickup peeled away from the curb, leaving the stench of burning rubber and the screeching of tires hanging in the air, along with Ricky Slater's wail that they couldn't leave his brother Donnie lying there on the sidewalk! If there had been anyone conscious or cognizant on that sidewalk the sudden silence would have been noticed. The amplified call to prayer had stopped, and though sirens wailed in the distance, they were not yet close enough to be considered loud.

But it was loud as hell inside the 911 call center. There had been a dozen calls to 911, most of them people screaming about men in a pickup truck slaughtering Muslim women walking to church. The cops were dispatched—a lot of them, because what the call center operators were hearing defied belief and understanding: a drive-by with Muslim women as the targets. Then came the additional information: The men driving the pickup truck were white. Cops were practically silent as their squads hurtled toward the scene. All drive-by shootings, by their very nature, were grim and gruesome and stupid examples of the brand of needless violence that was all too common in America's big cities. But this? "Sounds like the stories my great-grandpa used to tell about the KKK, except they rode horses in the dead of night, not pickup trucks at sundown."

The feet of the men from the mosque running toward the slaughtered women made virtually no sound on the sidewalk because most of them were barefoot, as they'd left their shoes at the front door of the mosque in their hurry to get to their women. They arrived at the same time as the police and the paramedics and the firefighters—more than a dozen carloads of them. The medical personnel and their equipment rushed to the bodies. The law enforcement personnel, weapons in hand, fanned out in search of perpetrators. It was one of the paramedics who first noticed the gun in the hand of one of the victims.

"You guys need to see this!" he called out to the cops, and several came running, guns drawn, eyes searching and scanning.

"What the hell—"

"I know her!" exclaimed another. "She's on the job! I know her!"

Their sergeant ran over, looked down, then up at the patrol officer who claimed knowledge of the victim who might also be a shooter, then back down at the young woman whose eyes were closed and whose hand still firmly held her weapon. "Who is she?"

"Cassandra something. We were at the Academy together. I was ahead of her but she was a star. She works Hate Crimes—" The patrol officer stopped talking because his sergeant seemed to be choking.

"Oh sweet Jesus!" the sergeant said, crossing himself, and ran to his car.

"Fuck!" the paramedic yelled at the same time. "She's alive!" And he and his partner knelt down beside Officer Cassandra Ali.

Lt. Gianna Maglione, head of the Hate Crimes Unit, was in her office reviewing the previous month's crime stats with her second-in-command, Sgt. Eric Ashby, when the phone rang.

"Lieutenant Maglione's office—" Eric began; then he went silent as all the blood drained from his face. He listened, hung up the phone, and stood.

Gianna had been watching him and she stood up, too, waiting for him to tell her what was wrong and knowing it would be worse than bad.

"A drive-by. A truckload of white guys took out a group of Muslim women who were walking to Friday evening prayers."

Gianna's brain was processing what Eric had said when the phone rang again. Eric grabbed it, and before he could speak, Gianna heard shouting on the other end, and Eric gave her the phone. She, too, listened without speaking, then she hung up the phone. "Cassie Ali is one of the Muslim women who was shot, and it's not clear whether she's still alive." Tears filled Eric's eyes and spilled out. Gianna grabbed his shoulder and her fingers dug

5

in until he got control. "I'm going to the hospital. You gather the rest of the team and go to the site. I'll let you know about Cassie when I know anything."

"What do you want us to do at the scene?"

"Support, until you hear differently. The Chief will be there. He'll let you know. And Eric? Take care of 'em, especially Tim. And if he can't control himself, send him home."

And they were out the door, Eric heading downstairs to the Think Tank where the HCU team members were gathered. As he ran he wondered if they had heard any of the radio calls and if so, if they had any idea how soon and how closely they'd be connected to what sounded like a massacre.

Gianna tried not to think at all as she ran down the steps to the underground garage. She focused on driving. Friday night. Rush hour traffic. Downtown D.C. Lights and siren. Cassie maybe not alive . . . Cassie, the baby of her team who had endured more than enough tragedy and suffering for one young life. But how much was enough? How much was too much? She was all too familiar with all the existential and philosophical questions of life—as well as with the answers: There weren't any. So, *just drive*, she told herself. *Don't think, don't feel. Just drive.*

Don't talk, Mimi Patterson told herself. *Don't say a word*. She and her editor, the one she called the Weasel, stood staring at each other. He had just spiked her story on Eastern Shore migrant farm workers because he said it was biased against the president. She said he should get a job at one of the fake news sites where he could peddle alternative facts to people who would believe them because real news stories based on real facts seemed to elude him. He threatened to fire her. She told him to go ahead. They were in his office—he behind his desk, she in front of it—and they stood staring at each other, she waiting to be fired, he, as always, intimidated by her and terrified of her. He didn't know if he had the authority to fire her and even if he did, he'd be costing the paper one of its best reporters. But they detested each other, neither had a shred of respect for the other, and it was pointless to think that he'd ever bend her to his will. He might as well let her work for another editor, as she'd asked to do half a dozen times.

"You gotta come listen to the police scanner!" A reporter the Weasel did like rushed in, flushed and breathless. Mimi thought of him as Weasel Boy, because the Weasel had hired him and he definitely was the Weasel's boy. "Some kind of terrorist action over on the East Side!" he yelled as he rushed back out. Mimi could see that a crowd had gathered in the vicinity of the police scanner, and that the Weasel was half-tempted to see what the excitement was all about. The truth was that he didn't care for stories that were exciting or emotional, especially if they were in any way related to violence. But Weasel Boy was his creation—his hire—and it would be bad form for him not to appear interested. Without another word to Mimi, he left his office and headed across the newsroom toward the crowd. Mimi went to her desk where she retrieved her Eastern Shore migrant worker story from the sent queue. The Weasel would never miss it. Then she pulled up one of the twenty-four-hour internet news programs on her computer and stared in shocked disbelief and horror at what she saw and heard.

Anyone who'd ever wondered whether the Chief had earned his job had that question answered when he arrived on the scene of what could only be described as uncontrolled mayhem. He instantly took control easily and calmly by asking questions: Which victims needed transporting? Who was taking the crime scene photos? Were there eyewitnesses and, if so, who was inter-viewing them? The mayhem became controlled. He knew that Cassandra Ali was already en route to the trauma center. He had not known that her mother was another of the victims and that she was still alive, and he made certain that she was the next to be transported—and that her husband would ride with her when he recognized the man. He'd met Officer Ali's parents a year before when she'd been brutally attacked and beaten by a neo-Nazi skinhead asshole. The young officer had lost sight in one eye as a result of the beating, and he'd had to force Lt. Maglione to put the girl on waivers. She couldn't function in the Hate Crimes Unit blind in one eye, not to mention the fact that she had no memory of the incident. In the more than twenty years that he'd been Maglione's mentor and friend, it was the first really bad time between them.

"Lieutenant Maglione's already on her way to the hospital to be with your girl," he told the Alis. He did not tell them that their daughter was feared dead.

They thanked him though he knew he didn't deserve their thanks due to the truth that he was withholding from them, so when he slammed the ambulance door shut, he was relieved to see Eric Ashby barreling toward him, red hair and blue eyes blazing. He was as loyal to Lt. Maglione as she was to her Chief. Ashby sketched a hasty salute.

"Where do you need me, Chief?"

"Right here with me for now, until the terrorism task force gets here."

Eric's eyes went wide. "You're calling this a terrorist act?"

"Damn right! As well as a hate crime!" And he looked over his shoulder at the two men lying dead on the sidewalk with bullets in their heads, the two men that Cassandra Ali had shot in what might well have been her last conscious act on the planet. "I'm calling those two terrorists and I'm accusing them of a hate crime and I intend to use the letters KKK in the same sentence!"

Eric knew from his boss that the Chief of Police could, in her words, get mad enough to chew nails and spit out tacks, but he'd never seen it firsthand. Until now. He was imagining how the media would respond to hearing "hate crime, terrorist act, and KKK" in the same sentence when he saw the big SUV that was the operational unit for the Anti-Terrorism Task Force arrive.

"Come on," the Chief barked as he hurried toward the ATTF team as their doors opened and they spilled out of truck.

"Turn left at this corner," Mike Holton barked at Sammy, "and keep going until you see the Capitol dome. It'll be right in front of you!"

"Why are we goin' to the damn Capitol? We oughta be goin' back there to get my brother!" Ricky Slater had been crying and wailing the whole time that Mike Holton had been trying to read the map on his cell phone. Now that he had found where they were and where they were going, he had some space in his brain for Slater; indeed, he understood what he was feeling. He wanted to wail and cry, too, for the son he had left lying on the sidewalk, but wailing and crying didn't win you any points in the game.

"We're goin' to the Capitol 'cause we'll be safe there," he said. "Once we tell 'em what we did and why, they'll take care of us. They might even call us heroes! And goin' back will just get us arrested. The cops'll be there by now."

"That's why we never shoulda left without 'em! I told you that!"

"You don't tell me what to do, boy!" Mike Holton snarled at Ricky, and the young man saw clearly what his big brother meant when he would say that old man Holton was a mean bastard. Ricky didn't know about old man Holton firsthand because it was his big brother, Don, who was Army buddies with Mickey Holton. But to Sammy's eyes, the old man was more than just mean; he was crazy, too! There was no way that the church where the Muslim women were going was close enough to the president that he could hear the loudspeaker on top of the Muslim church. They were half a block away and could hardly hear it. He picked up the articles that Holton used to back up his claim about the Muslims, which he had printed from the internet. Passages he'd underlined: *The muslims' call to prayer disturbs the President.* No way. No damn way! The old man was crazy as hell and now his big brother was dead for no reason. What was going to happen to them now?

Gianna screeched into the Ambulance Only parking lot at the emergency room entrance of University Medical Center, threw the car into gear, and jumped out. She opened the back door of the unmarked cruiser to grab her jacket. She was pulling the jacket on when the security guard, on his way to tell her to move her damn car, noticed her shoulder holster and stopped in his tracks. She nodded to him and ran up the ramp and into the ER. She was about to ask for Cassie when she saw her, strapped to the ambulance gurney, a paramedic on either side, shouting information to the ER doctors. Actually, she saw the blood first, dripping onto the floor. A lot of blood. Too damn much blood.

"Lieutenant!"

She tore her eyes away from Cassie and raised them to take in the two patrol officers who no doubt had accompanied the ambo—had more likely led it through the traffic to the hospital. She hadn't noticed their unit in the parking lot. Walking toward them meant walking toward Cassie, so that's what she did. "Any word?" she asked.

"Maybe," one of them said.

"One of our patrol units may have spotted the truck," the other one said.

Before Gianna could query further, two things happened simultaneously: She heard her name called, and Cassie grabbed her hand. She focused on Cassie, whose eyes were flickering open and closed like a blinking neon sign with one of its bulbs burned out. As she leaned down close to Cassie, she saw who'd called her name—the young doctor who had operated on Mimi last year after she was attacked in the lobby of her newspaper. Perversely, Mimi's attacker had been a Muslim who objected to stories she was writing about lesbians.

"We must stop meeting like this, Lieutenant," the young doctor said, and she didn't mean it as a joke.

"Officer Ali is a Muslim. She'll need a female physician," Gianna began but the doctor was already nodding.

"We know and we're ready." She looked down at Cassie. "We need to take her right now."

Gianna leaned in close to Cassie. "I'll be back later, Cassie. You hang in there." She started to stand but Cassie pulled her down with surprising strength and whispered something. Her eyes flickered closed, then back open.

Gianna leaned in closer to hear and wished she hadn't. "I love you, Gianna," the young cop whispered as blood gurgled up her throat and out of her mouth, causing the medical personnel to spring into action. Somebody pushed Gianna out of the way, and the gurney bearing Cassie headed toward the surgical suite at breakneck speed. Then the young doctor hopped on, straddling Cassie, and began chest compressions.

Gianna couldn't watch any longer and sped down the corridor in the opposite direction, toward the parking lot. Then she heard the doctor yell, "Come on, goddammit, come on!" and turned to see that the doctor, still straddling Cassie and pumping on her chest. "Come on, come on, come on!" The young doctor was still yelling and pumping as the gurney disappeared through the swinging doors, but Gianna knew it was too late. She knew that Cassie was gone and she almost smiled to herself because she knew that Cassie would never have said what she said if she knew she'd have to face her boss again.

"Lieutenant Maglione!"

Oh God, would people please stop calling her name! Who was it this time? She looked up and into the face of Cassie's father who was climbing out of the back of an ambulance and following close behind another gurney. What the hell . . .?

"My wife!" he exclaimed. Then, "You've seen Cassandra?"

She could not tell this man that his only child was dead. "She's in surgery. They made me get out of their way," she added.

He nodded. "Hopefully I can check on her when they take Aisha back." He touched his wife's shoulder. She, too, was bleeding, though not as severely, it seemed, as Cassie had been. "Cassandra saved her life, Lieutenant."

"What?"

"She and her mother and three other women were walking to the mosque for evening prayers. Aisha said that Cassandra heard the truck coming and she knew something was wrong. She told the women to get down; then she pushed her mother down and fell on top of her." He stopped talking because the gurney carrying his wife was speeding down the hall toward the same surgical suite where his dead daughter was. He nodded at Gianna and took off after it.

"Mr. Ali! Why are you barefoot?!"

The man skidded to a stop and gave an astonished look down at his feet in their black nylon socks. Then he almost laughed. "We all ran out of the mosque when we heard the gunfire. We're all barefoot, I'm sure."

"What kind of shoes, Mr. Ali?"

"Black loafers," he called out, and disappeared behind the swinging doors.

She should have told the man his daughter was dead . . . but then she didn't know for certain that she was . . . yes, she did. She inhaled deeply when she got outside, surprised that it was fully dark. She pulled out her phone to call the Chief. He'd be beyond furious. Then she'd call Eric. He'd be inconsolable. And Mimi. She had to call Mimi, who must be sitting at her desk watching the story unfold on the television stations, and they all must be weighing in—from Al Jazeera to the BBC. The reporters would try valiantly, and in vain, to have something new to say from minute to minute but the cops had sealed off the site and any and all information related to it. It was looking to be a long night for cops and reporters alike—unless the cops caught a break.

"We got 'em, Chief! We got the bastards!"

"Tell me," the Chief said, almost quietly.

"First and best, the eyewitness descriptions were damn near perfect for a change: Silver or gray pickup with a double cab and Indiana plates, though the wits didn't know the Indiana part—they just knew out of state. Three perps inside, two of 'em refusing to talk, the third unable to shut his mouth."

"Where were they?"

"They had just turned off of Brook Parkway onto Capitol Hill Drive."

The Chief looked perplexed. "Why the hell were they going that way? Every cop in D.C. is in that direction. Even being from

Indiana they'd have to know that. Why weren't they headed for the interstate?"

The Anti-Terrorism Task Force cop who was relaying the info to the chief now looked perplexed and confused himself—as well as slightly amazed. "It seems they thought they'd be safe if they could get close enough to the White House to tell the president that they had just helped him make America a better place for Americans."

The Chief's phone rang, saving those close to him from the eruption that was coming. The look on his face when he saw who was calling caused everyone but Eric Ashby to take a step back. Eric moved a step closer. When he saw the Chief's eyes close for a moment after he listened to the caller, Eric grabbed his own phone and waited for Gianna's call.

"Everybody," the Chief said, and he didn't shout. He didn't need to. Every pair of eyes and ears were his. "Those bastards have killed a member of the D.C. Police Force. Officer Cassandra Ali, a member of the Hate Crimes Unit, just passed away at the University Hospital Trauma Center."

Eric's phone rang at that moment. He met the Chief's eyes. The Chief nodded and Eric stepped away.

"What do you need me to do?" he asked his boss and good friend.

"Come here to be with Cassie's parents. But first, Eric—please go get Jamal Ali's shoes," and she explained how it happened that the man had arrived in an ambulance with his wife without shoes. Then she told him that Cassie had, in all likelihood, saved her mother's life at the cost of her own. Then she called Mimi.

Mimi could almost feel the energy shift through the computer screen as all of a sudden cops and reporters were in motion—the cops first, then the reporters as they tried to surge past the police barricade that was keeping them far away from the scene of the massacre. The long lenses of the television cameras were able to capture the image of the cops as they gathered in front of and around the Chief, but no matter how they tried, their microphones could pick up only ambient noises. Then her cell phone rang. It was Gianna. She grabbed it and ran out into the hallway near the water cooler. It was understood that when a person was back here, privacy was required.

"Sweetheart?"

After the briefest second in which she heard Gianna inhale: "Cassie Ali is dead. Some dumb fuck killed her and at least two other Muslim women as they were walking to their mosque for Friday evening prayers. Cassie's mother is injured but, Mimi, Cassie knocked her mother to the ground and covered her with her own body. She probably saved her mother's life."

Mimi couldn't speak. There was nothing to say. She held the phone and they listened to each other breathe for a moment. "Where are you?"

"I just left the hospital and I'm heading to the scene."

"What do you need me to do?"

"You won't be assigned to cover this?" Gianna was genuinely surprised. Mimi was a top reporter and got assigned to cover top stories. Usually.

"Nope. Weasel Boy is all over it."

Gianna snorted a laugh. "I met him. That new guy, right? He's an idiot."

"No shit, Sherlock . . ." Mimi stopped mid-sentence when she heard a sharp intake of breath from Gianna. "What is it, Gianna?"

"That's . . . that was one of Cassie's favorite expressions: 'No shit, Sherlock.'" She signed deeply. "That kid is really going to be missed."

"I know," Mimi said. And she did know. She'd met Cassie Ali several times and she knew how protective Gianna was of her—the youngest member of her Hate Crimes team. She also knew that the young cop harbored a secret infatuation with her boss and she wondered if Gianna knew, and thought that she probably didn't. Gianna probably also didn't know that Cassie Ali wasn't the only woman on her HCU team who had the hots for the boss, Detective Alice Long being the other. Of course, Alice also had made a play for Mimi a while back. . . . Gianna said something that Mimi didn't hear. "I'm sorry. What did you say?"

14

"I said I have no idea what time I'll finish tonight, or even if I'll finish."

"Whenever," Mimi said. "I'll be waiting for you at your place."

Sergeant Eric Ashby walked slowly through the front door of the University Hospital Center. There was no need to rush. Cassandra Ali was already dead and he was in no hurry to talk to her parents. Even if there existed some appropriate words for them, he didn't know what they were. He knew he could proceed directly to the ER and the administrator would meet him. Like practically every cop in the city, he knew exactly where the ER was, and the closer he got the larger the lump in his chest grew, so that by the time he got there, tears swam in his usually bright blue eyes, dulling them.

"Sergeant Ashby."

He turned around to see who was calling him and when he recognized Cassie's father, the tears spilled out and down his face. Mr. Ali was weeping, too, and he grabbed the cop and they held each other tightly for a long moment, their love and respect for their daughter and colleague their bond.

"Thanks," Jamal Ali said as he pulled a handkerchief from his pocket and wiped his face and blew his nose.

"For what, sir?" And Jamal Ali pointed to the black loafers that Eric had forgotten he carried. He gave the man his shoes and then supported him as he stepped into them, one foot, then the other.

"Have the reporters showed up yet?" Eric asked.

Ali nodded and scowled. "Thank heaven they can't get in."

"Even if they do, you don't have to talk to them."

"I know. The Chief told me. He called a few minutes ago to tell me that he planned to make the announcement about . . . Cassandra . . ." He tried to take a deep breath but it got caught somewhere in his chest and he started to cry again, which caused his chest to constrict even more. Eric clapped him on the back, hard, until he was breathing again and could talk. "He's a very decent man, isn't he? He said he wouldn't talk about Cassandra if I didn't want him to."

"Yes, he is a very decent man, and he meant what he said: If you asked him not to speak of your daughter tonight, he won't and he'll let the reporters howl at the moon. He knows you need time."

"But he has a job to do. I could tell he was mad—"

"You have no idea!" Eric hadn't intended to speak but the words were out before he could control them.

"I'm mad, too, and I want people to know what happened to my daughter. But I would like for her mother to be left out of it—at least for now."

"Did you say that to the Chief?"

"Yes, I did."

"Then he will honor your request—" Eric saw the head of the emergency department coming toward him as if the hounds of hell were on his heels. And perhaps they were: dozens, perhaps hundreds of reporters and cameras, clamoring for information.

"I gotta tell 'em something, Sergeant Ashby!"

"I know you do. Put 'em in a room with a TV and tell 'em the Chief is about to make a statement. Then I'll come in and tell 'em what the Chief told 'em, and I'll say the same thing a dozen different ways until they get tired of hearing it. Or until I get tired of saying it—whichever comes first."

The administrator nodded his thanks and hurried away. Eric gave Jamal Ali his card. "My cell phone number is on the back. You call any time. I'll be here in the hospital, probably most of the night—at least until we know for certain how Mrs. Ali and the other women are." And after a brief hug, he left Jamal Ali to his grief and followed the hospital administrator so he, too, could watch the Chief on TV.

Between the lights of the crime scene investigators and those of the TV cameras, the area where a massacre had taken place less than four hours ago was lit up like it was the middle of the day instead of the darkness an hour past sundown dictated. All of the women's bodies had been removed, but the two assailants still lay on the sidewalk, covered, while the techs continued collecting evidence, so all of the reporters—dozens of them—were still being kept a good distance away. The Chief stood in front of the ATTF SUV, a very impressive-looking vehicle, on top of a step stool, so everyone could see him, looking very impressive himself. He was not a tall man, but he was muscular and he exuded both physical and mental strength and confidence. He looked out at the assembled reporters, not recognizing just as many as he did recognize. This was, he knew, an international story and he was about to make it bigger.

His Public Affairs Officer had printed out and was distributing the single-page statement that he would make. They had agreed on the language and on which facts would be made public. There was still too much that was unknown for him to say more, but he knew from personal experience that not giving reporters even a small bone to chew on only served to make them more ravenous. And now, with a government in Washington at the federal level that cared nothing for truth and facts, he was determined that every word that came out of his mouth would be verifiable.

He raised his hands, and the crowd before him immediately silenced. "I wish I didn't have to be out here with you on a Friday night with the kind of bad news that I have for you. Something terribly ugly happened at this location several hours ago. We don't know all the facts yet, so what I'm able to share with you is, of necessity, sparse, and it comes with some rigid ground rules that I'm going to insist that you respect. Are we clear?"

He waited for the answer, and he waited long enough that the reporters finally understood that if they didn't agree, he was done talking. They agreed. "First, the bad news: Five Muslim women were walking to their Friday evening prayers at the mosque over there when they were attacked and fired upon by five men in a pickup truck. As of this moment, two of those women have died and a third is in critical condition with a guarded prognosis—the doctor's words." He stopped talking and inhaled deeply. "One of the victims, one of the murdered women, was one of our own—"

Almost as if they were cued by a director the reporters started to yell out questions—so many voices raised at once that none of the questions could be clearly understood, but it didn't matter because the Chief didn't intend to answer them. He waited for five seconds, and then he raised his hands. Most of the noise stopped. One loudly insistent questioner did not.

"Why won't you answer the question, Chief? Are you hiding something?"

"I don't answer stupid questions," the Chief snapped. Then: "I'd like to finish if you all would like me to finish. If not, I'll go back to my office and get the latest reports from the arresting officers."

Arresting officers. The reporters heard those two words and silence fell as if it were an animate object. "The murdered officer was Cassandra Ali of the Hate Crimes Unit who was walking to the mosque with her mother—"

"You allow Muslims in the D.C. Police Department?" This from the same loudly insistent questioner, the one the Chief had implied was stupid.

"Do they pay you to ask stupid questions or is that your idea?"

"It's not a stupid question; it's a legitimate one! Do you allow Muslims on the D.C. Police Department?"

"Same as we allow Baptists and Catholics and Buddhists and Methodists and Episcopalians and Presbyterians—who am I leaving out?"

"Quakers!" somebody called out.

"Lutherans!" somebody else said.

"Hindus!" somebody else said.

And the Chief said, "The way it works in this country is that people can be free to worship their own god in their own way. That's the American way, no matter how desperately some people are trying to redefine what it means to be an American. Like the people who murdered Officer Ali this evening."

The Chief pointed at the reporter who had interrupted him twice and who was preparing to do it again. "Do not interrupt me again. If you do, I'm done talking and you can get all further information about this incident in the form of press releases from the Public Affairs Office."

"What are you hiding, Chief?" the reporter yelled out.

"Shut up, motherfucker!" one of the other reporters called out.

There was a scuffle that lasted several seconds, followed by calls from several reporters for the Chief to continue. He did.

"You will have noticed the presence of Lt. Andrew Page of the Anti-Terrorism Task Force and Lt. Giovanna Maglione of the Hate Crimes Unit. That's because this brutal and cowardly attack on five women who were walking to a church service is being considered both a hate crime and a terrorist attack. Five men, shouting and yelling and firing weapons and driving one of those big pickup trucks came riding down the street behind unsuspecting women, like the KKK, firing into their backs. All of the victims were shot in the back. The fact that the victims were all Muslims makes it both terrorism and hatred, and the fact that all were shot in the back makes it cowardly. Just about an hour ago, patrol officers from our Department, with assistance from the United States Capitol Police, arrested several suspects. We will not release any information about them until our investigation proceeds and progresses. That is, until we have all the facts. Suffice it to say, however, that we are confident that we have the people who are responsible for tonight's horrible tragedy. You all know Sgt. Jerome Gregory from the Public Affairs Office. He will provide hourly updates throughout the night, and I'll hold a formal briefing in my office at 9:30 tomorrow morning. Thank you all for yo—"

"Chief! Please! Just one question: about the KKK reference!"

"Why don't you read up on that particular group of cowards and then ask your question in the morning?" And with that he stepped down from his step stool to stand close to his two lieutenants.

"We've already got a dossier being compiled on these guys, Chief," the ATTF lieutenant whispered. "We've made contact in Indiana where they're from, and the authorities there are being cooperative. We'll make damn sure you're ready for that morning briefing."

The Chief nodded his thanks, and Andy Page followed his

troops as they all piled into their SUV. Page might or might not have heard the questions yelled at him by the reporters but he never looked in their direction. He looked instead at his colleague, Gianna Maglione. "I can't imagine how you're feeling," he said to her, moving his eyes from hers to peer at his team.

"I'm still numb from shock, thank goodness, so right now I'm not feeling much of anything. But I know that can't last forever."

He stuck out his hand and she shook it, and he climbed into his SUV with his team. She searched out and found her team and she reached out an arm to them while she leaned in to listen to the Chief.

"I don't have to tell you how sorry I am about Officer Ali."

"No, sir."

"I wish I could let you all go home but I can't."

"I know, and we don't want to go home."

"And I know that," he said with a sad grin. "Some of you at the hospital and some of you at the office—you decide who— but I want the Hate Crimes and the ATTF offices staffed around the clock until this thing calms down."

"Yes, sir," she said, and when he was gone she and her team wrapped their arms around each other and stood together in a tight circle for a long while without speaking. Then she let them decide who would join Eric at the hospital and who would stay at the office with her, and she was not surprised that the guys opted to join Eric and the women to stay with her.

She pulled some bills from her pocket and gave the money to Bobby. "The food is pretty good in the hospital cafeteria and it's open all night, but order out if you'd rather. I want somebody with the Ali family at all times—you all can decide who. And I want constant updates on the woman who's critical. We'll meet at the office at eight. I'll provide breakfast. Then, after the Chief's press conference and unless something major has occurred, half of you will go home and get some sleep; then you'll relieve the others. Am I clear? I don't want to hear any arguments and I don't want anybody to disobey me."

They hugged each other then, individually. "Anybody who wants to ride with me can do that. And somebody call the Chinese place and order enough food to last us all night. I'm buying." Too bad alcohol isn't allowed in the police station, was her final thought before shifting into what Mimi called "Lieutenant Mode," because the lieutenant needed a drink. A strong one.

Mimi, who had joined her colleagues to watch the Chief's press conference on the big-screen television in the newsroom, was feeling the same need. She stood beside Joe Zemekis who she considered a friend and who'd been at the paper as long as she had, though he'd spent several years on the National Desk and therefore out of town more than he was in it. When the paper cut back not only on the number of reporters it employed, but on the nature of the work those who remained would do, Joe came home. He still looked like Tom Hanks, only with more salt than pepper in his hair and beard. They spent a quick moment whining about being on the sidelines while a potentially huge story was developing. They also agreed that they'd never seen or heard the Chief so controlled and so solemn. There was the to-be-expected mumbling and grousing at the announcement that this was to be a statement only, no-questions event, but it was halfhearted at best. The current White House shenanigans notwithstanding, nobody could realistically expect facts in such a short time. The fact that the Chief announced that one of the victims was a D.C. cop and a member of the Hate Crimes Unit stunned the newsroom staff, half of whom snuck surreptitious glances at Mimi to see whether she already knew about Cassandra Ali, but only city editor Tyler Carson knew her well enough to be able to read the truth behind her blank stare: Gianna had already told Mimi. It was the Chief's stinging rebuke of their colleague, though, that really galvanized the room.

"Holy shit! I knew Carl was aggressive but that's ridiculous!" Joe said.

She frowned. "That's not his name, is it? Carl?"

Joe laughed. "No. We just call him that. For Bernstein, you know? 'Cause he thinks he's such a badass."

The room erupted when the Chief leveled his second salvo at Weasel Boy, the "do they pay you to be stupid" one, the one that brought the executive editor out of his office to glare at metro editor Todd Wassily, Weasel Boy's mentor and protector. Then it got deathly quiet, first watching the scuffle that quieted their colleague, and then tuning in to the several bombshells dropped by the Chief: that suspects were in custody; that the attack against the women was being treated as both a hate crime and a terrorist act; and his comparing the men who committed the crime to the KKK.

"Holy shit!" Joe exclaimed again and rushed over to his desk.

"You don't want to miss this," Mimi called out to him as the executive editor stalked to the front of the room, veins bulging in his forehead.

"What a fucking clusterfuck! Was what's-his-name, the new guy, our only reporter on the scene? Somebody answer me, goddammit!" And here Mimi had thought the Exec had calmed down in his old age.

"Yeah, Stu, he was," Wassily managed.

"Who's at the hospital? Who's following up on the arrest? Who's inside that mosque? Who's following up with Hate Crimes and Anti-Terrorism? Who's canvassing the neighborhood?" He looked all around as he waited for answers, the vein throbbing and pounding, his eyes wild and bulging. "All editors, my office, now. All reporters, be ready to deploy. And when what's his name gets back, send him to my office."

Mimi met Carson's eyes as he followed the other editors into the Exec's office, and his look told her to get ready for major action. She pulled her phone out of her pocket to call Gianna though she was certain that neither of them would get home this Friday night. She felt Joe materialize beside her. "Looks like we might get to suit up and play after all," he said.

"I hope so," Mimi said. "It would be nice to function like a real newspaper again," and they both indulged in a back-in-the-day moment.

"Patterson! Zemekis!" They heard their names shouted and

followed the sound to see city editor Tyler Carson waving them over, and they sprinted toward him like young reporters, not caring what their assignment would be as long as they had a piece of this story. There was more than enough to go around.

Mike Holton and his son, Samuel, had stopped talking. Had refused to say another word without a lawyer present, and that was all right with the cops who had stopped them, arrested them, and impounded their truck. Ricky Slater *was* talking. He was talking enough for both the Holtons. In fact, they couldn't get Ricky Slater to stop talking, and the more he talked, the more bizarre the story he told. Bizarre and unbelievable. Incredible. It seemed that the lawyer Mike Holton was asking for—the "general lawyer" was what he kept saying—was the attorney general. The man thought the attorney general of the United States was a lawyer for hire by citizens—holy shit!!! Wait until Captain Healy heard this! A man of moderate imagination on a normal day—this would crash his internal hard drive.

CHAPTER TWO

Arrests Made in Murders of Muslim Women
Police Call Attacks Terrorist Hate Crimes

By J.J. Zemekis Jr.
Staff Writer

Less than an hour after five Muslim women were
mowed down in a hail of bullets while walking to
evening service at their midtown mosque, three
men were arrested while apparently driving to
the White House to see the president. Police
Chief Benjamin Jefferson quickly called the attack
an act of terrorism as well as a hate crime, and he
likened it to the actions of the KKK. "It also is an
act of almost unimaginable cowardice," Chief
Jefferson said. "What other kind of person would
attack a group of women walking to church from
behind? It's the kind of thing cowards do."

Police would not release any details of the
arrests but did confirm eyewitness accounts that
the assailants were driving a silver or gray pickup
truck with out-of-state license plates, and that all
of the occupants of the truck appeared to be
white males. All of the Muslim women were

Black. At least two of the women were pronounced dead at University Hospital Trauma Center. A third is in critical condition, while the condition of the other two was withheld in accordance with the wishes of the next of kin.

The alleged assailants were arrested by the SWAT team after their truck was spotted by patrol officers near the Capitol. "Every cop in D.C. was on the lookout for this truck," said Lt. Andrew Page of the SWAT Unit. When asked why he thought the men were headed to the White House, Chief Jefferson replied, "Why did they do anything they did here this evening?"

Muslim Women's Walk to Mosque
Act of Defiance and Faith

By M. Montgomery Patterson
Staff Writer

Aisha Ali and her best friends are devout Muslims, but walking to their mosque for evening prayers last night was a departure for them because women traditionally do not attend evening prayers at the mosque. Men do. Women pray in the home. "But we became so distressed at the anti-Muslim language and behavior, especially coming from the highest levels of our government," she said through her tears. "We spoke to our husbands and told them we wanted to attend evening prayers as a way to protest the hatred directed toward us as much as to practice our religion in public and with pride."

"They had our support," said her husband, Jamal Ali, through his own tears. "Our mosque is more progressive than some and we don't ban women. We welcome them."

Mr. and Mrs. Ali wept throughout our interview because their 25-year-old daughter, Cassandra, who was walking to the mosque with her mother, died from the wounds she suffered in the attack. But they wanted to talk about her, and they wanted to ask why so many people seem to be so willing to deny them their right to freedom of religion. "We are American-born," said Jamal Ali, "as are our parents and grandparents and great-grandparents."

"We live our Muslim faith," Aisha Ali said, "but we have been questioned about our daughter's name. Cassandra is not a traditional Islamic name." She had to stop speaking so her husband continued for her.

"Both our mothers are named Cassandra. How unusual is that? So when our daughter was born, it seemed so logical to name her after her grandmothers. Now we must tell them that she is . . ." And he had to stop speaking.

Violent History of the KKK

By J.J. Zemekis Jr.
Staff Writer

The letters stand for Ku Klux Klan and they were once as well-known as other groupings of three letters, like FBI or CIA. The Southern Poverty Law Center calls the KKK the oldest American hate group. It was formed in 1865 specifically to harass, intimidate, and lynch freed slaves primarily in the South, but it quickly spread throughout the country, and its hate tactics expanded to include Jews, homosexuals, and even Catholics. They were also called night riders because of their habit of galloping their horses in the dead of night to the homes of rural Blacks. The Klansmen wore hoods that covered their faces and often carried fiery torches that they threw into the homes of their targets. They would also shoot into the homes of targets, or fire at them as they ran.

"That's what that big pickup truck reminded me of," said 89-year old Arthur Crawford, an eyewitness to the attack on the Muslim women. "I grew up down South and I remember seeing them as a boy, but mostly I remember my parents telling me how they'd ride up on their horses, whooping and hollering their rebel yells, shooting people in the back as they tried to escape. I thought I'd seen the last of that kind of thing."

They weren't just cops; they were elite cops, among the best of the best, so of course they were at work. All of them—except the one who'd been so brutally and stupidly murdered the previous day. They were in their private place, their sanctuary—the Think Tank they called it—where they would usually sift and sort and talk through the information and evidence that would lead them to the perpetrator of the hate crime they were charged with investigating. But they knew who'd murdered the absent member of the Hate Crimes Unit. Other cops had caught them and arrested them and charged them with the murder of Cassandra Ali and two other women. Charged them with committing a hate crime and a terrorist act. But that knowledge did nothing to soothe or comfort the remaining members of the Hate Crimes Unit of the D.C. Police Department: Lt. Gianna Maglione, the boss; Sgt. Eric Ashby, her second in command;

detectives Alice Long, Bobby Gilliam, and Kenny Chang; and officers Linda Lopez and Tim McCreedy. No more Officer Cassandra Ali.

Everybody had a newspaper and had read the articles about the men who had murdered their Cassie, and their disgust at the hatred that had bred and fostered the level of stupidity that led five men to leave their homes and drive across four states to attempt the murder of five women, knew no bounds. But it was the story written by M. Montgomery Patterson that captured them. After reading almost every one of her stories they always asked the Boss, "How does she know the stuff she knows?!" and the reply always was, "Reporters have sources, too, just like cops do." They asked the Boss because the reporter was Mimi Patterson, the Boss's partner in life and love, and they never quite believed that Patterson the journalist didn't get at least some of her information from Maglione the lover. But if they really believed that, they'd have to believe the Boss was lying when she always denied advance knowledge of Patterson's stories—and the Boss didn't lie.

"That was really interesting, about how Cassie got her name," Bobby Gilliam said sadly. "I used to wonder—" he began, but the sadness overcame him and he couldn't finish.

"People must really trust her to tell her the things they do," Linda Lopez said. "I mean, I bet they've never told anyone else how Cassie got her name."

"You're probably right," Gianna said, "but don't look at me for answers. I was here with you guys all night. Ask Eric—he was at the hospital with her." And all eyes turned to their sergeant. He shrugged and yawned and was about to ask his boss if she was certain that she ordered breakfast when there was a knock at the door and it opened before anyone could respond. The food had arrived—three carts' full—accompanied by two of the staff of the Phillips Family Diner and followed by Delores and Darlene Phillips. The spirits inside the Think Tank almost lifted.

Gianna stood up to greet the Phillips sisters and was surprised and pleased to receive hugs from both of them, along with their condolences. They had met several months ago when the women's bar the sisters owned had been targeted by right-wing religious extremists, with the cooperation of a cadre of anti-gay cops. To Gianna's everlasting dismay, the Phillips sisters had never heard of the Hate Crimes Unit, had no idea that there were cops whose job it was to protect them, and Officer Cassandra Ali was one of the first HCU cops they encountered. Since then, Mimi and Gianna had visited the club, called the Snatch, and not only had Cassie become a regular but she'd also become good friends with Darlene Phillips, whose red-rimmed eyes testified to how deeply she was feeling the loss of her newfound friend.

"Thank you both for coming," Gianna said.

Dee Phillips shook her head. She was the younger of the sisters, but was the face of their business. Impeccably dressed as always, businesslike as always, she made it clear that no thanks was necessary. "We will always be grateful to you, Lieutenant, for standing by us, for standing with us, for standing up for us when no one else would."

"We were just doing our jobs, Ms. Phillips. You know that."

"You did more than just your job, Lieutenant, and you know that," Dee said. "You and your people gave hatred a hard kick in the ass. You let people know that they couldn't treat us like we were less than nothing. And now for that same kind of stupid, ugly shit to take the life of Officer Ali—that sweet, kind young woman—it makes me mad as hell, Lieutenant!"

Dee had raised her voice and everybody stopped eating and looked their way, ready to spring to the defense of their boss if necessary. They were on edge. It would take very little to tip them over. "I'm just glad we're not the ones who had to find the killers. I couldn't be responsible," Gianna said.

Dee looked at the cops she'd come to respect and knew without a doubt that if any one of them ever laid hands on the men who murdered Cassie Ali there would be another murder. "Breakfast is on me, Lieutenant—and please don't resist me. I'm glad you chose us to serve you this morning, and it seems that you need the nourishment. I can tell that nobody in the Hate Crimes Unit got any sleep last night."

"Do we look that bad?" Gianna asked.

"You look worse than that!" Dee said with a small smile, and she looked as if she wanted to say something else, but she turned toward the door. "And will you let us know about the funeral arrangements? Darlene especially. I read up on Muslim funerals and, like the Jews, Muslims require a pretty quick burial. None of that wait a week stuff we Black Baptists do."

Gianna realized that she had absolutely no knowledge about Muslim ritual and said as much. Then she realized that the department would want to honor one of its own in some way, and the sorrow that she had been fighting to keep at bay overtook her. At that moment Eric handed her a cup of coffee in one hand and a glass of orange juice in the other. Then he led her to her place at the head of the table where her breakfast was waiting. She looked down at her watch, then up at the wall of clocks to confirm that they had exactly thirty-seven minutes to eat and get downstairs to the press room.

The Chief's press conference was standing room only. There were even more reporters and camera crews crowding the press room than there had been on the scene last night. The Chief was the only cop in the room who didn't look like he'd been up all night, though he had. He also looked angrier than he had the previous night, and that was saying something.

Mimi and Joe stood at the back of the room. Everybody had already read their stories and unless something major was announced now, they both stood a good chance of being able to go home and grab a nap though they both had pens and notebooks at the ready. Mimi didn't really care if she got to sleep, but if she didn't eat soon she'd kill somebody. And coming toward them was the perfect candidate: Weasel Boy, with a face full of hostility and anger. He opened his mouth to speak at the same time the Chief did. It was the Chief who got listened to.

"Good morning and thank you for coming. There are a few things that I can tell you now that I couldn't tell you last night.

First: the names of the five men who came here to my city to commit hate-based murder," and he waited until the collective intake of breath was released before he continued.

"Their names are Michael Holton, age fifty, and his two sons, Mickey, twenty-three, and Sammy, nineteen, and brothers Ronald Slater, twenty-three, and Richard Slater, seventeen. They are from Pinetree Valley, Indiana, and according to an official of the state police there they left home sometime before sunrise yesterday and arrived in our city at approximately 6 p.m. They were driving a 2014 silver Ford F-150 registered to Michael Holton. Based on information recovered from the pickup truck and from the cellular telephone belonging to Michael Holton, it is our belief that these men came here to help 'Make America Great Again' by, in their words, putting an end to the call to prayer that emanates from the mosque on Temple Boulevard. The mosque that was the destination of the five women who were mowed down by the five men in the pickup truck."

The Chief stopped speaking while the Public Affairs office staff passed out press releases containing what the Chief had just said in language that was more inflammatory than Mimi had ever heard him utter. Deliberately inflammatory and everybody in the room knew it. Mimi was writing so fast her hand was starting to cramp. So was Joe and every other reporter in the room. Except for Weasel Boy. What the hell was wrong with him?

"Another thing that I can tell you now that I couldn't tell you last night," the Chief said, "concerns Officer Cassandra Ali. And I suppose I should be grateful that Montgomery Patterson left something for me to say."

At that Mimi looked up, surprised at the Chief's sarcastic criticism. So did Gianna. Mimi could see the shock and irritation that crossed her face, but left in an instant. Nobody but Mimi would have noticed it and nobody but Mimi would have known what a rarity it was for Gianna to harbor any negative feeling for the man who was more than her boss; he was a mentor and her friend. Mimi was wondering what shape Gianna was in. Now she knew. They hadn't had significant contact with each other in more than twenty-four hours. She knew that Gianna, no stranger to long, hard hours at work, could and would hold it together under normal circumstances. The murder of one of her team—the one who, if pressed, Gianna would own as her favorite—was not normal. Gianna's face was back to blank, expressionless.

"Many of you may not know that Officer Ali was attacked and savagely beaten on her way home from work last year. That beating left her with some memory loss and the total loss of sight in one eye. Despite intensive therapy and hard work, Officer Ali could not continue as an officer in the Metropolitan Police Department."

The silence in the room was heavy, not least because no one had ever seen the Chief so emotional. "Officer Ali believed that she could perform her duties and her boss, Lieutenant Maglione, gave her every opportunity to prove it. But in the end, we both agreed that, her hard work notwithstanding, we'd have to let her go. In what most probably was her final conscious act, Officer Ali, who already had her service weapon in her hand, fired two rounds each into two of the murderers who had exited the pickup truck for a closer look at their handiwork. The dead men are Mickey Holton and Ronald Slater."

Half the reporters in the room, including Mimi and Joe, were on the phone to their editors. Even Weasel Boy, Mimi noticed, was talking animatedly to his editor, or so she assumed, but she couldn't give him any more thought. She had to focus on the follow-up to her story in the morning paper: the real reason that Cassie Ali was dead and her mother alive.

But the Chief wasn't finished with them yet. "You know that two women died yesterday—our own Officer Ali and Mrs. Wanda Muhammad. A third woman remains in very critical condition. Her family has asked that we not release her name at this time. We will update her condition as we get information. We also will tell you when formal charges are filed against the assailants and what those charges are—"

"Are they represented by an attorney?" Weasel Boy asked.

"Not yet," the Chief answered.

"Why not?" Weasel Boy asked.

"Mr. Holton wanted to be represented by the attorney general, and he had a hard time understanding why that wasn't possible—"

"What do you mean he wanted to be represented by the attorney general? The attorney general of the United States?" Weasel Boy was both incredulous and amused.

"It seems that Mr. Holton thought the attorney general was the lawyer for the people of the United States. We think he now understands that's not the case and he has asked for a lawyer from his hometown. We're waiting to learn the outcome of that—"

"Where are these men being held? Are they still in central lockup?"

"If I may finish my statement—"

"We have questions, Chief! You can't just talk like you're in a lecture hall and not expect to be questioned!" Weasel Boy was on a roll.

"He's nuts," Joe whispered to Mimi.

"The Chief's gonna walk out in a minute," Mimi whispered back.

"But he's not finished—" Joe was whispering to Mimi when the Chief stood down from the podium and stalked out.

The assembled reporters let out a howl that was ear-piercing. The Public Affairs sergeant pretended not to hear as he and his staff continued to hand out their pile of press releases.

Joe pocketed his notebook, grabbed a stack of press releases, and started to read. "Will you introduce me to Lieutenant Maglione?" he asked Mimi, and when she nodded, he followed as she worked her way through the crowd toward the front of the room where Gianna was standing next to Andy Page from ATTF. Both were now surrounded by reporters shouting questions, which Gianna was happy to let Page answer. She spied Mimi, headed toward her, slowed when she saw Joe. Then Mimi smiled and Gianna almost did.

"How are you, Lieutenant?" she asked Gianna.

"I've been better."

"This is my colleague, Joe Zemekis."

Joe stuck out his hand. "I'm so very sorry about what happened to your Officer Ali, Lieutenant."

Momentarily taken aback, Gianna shook his hand and then thanked him. "Those were good stories, Mr. Zemekis," she said, and it was his turn to be back-footed. He was as unaccustomed to receiving compliments from cops as she was to receiving condolences from a reporter.

"Can I get some more information about the attack on Officer Ali?"

"You should talk to Detective Jim Dudley in the Gang Task Force. That was his case. Then you can talk to me."

Joe thanked her, then asked, "Can I tell him you sent me?"

Gianna nodded, he saluted her and turned away. "Later, Patterson," he said over his shoulder, and disappeared into the crowd.

"Nice guy. Where'd he come from? And that other ass? What's his name? Where'd they get him?" Mimi shook her head, suddenly tired, and her stomach growled loud enough for Gianna to hear it. "You haven't eaten?"

"Have you?"

"Dee and Darlene brought food from the diner," Gianna began but Mimi didn't hear the rest, didn't want to hear the rest. She stalked off, hoping the food in the hospital cafeteria was as good as she'd heard. But first she needed to find a quiet corner to call Tyler, hoping that the executive editor wouldn't be annoyed with her about the Chief's comment.

"He got a kick out it!" Tyler told her. "He loves everything you and Joe are doing, which Wassily isn't loving."

"What's wrong with that guy? Can't he see that pissing off the Chief isn't the way to go?" She meant the reporter, she told him, not the editor.

She heard Tyler sigh and he lowered his voice. She could picture him at his desk, his back turned to the newsroom as he practically whispered into the phone. "I know, and Wassily tried to get him to follow up on the Cassie Ali story but he didn't want to do that—Joe called and asked to do it—you know what he wants to do? Find out why the family of the woman who's standing at death's door doesn't want to release her name. Know what he's trying to sell? That they're some radicalized Muslims who were hiding out in that mosque just waiting for their chance to . . . to . . . I don't know what!"

"He's nuts," Mimi said as her stomach growled again. "I gotta go eat, Tyler, before I expire."

"Where you headed?"

"The hospital, to see if Mr. and Mrs. Ali will talk to me again. Maybe I can feed Joe some information."

"Let's make it two separate stories. Just tell Joe about the story we did on the B-Moggers to go with his Cassie story," Tyler said, "and you keep with the up close and personal on the women, all of them." He hung up. Mimi looked around for Joe, forgetting her growling stomach for a moment as she called to mind the facts of the Black Men on Guard, known as the B-Moggers, a loosely organized group of men who annointed themselves the caretakers, guardians and protectors of their communities. Most of their successes involved banishing drugs and drug dealers, to the delight of the neighborhoods they helped and to the chagrin of the police, who considered them little more than vigilantes, given that their methods weren't always polite, to say nothing of legal. Once, at Cassie Ali's request, the B-Moggers came to the aid of an elderly Jewish woman, a concentration camp survivor, who was being harrassed by some neo-Nazi skinheads. Mimi smiled to herself at the memory. Then her stomach rumbled again.

Thankfully the taxi ride to the hospital was brief. It wasn't yet noon on a Saturday morning, which was considered early in D.C., relatively speaking. Rush hour lasted from about 6 a.m. until 8 p.m. during the week, but traffic didn't get dense on the weekends until noon because most people tried not to schedule work before noon on weekends. Except reporters and cops who, for the most part, didn't get to schedule their work. It happened when it happened and they dealt with it. Mimi would deal much better with whatever the day had in store for her when she'd eaten.

The cafeteria line was long—it was lunch time, after all—but it moved quickly thanks to the three cashiers at the end of the room. Mimi and her tray were almost at a checkout when she saw Detective Alice Long exiting the cafeteria, and she knew it was Alice only because few women on the planet were that gorgeous. But today Alice's beauty was weighed down with grief and Mimi knew why. Alice was to be Cassie's replacement in the Hate Crimes Unit, a job Alice wanted and welcomed but one that Mimi knew she'd take no joy in having now that Cassie's young life had ended so horribly.

For her part, Alice Long would gladly return to undercover Vice duties, a job she hated more than any other, if it would return Cassie to life and health. She had been the temporary replacement in Hate Crimes while Gianna gave Cassie all the leeway possible, hoping and praying, along with the young cop, for a miracle, even as the Chief was warning Gianna that he no longer could—or would—carry a cop on his roster who couldn't function as a cop. Now she had to go upstairs to the hospital room and be an official presence for the mother of the woman whose job she now held. What on earth could she say?

At that moment there was nothing Aisha Ali wanted to hear except that she could get out of the hospital bed and go to wherever it was they were holding her daughter's body so that she could bathe her and dress her and prepare her for burial. And at that moment Lt. Gianna Maglione was in the unenviable position of having to deny Mrs. Ali permission to get out of bed as the doctor had ordered. Besides, Gianna tried explaining—again—Cassie's body could not yet be released. Nor could Mrs. Muhammad. And furthermore, Gianna said, Mr. Ali had told her that Cassie's aunt, Mrs. Ali's sister, would prepare Cassie for burial.

"She's my daughter! It must be me! I must do this!"

The woman's wails were breaking Gianna's heart. They also

were costing her every ounce of her strength. She would weaken and collapse into sleep in a moment. The doctor had said to Gianna, "Just because she isn't dead doesn't mean that she's all right. Her wounds, while not life-threatening, are serious."

"Please let me get up." Aisha Ali's wail had become a weak whisper, and her eyes closed as the door opened. Gianna frowned at the doctor who entered. He wasn't supposed to be here; he was a male. Then she looked more closely at him, past the white coat and the stethoscope draped around his neck, and fury rose within her unchecked.

"You bastard! Get out of here!" Gianna was on the reporter before he had time to backpedal. She had him on the floor and was straddling him, trying to grab his arms, when the door opened again.

Alice Long hesitated not an instant. She grabbed Weasel Boy's wrists and yanked them behind him. He yelped, waking Mrs. Ali. Gianna cuffed him, got him on his feet, and Alice hustled him out into the hallway as Gianna turned her attention to Mrs. Ali.

"Who was that? Was that a doctor?"

"That was a reporter pretending to be a doctor," Gianna snapped.

"Why was he here? What does he want?"

Gianna shook her head, smoothed the covers over Mrs. Ali, and urged her to go back to sleep, which she did almost immediately. Gianna rushed out into the hall where Alice was making Weasel Boy's life a misery. Gianna got in his face. "What is your name?"

"I'm a reporter for the—"

"What. Is. Your. Name?"

"Ian Williams. I'm a reporter—"

"You're not a doctor, which is the only thing that interests me," she said as she headed toward the exit. Alice pulled Ian "Weasel Boy" Williams along behind. "Where's Linda?" she asked Alice.

"Out back here, with Bobby."

Gianna stopped in her tracks. "What's Bobby still doing here?"

"Lots of reporters and cameras. He stayed behind to help Linda control it before it got out of control."

"That many?" Gianna asked, dismay heavy in her voice along with the fatigue. God, how she wanted to go to sleep. Preferably beside Mimi. As she stepped on the pad and the Patient/Visitor door swooshed open, the reporters saw her and started yelling. Then they noticed a handcuffed Ian Williams—one of their own—and confusion quieted them. Though most of them harbored no love for Williams, the sight of a handcuffed reporter made them more than just a little uneasy.

"Who's he, Boss? And what did he do?" Detective Bobby Gilliam asked.

"He's one of them, and he was in Mrs. Ali's room impersonating a doctor. And speaking of which, Alice—"

"On my way, Boss," she said, turning Ian Williams over to Bobby and heading back into the hospital to Aisha Ali's room. They were under orders that none of the women should be without a police guard.

"Uncuff him and relieve him of his disguise," Gianna said as she took out her phone and pressed a button, noticing that she had several text messages from Mimi. She stepped away from Bobby and Linda as she heard the Chief answer. She told him about Ian Williams and listened to him yell for a minute before he hung up on her. She was grinning when she turned back to Bobby, Linda, and a no-longer-smug Ian.

Reporters were yelling at her again, this time their questions relating to their colleague instead of the issue that had consumed them all for the last sixteen or seventeen hours. "You should leave," Gianna told Ian.

"I don't answer to you," he replied.

"That's true, but I expect you'll be hearing from your editor shortly."

He gave her a startled look then turned and rushed back into the hospital, no longer dressed as a doctor. Gianna looked at Linda. "Make sure he doesn't do anything else stupid, then link up with Alice."

Linda threw her a salute and hurried to catch up with Ian. Then she turned to Bobby. "Go home and get some rest."

He looked about to cry. "I can't, Boss. I don't want to. I just want—I don't know what I want! I want Cassie back is what I want!"

And if they couldn't have Cassie back—which they most certainly could not—then she would have to do. "Think Tank, Bobby. Tell the others. I'll meet you there at five o'clock. But I insist you get some rest first."

"Thanks, Boss," he said in so low a voice it was almost a whisper, and he went back into the hospital leaving Gianna to face the crowd of reporters.

They started yelling questions as soon as she came into view and she raised her hands to quiet them—and they quieted. "I really and truly and honestly have nothing new to tell you," she said. "If and when there is anything new to report, you'll get it from the Public Affairs Office, and I promise there is no reason or intent to withhold information from you."

"Why was Ian Williams in handcuffs?" one of the reporters called out.

Well, damn. That certainly was information she wanted to withhold.

"It's not illegal to wear a white coat and a stethoscope, is it?" another one of the reporters yelled out.

"You could probably get a better answer from the hospital PIO, but from where I stand, wearing a white coat and stethoscope into a barely conscious patient's room is, if not illegal, certainly unprofessional. Which one of you would do the same thing?" And without waiting to hear a response she turned and went inside to look for a quiet corner to have a quiet, if brief, conversation with Mimi. Not to talk hatred and murder—the exact opposite—and the loving, soothing words, as they always did, helped to calm and focus her. For the same reason, depleted as she was mentally, physically and spiritually, she knew calling the team meeting in the Think Tank was the right thing to do. While they were as depleted as she was, they were also bewildered and confused. Their body language and facial expressions begged for an explanation, for help understanding what had just happened to them. Gianna wasn't that much older than most of them—Cassie had been the youngest—but she had experienced sudden, violent, tragic loss, and while that experience didn't lessen the shock to the system, it did—it sometimes could—provide a way to manage it. That was to be her mission this evening and, given Eric's red-rimmed eyes, she'd be pretty much on her own.

As usual, they were seated around the long table with her at the head. She stood up and walked to the front of the room. Their eyes followed her, hopeful expectation blooming in every pair of them. "I wish I could say something to make what happened to Cassie make sense," she said, and watched the expectation dim. "But it doesn't make sense. There's no sense to stupid, ugly, violent hatred, and that's what killed Cassie, and you all know there's no sense to be found in it. If there was, you wouldn't have the jobs you have and I wouldn't be your boss because I wouldn't have the job I have."

They looked numb. Shocked. Then as her words took hold, the pain took over, followed by the tears. And that's when they began to manage it. Tim broke first. He and Cassie had been best friends, and he was just beginning to get over the trauma of her beating at the hands of the neo-Nazi skinhead, the one that Tim had gone rogue to find. He could have been fired and arrested for what he had done but Gianna protected him, making certain that Detective Jim Dudley received credit for the bust. Cassie had lived with Tim while she healed, as she realized that her memory of the beating probably would never return, nor would the sight in her left eye. Tim had been there for her, and now she was gone and he didn't know what to do. So he wept like a baby, and it was Bobby Gilliam—big, tough, macho Bobby Gilliam—who wrapped his arms around Tim McCreedy and held him and let him cry.

Then Alice Long lost it. Smart, gorgeous, tough Alice Long who ran marathons for fun, who had more experience as a street cop than the rest of them combined—with the exception of Bobby—who came to Hate Crimes first on loan and then as the eventual replacement for Cassie; Alice, who wanted permanent assignment to the HCU more than she wanted to come in first in the Marine Corps Marathon and who would give it up in a second if it would return Cassie to them. Alice sagged and sobbed and Kenny Chang caught her. She tried to pull away but Linda Lopez piled on, wedging Alice between them, and it was several seconds before they fully understood her tear-stained words: "I'msorry, I'msorry, I'msorry," she wailed over and over, as if any one of them could or would blame her for the loss of their Cassie.

Bobby was crying with Tim, and Linda and Kenny were crying with Alice, and Gianna let them, waiting until they cried themselves dry. And when they did she got a roll of paper towels from the supply cabinet, and a couple of bottles of water, and rolled off bunches of towels, soaked them, and handed them out. She did this until the roll was empty, until all eyes were dried and noses blown. And as if it were timed and planned, a loud knock sounded on the door and before anyone could open it, it swung open and two uniformed patrol women entered carrying boxes and bags of food. From the Bayou.

"A lady parked out front asked us to bring this up here," one of the officers said, K. WILSON, according to her name tag. "She said to ask for Lieutenant Maglione?"

"I'm Lieutenant Maglione. Was she driving a white Audi convertible?"

"Yes, ma'am," the other officer, M.A. STEVENSON, replied.

"Ah, ma'am? Lieutenant? We know who you are, who all of you are, and we just wanted to say that we're very sorry for your loss," Officer Wilson said, as she and Officer Stevenson started to back their way out of the room.

"Thank you," Gianna said, thinking that the two officers probably were only a couple of years younger than Cassie. And then they were surrounded by the HCU team shaking their hands and thanking them for their words of condolence, and

Gianna realized that they hadn't received many of those kind words, not from the rank-and-file officers.

Wilson and Stevenson left, and Gianna opened the Bayou bags and the scents sprung out like a genie from a magic lantern. There were large containers of gumbo and of red beans and rice, and there were shrimp po'boys—big ones—for everyone. Eric handed out bowls and plates and forks and spoons, and the feasting began. They ate every bite of the food Mimi very generously had delivered, and all of them asked Gianna several times to make sure to thank her for them.

"How about I give you her number and you can thank her yourselves?" a tetchy Boss snapped, raising a grin on all their faces.

Tim stood up and compressed his six-foot-four-inch muscle-bound body into what he called his high queen posture to deliver, in high-camp, mincing caricature, "Lieutenant, ma'am, I'd just looove to have that sexy Ms. Patterson's private telephone number."

The laughter started, but before it could really pick up steam Alice deadpanned, in a perfect imitation of Cassie at her driest, "I wouldn't mind having that number myself." And then they all were howling with laughter, Gianna included, though she knew full well that Alice was only half-teasing and that she already had Mimi's telephone number.

"Let's clean up," Gianna said through her laughter, not needing to remind them of the mouse problem they had despite the claim by the maintenance department that there were no more mice. They knew better. "And somebody take these bags down to the dumpster," she added as she sprayed the room with pine-scented freshener to eliminate any mouse temptation.

Mimi had included coffee, tea, and soda and everybody had something to drink when the door flew open without a knock and the Chief blew in. "Sit down, sit down," he said, waving them back down as he began his customary pacing about the room. "I know there's no point in telling you all to go home. I don't feel much like going home, either, but try to stay focused on the positive, and yes, there are positives: We have the murdering scumbags in custody and your Cassie Ali managed to take down two of 'em. Cut short their evildoing ways." He looked at them, met every pair of eyes. "Don't let your hurt and anger steal these positives from you." He turned toward the door, then turned back. "You were right, Maglione. She could have qualified at the range with sight in only one eye. Two shots to the head to both the bastards," he said, and left them as quickly as he'd arrived, having put a huge dent in their sadness.

Another knock at the door and Eric's "come in" overrode Gianna's "what the hell!" She shot Eric a look of thanks when Lt. Andy Page, followed by the members of his Anti-Terror Task Force, entered with armloads of pizza, followed by Detective Jim Dudley with armloads of beer. There was lots of hugging and back-slapping and Gianna felt a real sense of validation: These cops were here to pay homage, not just to another cop, but specifically to Cassandra Ali of the Hate Crimes Unit.

The cops of HCU and ATTF didn't really know each other, nor did their lieutenants, so while this gathering was friendly and spirited, there was a standoffish quality to it as the officers took tentative steps to get to know each other. Gianna did, however, know and like Jim Dudley and their greeting was both genuinely warm and sadly nostalgic. "How're you holding up, my friend?"

"I've got people depending on me, Jim, so I'm keeping it together. But I'd love to be able to go out to the woods and howl at the moon."

He gave her an understanding pat on the back. "I saw the Chief in the hallway, invited him to come back for pizza and beer but, as usual, he's moving at a hundred miles an hour. Makes me want to take up boxing." A mid-weight Golden Gloves boxer in his youth, the Chief regularly sparred with men half his age—and held his own according to those who knew.

"Did he see the beer?"

Dudley nodded. "Yeah he did, though he pretended not to."

"He'd never admit it out loud but Cassie was a favorite of his, too."

"I admired the hell outta that kid. I wish all young cops were like her."

Andy Page approached them in time to hear that last comment. "That's what I keep hearing about her. I sure wish I'd known her." He looked across the room at his own team. "And I wish to hell I had one like her."

Gianna looked toward Andy Page's team, too: eight of them, two women, none appearing as young as Cassie had been and, surprisingly, all appeared to be white. Given the makeup of the D.C. Police Department, it seemed to Gianna that it would be almost impossible to put together an all-white unit—unless, of course, that's what the head of that unit wanted. Gianna gave Page a speculative look, then told him if he wasn't careful all the pizza would be gone before he could get a slice, and he hurried to the table where all the pizza boxes were open. She didn't expect that any of her people would want to eat again after all they'd just eaten, but every one of them had a slice and a beer. She turned back to Jim Dudley. "What do you know about Andy Page?"

He shrugged. "Just what I hear but nothing firsthand. Like you, he's a lot younger than I am."

"You putting me in the same box with Page?"

"Not hardly! You're real police, Maglione. I'm not so sure about Page." He gave her a speculative look. "You notice how homogeneous his team is?"

Gianna laughed out loud, and a couple of her own not-so-homogeneous team stole a glance at her. "You do have a way with words, Detective. Let's go get a beer, why don't we?"

He followed her to the pizza and beer with a final *sotto voce* comment: "I'm surprised the Chief let him get away with that." Gianna was thinking the same thing.

She opened a beer that she didn't really want, but turned down the pizza. She'd be full for a week after the food Mimi had sent. It must be nerves and adrenaline, she thought, that allowed the rest of them to eat. She mingled, introducing herself to the ATTF team, thanking them for their takedown of the killers, accepting what felt like true condolences for Cassie, and confirming their homogeneous nature. Then she noticed two things: that one of the

ATTF women, a very pretty green-eyed brunette, was exchanging surreptitious glances with Alice Long; and that the HUC team were talking among themselves and the ATTF team were talking among themselves. Eric Ashby and Jim Dudley were also talking with each other so she joined Andy Page, separating him from his team. The feeling of undefined unease she had about ATTF was replaced with the strong sense she had about her own team: They were going to be all right once they cleared the hurdle of Cassie's funeral.

CHAPTER THREE

Mimi had begged—literally—not to be assigned to cover Cassie Ali's funeral. Her editors wanted her to stay on the hate-based murders of the Muslim women, but Mimi wanted to be inside the mosque for the funeral service and the imam had banned reporters and cameras. Mimi had known Cassandra Ali. Not well enough to call her a friend but well enough to like her. However, her real reason for wanting to be inside the mosque was because that's where Gianna was, Gianna who was gutted by the murder of her young protégé and in more pain than she was able to express. Of course that wasn't saying much. Gianna didn't express her innermost feelings on a good day without a lot of pulling and prodding, which Mimi had learned how and when to do—and when not to—and now was not the time to talk to Gianna about releasing her feelings about Cassie's murder. She was too focused on being stoic and strong for the other members of the Hate Crimes Unit. She was their boss and had to behave like it. Still, Mimi wanted to be inside the mosque. Wanted Gianna to see her there, and when she did, know what kind of effort Mimi had put forth to be present. A reporter like M. Montgomery Patterson didn't relinquish a big story easily.

Though Mimi understood why the imam didn't want the distraction that reporters and cameras too often were at solemn events, she also wished that the world could see what she was seeing: the level of honor and respect being paid by such a diverse population to a twenty-five-year-old cop who was Black, female, lesbian, Muslim. She knew that the television cameras had recorded the crowd entering the mosque: the casket, borne by three Muslim men on one side and three uniformed D.C. cops on the other—Cassie's comrades in the Hate Crimes Unit—as it exited the hearse and entered the mosque; the two dozen uniformed Washington, D.C., police officers, led by the Chief, two assistant chiefs, two commanders, a captain, and two lieutenants (Gianna being one), sergeants, detectives and rank-and-file officers; the dozen lesbians, Cassie's friends, led by the Phillips sisters, all of their heads covered with shimmering silk scarves; a dozen members of Black Men on Guard, known by citizens, reporters, and cops alike as B-Moggers—young Muslim men who dressed like the Black Panthers of a previous generation and, like them, who saw it as their mission to guard and protect their community. In their minds that meant from white people, an attitude that kept them on the radar of the police department in general, and the HCU in particular. A tenuous truce between cops and Moggers was born when the men came to Officer Ali's aid the time she was attacked and beaten by neo-Nazi skinheads. That truce evaporated when, at the insistence of Cassie's parents, cops were chosen over Moggers to help carry their daughter's casket. Nevertheless, the Moggers showed up in force to pay their respects to a woman they admired and respected despite her choice of profession and sexual preference.

If Mimi were the reporter this day she'd write that the mosque, though not ancient by any stretch of the imagination, was nevertheless stately and beautiful in its Moorish design and appearance, that those within were not traditionally Muslim by any stretch of the imagination but that the intensity of the emotion displayed on their faces transcended religious belief. Though they did not know the words of the Muslim prayers, she'd write, they fully understood the intent.

At the end of the service only the Muslim men carried the casket to the hearse and only the Muslims followed it to the cemetery, as was the wish of the imam. The non-Muslims, who were grateful to have been allowed to participate at all, especially those who were Cassie's colleagues, did not protest. Many of the more traditional and conservative members of the mosque hadn't wanted them there anyway, but Cassie Ali's parents were proud of who their daughter was and what she did and were unwilling to conceal or minimize it, and those who knew her were grateful.

Most of the crowd outside the mosque following the service dispersed quickly: the B-Moggers to the cemetery, everyone else to work. A handful remained to greet friends and colleagues. Mimi hugged Marlene Jefferson, aka Baby Doll, who was almost unrecognizable in a peach-colored ensemble that covered most of her from head to toe. Mimi probably was the only person there who knew that in her former life, Baby had worked the streets of downtown D.C. in so few clothes that a sightless person could have guessed her profession. "You look fabulous, Baby," Mimi whispered.

"I feel stupid," Baby whispered back, "and I ain't never wearing these clothes again!"

"But you wore them today to honor your friend, just like Darlene did," Mimi said, and realized, as she studied the emerald-green ensemble worn by Darlene Phillips, that Dee most likely had purchased both. Her respect for the woman increased a notch.

Baby's face clouded and crumpled. "You really think she was my friend? Why would she be?"

"For the same reason I'm your friend, Marlene Jefferson, and if anybody wants to know, I'm proud to be." And she was, but Marlene—Baby Doll—had a long way to travel to reach self-confidence. At least she was on the road.

Baby grabbed the ends of the silk scarf that was falling from her head and wiped her face as she rushed away from Mimi to join a group of friends, most of whom Mimi had met and interviewed for a series of stories about lesbians known as Doms and Ags, women who in the past were called butches. Mimi waved at them and they waved back. Then she saw Gianna at about the same time Dee Phillips saw her, but Dee got to her before she could get to Gianna.

"Ms. Patterson, I need to speak with you, please. May I make an appointment—"

"You don't need an appointment to speak with me, Ms. Phillips. Tell me when and where you'd like to talk and I'll be there."

Dee seemed to think for a moment. "My office at the club? Ten o'clock tomorrow morning?"

"I'll be there," Mimi said. Then, "that is a gorgeous dress," she said of the dove-gray ensemble the woman wore, and she walked away leaving Dee Phillips not only speechless but a little bit breathless as well.

"You look delicious," Gianna told Mimi in the brief moment they had alone outside the mosque. Gianna was waiting for Eric to pick her up and Mimi was waiting with her; her own car was in the lot.

"You look rather fetching yourself. I'm available to be arrested—"

Gianna was trying to control her laughter, and the effort was contorting her face in several odd ways. "You've really gotta stop reading those British mysteries. Nobody here says 'fetching.' At least not out loud." She finally gave in to the laugh, and her face relaxed and she was beautiful. Mimi told her as much, only to discover that perhaps her woman preferred being fetching. "Beautiful is all right, I suppose, but lots of women get told they're beautiful. Fetching, on the other hand, not so much."

"You have lots of women telling you how beautiful you are?"

"What was Dee looking so serious about?" Gianna asked, artfully changing the subject.

Mimi shrugged. "She wants to talk to me about something. We're meeting tomorrow morning at the Snatch. And she did look serious, now that you mention it. Sounded it, too."

Gianna looked thoughtful. "When she and Darlene brought the food the other morning I had the sense that Dee had something on her mind, that she wanted to talk, but realized that it wasn't the best time."

49

"So maybe she's going to tell me whatever she wanted to tell you?"

The answer was lost in the arrival of Eric Ashby, driving an unmarked cruiser. He got out of the car to open the door for his boss and threw Mimi a friendly wave.

"You're awfully cute in that uniform, Sergeant," she teased him, and he blushed almost as bright red as his hair. "See you later, Lieutenant," she said to Gianna.

"Yes, you will," Gianna said, and they drove off, followed by another unmarked car that held the rest of the Hate Crimes Unit: Detectives Alice Long, Bobby Gilliam and Kenny Chang, and Officers Linda Lopez and Tim McCreedy. They all waved at Mimi. She waved back. All of them heavily and painfully aware of the permanently empty space in the car where Officer Cassandra Ali should have been.

Mimi received a subdued welcome when she returned to the paper. Everyone knew where she'd been, and the newsroom televisions had been tuned to the channels that had carried as much of the day's event as was allowed. A couple of cameras had followed the hearse to the cemetery but were stopped at the gate by a contingent of B-Moggers and D.C. cops, once again working together in aid of a common purpose. Mimi dumped her purse and scarf on her desk and went looking for Tyler. He'd texted her during the funeral service, asking that she find him as soon as she returned. He wasn't at his desk, but signs of his presence were everywhere. He'd return soon and so would she, after a bathroom visit. She headed for the hallway.

"Patterson!"

She turned around to find Tyler standing at his desk, waving her over. He looked as if he hadn't shaved in days or slept in a week. "I thought you were going home last night. If not to sleep, at least to shower and shave. And change clothes," she added, giving him a top-to-bottom appraisal.

"So did I. Then we got the word that Papa Holton and the boys were being arraigned in federal court this morning."

"Ah! Who's on it, Joe?"

Tyler winced, then nodded. "And Ian."

Mimi was about to ask who Ian was when she remembered that was Weasel Boy's name. She made her face go neutral and stood looking at Tyler, hoping he'd say more before she had to speak. He didn't, so she did. "Who's writing the lead story?"

"Shared byline." And Tyler almost smirked when he said the words.

"That's a shitty thing to do to Zemekis. He's a good reporter, and he's done some really good work the last several days. He deserves better."

"Yes he has and yes he does, but it wasn't my call. After today, though—and this is what I wanted to tell you—after today, you and Zemekis belong to me, Ian stays with Wassily."

Mimi wanted to do a happy dance all around the newsroom while shouting, free at last! Instead she just nodded, as if Tyler had told her what time it was or what he'd ordered from the Chinese carry-out, and thanked him. "Does Joe know?" she asked, keeping her face straight and her voice down. She was aware that many pairs of eyes now were on them. "Does the room know?"

"Joe does not know, but some in the room may know. Todd was not quiet in expressing his . . . shall we call it unhappiness?—with Ian's performance over the last few days. When Ian found out you weren't covering the funeral, he wanted it but Todd nixed that. He said—and he said it loud enough for the people in the next block to hear—that he didn't want Ian anywhere near the Muslims. Then he—Ian—wanted the arraignment but Todd nixed that, too. Said it was Joe's story, but Ian could work it with Joe and they're to run it through him."

Now Mimi understood the smirk. Ian still had his job, but Todd had him on a very short, very tight leash. And after today, he'd have no cover. "And here I thought Todd was just counting down until he could check out and collect his pension. Glad I was wrong."

Tyler lost the battle to stifle a yawn and rubbed his badly-in-need-of-a-shave face. "Me, too."

"You've really gotta get home tonight, Tyler."

He nodded and let rip another yawn. "You, too, Patterson. I know you went home in the wee hours of this morning to shower and change—you look terrific, by the way; red suits you—but a small child could get lost in those bags under your eyes."

She punched him in the chest, told him pomegranate was the color of her outfit, and turned toward her desk but he called her back. "Do you have anything going that I should know about?"

She started to tell him no, but then she remembered her meeting tomorrow morning with Dee Phillips. She told him about it, told him that she didn't know what Dee wanted, but also that Dee wasn't the kind of woman to overreact or waste another woman's time.

"OK. After that, you and Joe and me. Noon. Lunch."

She opened her mouth to confirm the appointment, but a huge, face-cracking yawn emerged instead of words. Tyler told her to go home, and she didn't argue. She just hoped she could manage to stay awake until Gianna arrived. She turned to head toward her desk to collect her belongings; then her bladder reminded her that she needed to pee, so she turned back around— and there was the Weasel. Right in her face.

"A word please, Miss Patterson," he snapped nastily at her.

Then Todd came barreling out of his office and snapped even nastier at the Weasel. "I told you I'd handle this, Stu."

"I think I can ask what happened to the story," the Weasel said, displaying more backbone than Mimi would have given him credit for. "That Eastern Shore story—" he began, with a sour look at Mimi, but Todd cut him off hard and fast.

Mimi hadn't known the executive editor in his glory days, which occurred in Chicago when she was in high school, but he had one hell of a reputation. Nobody at this paper had seen it displayed before the last several days, and now they saw—and heard—a lot of it. "You'll do what the fuck I tell you to do!" the Exec bellowed. "I told you I'd deal with Patterson regarding the

Eastern Shore story and I will!" He looked at her and bellowed her name since he apparently was in a bellowing mood, even though she was standing next to him. "Where's the damn Eastern Shore story! What happened to it?"

"Stu spiked it—" Mimi began, and got cut off equally hard and fast.

"I don't give a goddamn what he did! I want to read it!"

"I'll shoot it to you right now," Mimi said, and headed for her desk, working hard to control the grin that wanted to spread out over her face. She woke up her computer, typed in her password, pulled up her story file folder, and sent the Eastern Shore story to the Exec. Then she closed the folder, locked it, and hurried to the toilet, a visit she no longer just wanted but very much needed to make. As she washed her hands, she peered at herself in the mirror and had to admit that Tyler wasn't too wrong about the bags under her eyes.

As she passed Todd's office he called out to her and she stepped in. He peered at his computer screen. "I like this story a lot. I've got a couple of questions and a couple of suggestions but we'll talk about them tomorrow. You look about ready to fall on your face. Really good work the last few days. It's very much appreciated. Now go home."

"Yes, sir. Thank you, sir," she said, and hurried out of his office and to her desk before he changed his mind or before anyone else called her name. Loudly or otherwise. She locked everything and grabbed her bag, hoping that Gianna wouldn't have too long and too tough a day.

The Hate Crimes Unit was in the Think Tank eating turkey and Swiss cheese sandwiches on whole wheat bread with lettuce and tomato, at the insistence of their boss. Wonderful as po' boy sandwiches and pizza were, they didn't rank very high on the "good for you" scale. Chips were allowed, iced tea or lemonade or water were the beverages on offer. Nobody minded. The deli the sandwiches came from was the best in town. Also on the menu: the quarterly crime stats, and hate crimes were up a very uncomfortable—not to mention a very unacceptable—31 percent.

"Most of that increase came against members of the Jewish community and the transgender community, though given that stupid is as stupid does, I fully expect an uptick in crimes against Muslims," Gianna said, and took another bite of her sandwich. "I don't understand the Jewish thing, though, and it bothers the hell out of me." She shook her head and glared at the report as if it were guilty of withholding the reason from her. She looked around the table, startled for an instant to find them all in uniform. "Anybody have any thoughts, ideas?"

"Only that hate crimes have been up everywhere, across the board, since the election," Alice said. "Not to mention around the world."

The scowls and dark mutterings that punctuated this remark spoke volumes about the sad, awful truth of Alice's words. The only good news was that their archenemy on the city council had stopped talking about eliminating them from the budget. Hate crimes were big business again. "As true as that may be, it doesn't help us deal with the problem," Gianna said. "And we've got to be proactive and preventive. I don't want to have to do any more after-the-fact cleaning up. And yes, I know that means we need more bodies. I plan to discuss that with the Chief tomorrow. In the meantime," she said, and began outlining assignments: Tim and Alice to monitor the transgender community, working through Metro GALCO—the Metropolitan Gay and Lesbian Community Center; Bobby to outreach in the Muslim community and to take the opportunity to build on the relationship he'd recently established with the imam of Cassie's mosque; Linda to be a presence in all segments of the Spanish-speaking community, making sure they remembered who the HCU was and what they did; Eric to strengthen ties already existing in the Jewish community; and Kenny to establish HCU creds in the Hindu, Sikh, and Buddhist communities. "Because I don't think we have any," she said.

Kenny looked comically aghast. "Do we even have Hindus and Sikhs? And why Buddhists?! They never bother *anybody!*"

"This is the nation's capital, dude! We've got everybody!!" Bobby said energetically. Then he frowned. "I know where some

Buddhists hang out. But Hindus and Sikhs? Not so much. Sorry, Kenny." Then he looked at Gianna. "Hindus and Sikhs, Boss? Really?"

Gianna never minded when they got loose like this. It broke the tension that came with the work they did, but it also helped them focus more tightly on the work. Right about now, Cassie would have had something caustic or silly to say—she'd have made fun of Bobby or Kenny or both, but especially Bobby. *(Dude! You know where Buddhists hang out?)* Gianna knew they all were thinking and feeling the same absence. "Sikhs and Hindus, really. Listen, folks: As much as we don't like it, we have to think like the perpetrators of hate crimes. *(She heard Cassie: I don't want to think like them, Boss.)* Most of 'em don't know what these different religions believe or how they practice. What they have in common is their dress. They look different. Not like us 'real Americans.'" Gianna said the words and let them sink in. (And heard Cassie again: *Nice to know I finally look like a real American, now that they have somebody else to hate.*)

"Do we have a priority?" Eric asked.

Gianna nodded. "I'd say the transgender community, and if you get any pushback from Metro GALCO, let me know immediately."

"Why would we get any pushback from them?" Alice and Tim asked almost simultaneously, both looking confused.

"Because like a lot of groups that serve a specific population, they don't want anybody else telling them what to do or how to do it. And as far as I know, they don't have any transgender people on staff though they do have a strong outreach effort." Gianna finally tired of the stricture of the uniform and loosened the tie and removed the jacket. Everybody in the room sighed in relief and followed suit. They'd had enough formality for one day, apologies to Cassie. "So talk to Jose Cruz. He runs the hotline and he has a few transgender volunteers. Eric, a couple of rabbis who'll be helpful to you: Annette Koppel and Henry Silver. Kenny: Samuel Hendricks, a professor of comparative religion at the Howard School of Divinity and Bill Kamal, professor of Middle Eastern Studies at GW. They can help with the Hindus, the Sikhs, and the Buddhists, though I know you'd rather rely on Bobby for help with the Buddhists—"

The hoots of laughter that produced once would have caused Bobby Gilliam deep embarrassment—the man did not like being in the spotlight—but now he just smiled and nodded, making Gianna think that perhaps he really did know where the Buddhists hung out. "But if it's all right with you, Bobby, stick with Muslims—unless you have a direct line to the Dalai Lama, in which case the Buddhists are yours! And yes, everybody, I have contact info, so check with me after the meeting."

Eric knew there was no point in wondering how she knew all these people. She was, after all, the Chief's protégé and one of his favorite sayings was, "I know everybody." The rest of the team just looked at her in amazement but nobody was brave enough to ask how she knew professors, rabbis, and hotline operators. Eric wished someone would ask so he could hear her say, "I know everybody." Maybe one day he'd ask . . . just for the heck of it . . . so they all could hear her say it with her face a mask of innocent inscrutability, just like the Chief.

Gianna stood up and began to pace, a sure sign that she was about to unload. "I don't want any of you stepping on any toes. That's my job. And the Chief's. Talk to people, reason with them. I think most of them understand that we're dealing with a new normal. *(Abnormal, Cassie interjected.)* And I think most of them want to do whatever it takes to make certain that we never have a replay of the events of Friday night in this city." She walked to the end of the room and turned her back to them as she struggled to get her emotions under control.

"How in the hell do we stop it, Lieutenant?" Alice was standing now, coldly angry. "Those women were walking to church! Are we supposed to tell people not to walk to church?" Alice was a South Carolina Gullah, and when she was emotional, the accent that she usually controlled was released, making it difficult to understand what she was saying, though her intention was never in doubt.

"Maybe, Alice. In fact, probably," Gianna said, turning back to face them. "Just as Metro GALCO is going to have to hire some transgender staff. Just like we're going to have to find out where transgendered people and Hindus and Sikhs hang out and suggest that they not be so open. Do I like this? I do not! It sucks! But we cannot stop the hate. We cannot stop people from wanting to harm those they hate. Therefore, those likely to be the victims of this stupidity will have to take steps to protect themselves, and they'd have to do this if we had sixty people in this unit instead of six." *Five, Cassie said in her head. Five, Boss.*

"How many extra bodies do you think the Chief is gonna give us?" Eric asked, and Gianna laughed.

"Go home, you guys, and get some rest. I mean it. However you wind down, whatever it takes—steam and a massage, two sets of tennis, a five-mile run, vodka, sex—wind down and get some sleep. It has been a god-awful few days. We will never get over losing Cassie. We will never stop missing her. But we have work to do, and people's lives depend on how well we do it. Take the crime stats report home with you. Anybody having trouble getting to sleep, reading it might help." They were laughing as they stood, and they cleaned up the remnants of their meal without her having to remind them.

"You're going to get some rest, too, right, Boss?" Tim asked.

"I only hope I can stay awake until I get home," Gianna said, and she was only half kidding. Mimi was already there; she'd texted when she left the paper, saying that she would stop at Tender Greens and pick up big salads. "I, for one, won't be reading crime stats until tomorrow morning. Eight-thirty, everybody. Promptly."

Mimi gave really good deep-tissue massages, and Gianna really needed one. Every muscle in her body was knotted and painful, from the top of her head to the soles of her feet. Mimi began by massaging her scalp, and just as Gianna was wondering whether there were muscles in the head, she swore she felt her brain loosen and relax. She was lying on a big beach towel on the bed so that the massage oil wouldn't stain the sheets. Mimi's hands moved smoothly over her skin, thanks to the oil, but their strength as they kneaded the muscles in her shoulders and back was as painful as it was welcome. She would gladly endure the physical pain if it would banish the emotional and mental pain of the last five days.

She groaned and Mimi's hands ceased their work. "I'm sorry. Did I hurt?" she asked, concern heavy in her voice.

"Please don't stop! I haven't been this sore since I fell on the ice while chasing those Irish gun runners. And I hurt pretty much everywhere then, if you recall."

As her knotted muscles relaxed, the accumulated stress and tension of the last five days began to drain away and Gianna began to relax. The pleasure of the moment gradually began to replace the pain brought on by the senseless slaughter of women walking to church. She was safe and secure, surrounded by the familiar: Mimi straddling her, Gianna sandwiched between her knees as she knelt over her, massaging the lightly sweet almond oil into her skin. She gratefully allowed all the ugliness of hatred to drain away and readied herself for the pleasure she knew was coming: Mimi's strong hands would slide off her shoulders and beneath her to caress her breasts before returning to the long muscles of her back with the strength and pressure needed to untangle the knots there. That would be painful, yes, but it was a necessary prelude to the downward movement of those wonderfully strong hands to massage her glutes, the only muscles that were not knotted and painful. Gianna waited for the hands to slide off her butt, down her thighs, to more gently but still intensely massage and caress her clit . . .

"Wake up, Gianna! Wake up, now! You're having a nightmare!" The light was on and Mimi was shaking her awake, rubbing her face and her arms.

"What is it?" Gianna groggily asked. "What's wrong?"

"You were crying out in your sleep."

"Really? What was I saying?"

"You were talking to Cassie," Mimi said. "You kept saying no, Cassie, no Cassie." Mimi held her close, massaging, gently now, her neck and shoulders and back. "Lie back down and go back to sleep. I'll hold you."

Because she'd not fully awakened, drifting back to sleep wasn't difficult, but the thought, the memory she took with her was Cassie's declaration of love as she died. That's what Gianna had been saying "no" to. Because she didn't want Cassie to have had those feelings, and because she couldn't believe that she, Gianna, the Boss, hadn't been aware that Cassie had them. And she should have been.

Mimi's meeting with Dee in her office at the Snatch was quick. What Dee wanted her to see was at the warehouse she'd recently bought, so they left almost immediately, treating Mimi to a first: a ride in a Bentley. She tried to be cool about it, to act as if it were no big deal. She couldn't pull it off. "This is some car, Miss Phillips."

Dee gave a slight smile of thanks, then said, "That Audi convertible is no rattletrap."

It certainly was not! After Mimi's classic Karmann Ghia convertible was stolen and wrecked and she accepted that she'd have to buy a new car, Gianna had pushed her in the direction of the Audi; she'd never have considered it on her own. She had realized why as she stood in the showroom, mouth agape in full-blown sticker shock. "Are you nuts?!" she practically yelled at Gianna, who laughed and told Mimi they'd be sharing the cost of the car since they'd be sharing the car. Driving a police department-issued Ford wasn't Gianna's idea of a driving good time.

Mimi was enjoying the elegance of the Bentley's interior, but she was also keeping one eye on where they were going and was not exactly surprised when Dee turned off a major thoroughfare into an industrial area of low-rise warehouses. But there was nothing run-down or derelict about the area, and there certainly was nothing run-down or derelict about the building they stopped before when Dee made a smooth, tight U-turn.

"We're entering the front of the building," Dee said. "There's also a back entrance with loading docks," she said as she pushed a button on a remote and the metal door of the building rode up smoothly and quietly. Inside, it was a warehouse—cinderblock and concrete, cool and quiet, but clean enough to eat off the floors. A row of stainless steel industrial refrigerators lined one wall, pallets of every kind of soft drink lined another. Mimi followed Dee to the middle of the room and an elevator, which opened immediately when she punched a button. Like the front gate, the elevator door opened and closed smoothly, quietly and quickly, and the box rose one floor the same way.

The back half of the second floor was filled with furniture—office furniture, home furnishings, patio and outdoor furniture—all of it new. The lights that came on automatically when they stepped off the elevator illuminated the entire floor. The front of the space was empty, and floor-to-ceiling windows made it almost too bright. Dee walked over to the wall of windows.

Mimi followed and looked out at another building that shared a parking lot with this building but was not connected to it. "Is that one yours, too?"

Dee shook her head. "That belongs to what I believe is a sex-trafficking operation." Before Mimi could formulate a response, a dark blue panel van pulled into the parking lot. Both driver and passenger got out, and the passenger slid open the side door, reached inside, and pulled out three young women—girls, really. They stumbled, seemingly unable to stand upright. The two men push-pulled them to the door where one of the men pushed a button. The door opened almost immediately. The girls were dragged inside and the door closed.

Mimi still struggled to find words. "That's ... I don't ... I can't ..."

"Men come at night," Dee said. "Lots of men. I stood here in the dark one night. I turned out the lights, and I stood at this window and watched cars of men come and go. Three times one of the men left with a girl, a really young girl. Children, really. I've done some reading and research. I believe they're selling some of the girls and just prostituting the others."

Mimi couldn't talk. She could barely breathe. She was still

looking out of the window, but in her mind she was feeling the impact of Dee's words: A version of the international sex-trafficking problem was playing out not a hundred feet away, and it *was* international because the girls she saw forced into the building across the parking lot were all Asian. "I'm speechless."

"I wanted to tell the lieutenant, but with all that's been going on with her . . . will you tell her about this?" Dee asked. "Please. Somebody has to do something." And there was only one some-body who could do something.

"Chief." Gianna said the word, and he stopped the pacing and the coin jiggling. He'd known her long enough and well enough to register that her tone of voice in that one word meant that she had changed the subject to something much more serious. More serious than hate crimes? To her? He came toward her, but instead of going to sit behind his massive, highly-polished desk he sat beside her in one of the chairs in front of his desk.

"What is it, Maglione?" He listened intently and without interruption as she told him what Mimi had told her. When she stopped talking, he asked, "Is this the Dee Phillips that owns that nightclub in Midtown and every other building in D.C. not owned by the federal government?"

She almost smiled at that. She and her team had met the Phillips sisters, Delores and Darlene, several months earlier when a young woman was murdered while walking to the train station after leaving the Snatch, the women's nightclub they owned. The murder was a hate crime committed by the victim's former brother-in-law who hated her and the fact that she was a lesbian. During the course of the investigation the HCU team had learned that the Phillips sisters and everyone related to them had a business degree and owned property and businesses all over D.C. "She just recently bought this warehouse and witnessed what she believes to be the sex trafficking of young girls from her window overlooking the parking lot of the adjacent warehouse."

"And Patterson is sure about what she saw from that window?" The Chief had known Mimi longer and better than he knew

Gianna, and he knew that she did not make mistakes, and Gianna knew that he knew how scrupulous and meticulous Mimi was about her facts. No alternative facts and fake, pseudo news for her. Still, he had to ask.

She had done the same thing, had asked Mimi if she was certain about what she saw, and Mimi had been still too shocked, too traumatized to get pissed off. "She called all of her contacts and sources in the federal government—at the State Department, at Justice, at the FBI, at the U.S. Attorney's, at the Attorney General's, at U.S. AID—everywhere somebody should be concerned about child sex trafficking in the nation's capital." Gianna stopped talking for a moment as she recalled the horrified sound of Mimi's voice: *Nobody that I knew still worked in any of those offices. I couldn't find anybody who was interested in or cared about the issue. And worse than that, Gianna. In half the offices I called, nobody answered the phone.* She told the Chief all of this and watched the expressions wander across his face and in his eyes: shock, disbelief, horror, disgust, and finally, anger.

He got up and began to pace again, but there was no jiggling of the change in his pockets. "They actually think they can do this kinda thing and get away with it. Like those fools who rode in here and shot up those women! They think they've gotten a free pass!" With every sentence his voice went up a few decibels until he was shouting. His aide opened the door, hand on his weapon, to see if his boss was in danger. He quickly closed it when he saw that his boss was pacing and that Lieutenant Maglione was sitting still as a statue. "They think a great America means they can come here and do what they damn well please. Well, not in my town, and it's been my town for a lot longer than it's been his, and it'll be mine when his large ass and nappy head depart."

Gianna almost smiled again. Large ass and nappy head indeed. She couldn't wait to share that with Mimi. "So . . . we're going to do something, Chief?"

He nodded and began the coin jiggling. "Oh, yes! We're definitely going to do something. I just don't know what or how since we can't count on any help or support from the feds these days. And that may be a good thing in the long run." He said the last sentence almost under his breath and with a definite edge to his tone. Gianna knew all she could do was wait—and hope he included her in his plan.

Meanwhile, a dozen blocks uptown from police headquarters, another boss was having a similar reaction to the news of the sex trafficking of young girls in the heart of the nation's capital.

Tyler looked at Mimi like she was handling snakes and speaking in tongues. He couldn't find words, either. They were looking at each other, speechless, until Tyler finally found his voice. "Child sex trafficking in the middle of the nation's capital, Patterson?! That can't be true! I hope to hell that's not true!" But he knew that if she said it, then it was true, and they looked stunned, shocked, and a little bit scared—not normal expressions for either of them.

"Are you guys all right?" Joe Zemekis asked, looking from one to the other of them. They hadn't seen him approach and hadn't smoothed their facial expressions back to something resembling normal. "We're still assigned to you, right, Tyler? Me and Patterson?" Then he cast a worried frown at Mimi. "You're all right with that, aren't you?"

"I'm fine with it, Joe. In fact, I'm looking forward to it."

"OK," he said warily. "We still doing lunch? I hope so 'cause I'm starving."

Tyler stood up, nodded. "Yeah, but we're seeing Todd first. He wants to make sure we're all on the same page—his words, not mine." And he led the way the few steps to the Exec's office. He saw them approach and waved them in, telling Tyler to leave the door open.

Todd led them to the round conference table and waved them into chairs. Copies of Mimi's Eastern Shore story were laid out like place settings, and their boss got right to the point. He liked how Mimi and Joe complemented each other, how their stories fed and strengthened and informed each other, and he wanted more of it. "Read these stories, Zemekis, and find me an angle that Patterson didn't cover and tell me how you'd do it. By the close of business."

Tyler got up first and headed for the door. Mimi and Joe followed. "Guess we'll do lunch tomorrow," he said, returning to his own desk, leaving the two reporters to cross the newsroom to their desks, stomachs growling with every step. "I don't write well hungry," Joe said, "and I'm starving!"

Mimi grabbed the menu of the Chinese restaurant from the top drawer of her desk and passed it to Joe, who waved it away. Like her, he had his favorites and she called to place their orders. Everybody in the restaurant knew her voice and her order so she ordered Joe's Mongolian Beef, extra spicy, then hung up the phone. It rang immediately. She answered and initially heard nothing, then a muffled sob. She waited for the person, who she was certain was a woman, to collect herself.

"Miss Patterson," the caller finally managed before a heaving sob stopped her words. Then the woman was hyperventilating.

"Miss?" Mimi said. "Ma'am!" she said authoritatively. "Take a deep breath right now and hold it! Right now! Take a deep breath and hold it!" She waited, then said, "Now release the breath and inhale deeply again. Right now! Deep breath in, hold it for a five count, release it. Do it again!" Mimi guided the woman through five deep-breathing exercises with Joe Zemekis standing beside her desk, watching intently.

"I'm OK now. Thank you, and I'm sorry."

"You don't need to apologize . . . what is your name, please?"

"Virginia Barrett. Virgie," she said, and Mimi wrote it so Joe could see.

"Why did you call me, Ms. Barrett? Virgie?"

Virgie Barrett inhaled deeply, held the breath for five seconds, released it. "You probably don't remember her, but you interviewed my sister when you were writing those stories about the Doms and Ags. She said you write about everything, not just gay people. Is that right? Because I'm not gay. Does that matter?"

64

"No, Ms. Barrett, it does not matter. Your sister is correct. I write about everything and everybody. What do you want to tell me?" And for the second time in two days what Mimi heard left her speechless.

Joe had pulled up a chair, taken out his notebook, and was taking notes, writing down things that Mimi repeated out loud, even though she, too, was taking notes. Even though she'd attached a recording device to the phone so she wouldn't forget or omit anything. She was silent for a long moment after Virgie Barrett stopped talking.

"Miss Patterson? Are you still there?"

"I'm still here. We need to meet in person. I can come to your home—"

"No!" Virgie Barrett cut her off quickly and sharply. "You can't go there!"

"All right. Where?"

"The hospital. I saw you there every day when those Muslim women were murdered. I knew it was you because my sister told me what you look like. I work there."

"Today. This afternoon. Tell me where and what time." Mimi had no intention of giving Virginia Barrett time to change her mind about talking to a reporter. She wrote down the time and place, hung up the phone, and locked eyes with Joe Zemekis.

"Holy shit!" he whispered.

"And you didn't even hear the whole thing," Mimi whispered back, disconnecting her recording device from the telephone handset and standing up. "Let's go find Tyler."

"And commandeer an office," Joe said darkly. "We can't let anybody hear any of this until we get it nailed down all nice and neat. Make sure there aren't any alternative facts lurking in there."

Tyler watched them approach his desk and thought for at least the one-millionth time how lucky he was to have them assigned to him rather than that twerp, Ian Williams. Then he read their faces—Mimi's he knew well, Joe's he was just learning—but what he saw caused him to hang up the phone and save and close the document he was reading on the computer screen. Tyler always did at least two things at once. When he focused on a single thing—in this case, Joe and Mimi and whatever they were coming to tell him—everyone who knew him and his work habits knew he was serious indeed.

"We need to talk," Mimi began.

"Behind a door that closes and maybe even locks," Joe added.

Tyler gave him a look and stood up. "The Exec's in meetings at the top. We'll use his office," he said, and led them into the executive editor's office, the one they'd just left, and closed the door. None of them really wanted to know what he was meeting about "at the top," in the publisher's office on the top floor of the building. "What's up?" Tyler asked. "And do I really need to lock the door?"

Mimi took a deep breath and held it briefly, much as she'd instructed Virginia Barrett to do. "I just got a call from a woman—"

"A source?" Tyler asked.

"No, not a source, a stranger," Mimi snapped, "and quit interrupting me, Tyler! I'm trying to keep this thing organized in my brain."

Tyler raised his palms in apology, removed his glasses and polished them on his tie, exposing bright green eyes, the best feature in an otherwise unmemorable face. Other than his brain, which couldn't be seen on visual inspection. "I'm listening. Not a source."

"Right. Virginia Barrett is her name. She's a dietician/nutritionist at University Medical. Her sister told her to call me because I could be trusted. I interviewed the sister during the course of the Doms and Ags stories. Didn't know her before then, have had no contact since. OK?"

Both Tyler and Joe nodded, and Joe made a note to himself to reread the Doms/Ags stories.

"Virgie, as she's called, lives with her children in an apartment complex called Sunset View. There are twelve units in three buildings, all of them two- and three-bedroom units: rare for D.C. as you know, so no surprise that the residents have lived there for a while. The residents are all women and children because, one by one, all the men either have died, been incarcerated, or just left. Virgie's husband and three of the other men were killed in a car crash on the Pennsylvania Turnpike last winter coming back from a Steelers game. More about that later. But here's where it gets— I don't know what to call it—Virgie calls it sick. A group of D.C. cops in the last two months have invaded—Virgie's word again— the complex. Four of them. They come most nights. She says they act like a gang, like they're in charge, like the apartment complex is their clubhouse. Two nights ago, one of them raped one of the women—"

"Stop!" Tyler was on his feet looking at them like they'd just sprouted horns and a tail. "Do you know crazy that sounds? A 'gang' of DC cops have 'invaded' an apartment complex, taken it over, use it as a clubhouse, and sexually assaulted a resident? Is that what you're saying?"

"I said raped," Mimi snapped at him, "and you can take your cute little euphemisms and—"

"I'm sorry! Raped! You're right. But Patterson!"

"I'm just telling you what the woman told me. May I finish, please? And yes, I know exactly how it sounds." And she did. It made her head and stomach hurt and her skin crawl. "There's a lot more but the one other big piece, potentially big piece, is that, according to Virgie Barrett, nobody from the Pennsylvania State Police will talk to any of the women about the crash that killed their husbands, and they—the women—haven't had the time or the money or the energy to pursue it. And their insurance hasn't paid out."

Tyler stood watching, looking from Mimi to Joe, getting back steady, serious looks in return. They believed this story. Believed in it. These were good reporters, two of the best, and they didn't get taken in by snow jobs. If they believed Virgie Barrett, so would he. "How do you proceed?"

"I'm meeting with her at the hospital in a couple of hours. The first thing I want to know is what brought the cops to their doorstep in the first place. Then Joe and I are going to check out the neighborhood and the apartment complex. We'll use the intervening time to check whatever records we can, like who owns the apartments, pays the taxes, whatever is in the public record—"

"And check out that car crash," Joe said. "If it happened on the PA Turnpike and killed four men, there's gotta be a record and a cause."

Mimi was nodding her head. "After I meet with Virgie and get more names of residents, we'll start a records check on them. But based on what she told me, Tyler, these are solid citizens. One of the women is a court stenographer, a couple are schoolteachers, a couple are nurses, and one is a teacher's aide."

"What happened to the men, Patterson? Did she tell you that? In addition to the four who died in the car crash. These women, these solid citizens, they had husbands or partners, right?" Tyler was still trying to wrap his mind around a situation that would permit a gang of men—cops or otherwise—to descend on and take control of a group of women and their children, but his brain was posing the questions of the ace editor who'd once been an ace reporter, questions that demanded answers.

Mimi was looking at her notes. "One was killed in Afghanistan. Another two are still deployed. Three are locked up. A couple of 'em just took off, walked away from their families. And one is in the VA Hospital." Mimi closed her eyes and shook her head. "Virgie called him a stump. She says that's what his wife calls him. She refuses to visit him. He has no arms and no legs. The Army sent him home from Afghanistan with no arms and no legs. And one eye."

Even wearing civilian clothes the Chief looked like a cop. It was the haircut, Gianna decided, though it may have been the fact that his jeans were starched and pressed and that not even a new tee shirt was that white. At least his sneakers and his hoodie were well-worn, probably part of his attire at the boxing gym. Gianna and Eric wore workout clothes that very obviously had seen more than a few workouts. Dee Phillips, as usual impeccably attired, observed them in amused amazement. The fact that the three of them were in her office in the Snatch, a nightclub that catered exclusively to lesbians, was amazing in and of itself. The fact that one of them was the chief of police boggled her mind. She started to tell him how much she appreciated Lieutenant Maglione and Sergeant Ashby but he wouldn't hear it.

"They were doing their jobs, Ms. Phillips," he said with a wave of an upturned palm. "You don't have to thank them or me."

"That's what they keep telling me," Dee said.

"Then listen to 'em," the Chief said, and turned the tables. "It's me who should be thanking you for giving us access to your warehouse."

Dee covered her face with her hands, and when she took them away, tears stood in her dark eyes, along with some heavy anger. "It makes me physically ill to imagine what's happening to those girls, Chief. You can have the damn warehouse if that's what it takes! I'm just so grateful that you care, that you want to do something. And Lieutenant, I'll thank you if I want to and you can't stop me!" She gave Gianna a defiant look and Gianna raised her hands in surrender.

"This is me not stopping you, Ms. Phillips," she said with a laugh.

Dee gave them the keys, the remote door opener and the passwords to the rooftop alarm system. She told them where all the light switches and fuse panels were. And she told them to do whatever they needed to do to set up surveillance on the warehouse adjacent to hers where they now all believed a group of Eastern European men were running a sex-trafficking operation. "Nobody will bother you because nobody will be in that warehouse except you until you tell me it's OK," she said, and she watched, filled with a range of strong emotions, as they drove away in Eric Ashby's SUV. She knew she had the respect of people whom she respected and that meant a lot. And she knew they'd do their damn well best to stop the ugliness happening in the next-door warehouse; but more importantly, they'd save those girls who were being brutalized day and night. But it was the big bunch of unresolved feelings that she didn't know how to manage. Dee knew that she wasn't a traditionally beautiful woman—never had been, never would be—and she'd learned to compensate, first by being smarter than everyone in all of her classes, including graduate school. Then she became rich. As far as she was concerned there was no such thing as enough money, and she used much of it to be exquisitely coiffed, bejeweled, and groomed at all times. She lived well and she drove that Bentley. But all those years of hard study and hard work hadn't left much time for learning social niceties, so what she didn't have in her life, and what she desperately wanted, was what the money couldn't buy: a Gianna Maglione. A Mimi Patterson. Even a Cassandra Ali. Dee knew that she had a bad reputation where women were concerned. She was called "The Pussy Pouncer" inside the Snatch due to her way-too-aggressive pursuit of women she found attractive. That behavior stopped *right now*, she decided. Given what she knew to be happening in the warehouse next to hers, the warehouse her cop friends were en route to at this very moment, Delores Phillips could not, in good conscience, ever disrespect a woman again, not if she lived to be a hundred and added a few more millions to her net worth.

Dee's cop friends were thinking and talking about her, too. She had insisted on telling the Chief how, under a directive of the lieutenant, Sergeant Ashby and Officer Linda Lopez had watched and studied the CCTV of her nightclub in action, seated at the console in her office. "They didn't move a muscle, Chief, neither of them, until they spotted that asshole who'd snuck in pretending to be a woman!" Then she described in equally vivid detail the takedown of the perp that was so quick and quiet and efficient that most of the women in the club didn't know it had happened. Now, as they drove toward Dee's warehouse, the place where she believed young girls were being held as sex slaves, the three of them quietly lost in their thoughts, the Chief spoke what was in his mind, and it wasn't sex trafficking.

"I don't ever tell any of you how much I appreciate what you do, and I should," he said. "I know I told Ms. Phillips that you all were just doing your jobs, and you were, but not many of our citizens would give us the keys to their property as a way of thanking us for doing our jobs. You all went above and beyond and I appreciate it. I'm honored to be your chief."

Gianna and Eric were speechless. The Chief didn't seem to mind, so they rode in silence for the final few minutes of their journey. Eric pushed the remote button as they approached the warehouse, and the door was sliding open when they reached it. They drove in, and as the door slid down behind them, the three cops shared a single thought: putting a stop to the horror transpiring on the other side of the adjacent concrete walls. Eric switched on the lights, and Gianna led them to the elevator. Mimi had described it perfectly. Nobody spoke on the short ride up, and they maintained their self-imposed silence until they were side by side looking out of the window, down to the parking lot where Delores Phillips and Mimi had seen women—girls—being forced into the adjacent warehouse.

"They can see us as easily as we can see them," Eric said.

"We'll have to install cameras on the roof," the Chief said as he turned from the window and headed back to the elevator. He studied the ring of keys Dee had given him, then looked at Gianna. "The elevator goes up one more floor, right?"

She nodded and pressed a button on the panel that proved her right. The door slid open to a space that was shorter, narrower, and not as clean as the two lower floors. Clearly Dee hadn't intended to use this area for storage, and that was fine with the Chief. He could deliver as much equipment as he wanted and needed. Dee already had installed an alarm on the roof. His cameras would be right at home. Then there were the drones, sneaky little buggers . . .

Mimi and Joe had wolfed down their Chinese food in the paper's cafeteria, not talking much but thinking faster than they could speak anyway. They tossed their empty containers in the trash and headed back to the newsroom, stopping in the back hall near the watercooler for a whispered conversation.

"I've got to work on that Eastern Shore piece for Todd or he'll think I'm as useless as your Weasel Boy," Joe said, leaving unsaid his real thoughts.

"Not a chance. And tell you what, so you can lose that long, sad face you're wearing, Zemekis," Mimi said. "I'll go see Virgie Barrett and record her every word, then I'll haul my out-of-shape carcass to the gym. This way we can start on the story together, first thing in the morning."

"You're the best, Patterson!" Joe Zemekis called out as he ran to his desk.

"And don't you forget it," Mimi said with a grin as she ambled more slowly back to her own desk. She had never had a writing partner before—had never wanted nor needed one—but it hadn't taken long for her to adjust to the relationship with Zemekis. If she had to have a writing partner, she couldn't ask for better than Joe. He was an excellent reporter, intuitive and thorough, and he was a fine writer. However, his approach to a story was almost the exact opposite of hers, which was what made them so compatible. The executive editor spotted this after, what, three stories? And all that time she'd wasted being assigned to the Weasel, him trying to force her into a box she never would or could fit into.

Mimi plopped down into her chair, unlocked her desk drawer, and retrieved her Virgie Barrett notes. She was glad he'd be otherwise occupied so she would not have to tell Joe that he couldn't accompany her to this initial interview with Virgie, though she knew he'd understand and agree completely that his presence would be unwelcome, at best. In fact, the only person Mimi would have felt comfortable having with her would be Gianna and, given what Virgie and her neighbors currently were enduring, a cop, no matter how compassionate, understanding and wonderful, would not be welcome.

"Now that you're here, I don't know what to say."

Mimi had looked at Virgie Barrett and seen a woman very close to the breaking point. She'd once been a very attractive woman but a figure that should have been merely slim was gaunt, a face that should have been easing gracefully into middle age was deeply creased by worry wrinkles and frowns. "Why didn't you want me to come to your home?" Mimi asked. The question surprised Virgie as Mimi had intended.

"Nobody knows I've sought help from outside, and I don't want anybody to know!" She'd whispered the words but they sounded like a shout. They had been in her cubicle of an office at the hospital with the door closed and locked. "I don't even know what I expect you to be able to do, Miss Patterson, to tell you the truth, but I always read your stories in the newspaper, and I read those stories you wrote about my sister and her friends, and I thought that if anybody could make sense out of what was happening to us—and make it stop!—it would be you."

Virgie Barrett apparently had more faith in her than she had in herself, Mimi thought, as her feet pounded out the rhythm of her anger and frustration on the treadmill. She was running as fast as she could. Sweat was pouring off her faster than she could mop it up with her towel, which was now too soaked to be of much use. Her face-to-face meeting with Virgie Barrett had accomplished what for Mimi was its primary objective: The woman was truthful and believable. There definitely was a story there, but Mimi wanted more than a story, and she knew Joe and Tyler would want more, too. What was happening to the women and children at the Sunset View apartments was all kinds of wrong and it needed it to get fixed, goddammit! Just like what happened to Cassie Ali and her mother and her friends was wrong. Just like what was happening to the women and girls in the warehouse next to Dee Phillips was wrong. There was more wrong than there were people with the will and the ability to make things right, and it seemed that it was getting worse—not just here in D.C. or in the U.S. but everywhere in the world. The thought exhausted her. She couldn't run another step. She slowed the machine to a trot, then to a walk, and finally turned it off. She had just enough strength and energy left to shower and then lie in the steam room. She saw familiar faces on her way to the locker room and she waved but she didn't stop. She didn't feel like talking to anyone. She prayed that she'd have the steam room to herself and said a prayer of thanksgiving when the first prayer was answered. She envisioned herself sinking deeply into oblivion, and she was almost there when she heard the door open.

"I'm sorry to disturb you, Mimi," she heard Evie say.

Then don't, she wanted to say. "Evie. How are you?" she said instead, but she did not open her eyes or sit up. Rude, she knew, but so was disturbing someone who clearly didn't want to be disturbed.

"I need to talk to you. Please."

Mimi heard the stress in her voice and sat up. "Are you still at the DOJ?" Evie and her best friend, June, were Justice Department lawyers, not a safe space these days for Black women who didn't look and dress like hookers.

Evie gave her a wry grin in which there was no trace of humor. "I'm not dangerous enough to be on anybody's kill list, but thanks for your concern, Mimi." She hesitated, inhaled, then plunged in. "Have you seen Alice?"

Mimi was surprised by the question, but mostly she was annoyed, and didn't mind showing it. "You're the one dating Alice. Why would I have seen her?"

"Because apparently I'm not. Not anymore."

Ah, hell, Mimi thought. "I'm really sorry, Evie, but I can't help you." She stood up, her intention clear. It was time to go.

"Please, Mimi. I just want to know. . . . I haven't seen or talked to her. She won't answer my calls . . ."

"I saw her at Cassie Ali's funeral, not since then." Mimi grabbed her towel and headed for the door. So much for oblivion.

"Will you ask Gianna—"

"I certainly will not!" Mimi snapped. "Gianna does not involve herself in the personal lives of the people who work for her, and I don't involve myself in Gianna's job. I'll see you, Evie."

"Wait, Mimi, please! I need some help here! I don't know how to be lovers with a cop!"

"I can't help you with that, either. There's no how-to manual I know of."

74

"But what do you do when they won't talk to you? What did you do when Gianna wouldn't talk to you? There must have been times when—"

"There still are and I wait until she's ready. That's all I can do. That's all you can do." And that was the truth, Mimi thought to herself: *You wait until she's ready to talk, and pray it'll be sooner rather than later.*

"What if the waiting looks like you don't care? Isn't that worse than not trying to talk?"

Mimi almost felt sorry for the woman. She had a lot to learn about cops. "One thing that cops do better than most is read people. They can tell when you don't care and when you're being considerate."

Evie considered this, but only for a moment. "Would Gianna know if Alice is seeing someone else?"

"I doubt it, but I'm certainly not going to ask her," Mimi said, and left the steam room. She showered and dressed in record time, and all but ran to the parking lot. She didn't want to talk to Evie or any of the others about Alice or any of their lovers. She wanted to talk to her own. Or listen to her. Or just sit in silence with her: whatever she wanted or needed. Gianna hadn't yet talked about Cassie, but she'd had a couple of sweat-drenching nightmares about Cassie's murder. She'd talk when she was ready. Until then, Mimi was happy to just be with her, to share the things they enjoyed sharing—good food and drink, passionate lovemaking, soaking in the Jacuzzi, spirited and opinionated conversation about everything except police-related matters, movies and some of the better cop shows on TV. The being together was what mattered most.

CHAPTER FOUR

"I'm not calling down anything on anybody!" Gianna was pissed at the Chief and she didn't mind letting him know it. She was up and pacing—not something she'd ever done to or with him, and especially not in his own office. The fact that he let her get away with it spoke to how well he understood her frustration.

"You can't make 'em do something they don't want to do, Maglione, even if you are the law."

"I want them to keep safe, Chief! I shouldn't have to *make* them do that!" Metro GALCO was the focus of Gianna's ire. That known-by-everybody organization had been the city's— and the Metropolitan Washington, D.C., area's—lesbian and gay social and cultural hub for more than two decades, since before bisexual and transgender were added to the mix that became LGBT. And the people who ran it had told Gianna in no uncertain terms that they didn't want "armed guards all over the place scaring the shit out of people."

"I take it you explained to them that you weren't advocating armed guards all over the place," the Chief said.

"Of course I did," Gianna snapped at her boss. Then she apologized and sat down and was surprised at how relieved she was to be off her feet. She calmly told him all about her not always polite conversation with the co-executive directors of Metro GALCO . . . not always polite because Gianna could not refute any of their arguments against heightened security, and that made her angry with herself. No, she'd had to admit, heightened security would not have prevented the slaughter of forty-nine people at the Pulse nightclub or the slaughter of five Muslim women walking to evening prayers at their mosque. And who would have thought that a baseball team composed of Republican members of Congress would not be safe on a ball field within eyesight of the Capitol? And the terror attacks around the world—terrorists using trucks and busses to mow down people like bowling pins, shooting people at cafes and theaters—what could have prevented those murders? The honest answer was what pissed Gianna off. It was her job to try, dammit! That's what she was trying in vain to convey to the other people tasked with keeping Metro GALCO safe.

"Why are you so afraid that something ugly is going to happen there, Maglione?"

Gianna closed her eyes and rubbed them. She certainly couldn't tell him it was because Cassie Ali had told her so, but that was why. *You have to keep our people safe! They know where to find us, and they're coming for us!* Instead, she told him a version of the truth: "Tim says there's been an increase in visits by the leather, chaps and chains fellows, and he's noticed them giving what he called hard, ugly, menacing looks to some of the transgender people." *If looks could kill* was what Tim had said.

"But nothing verbal or physical?"

Gianna shook her head. "Just the dirty looks."

The Chief shook his head. "Nothing illegal about giving dirty looks, even if they are directed at a target population of hate crimes. We just have to wait—"

"I know. Until they act on their hate. And speaking of which—"

"And I know what you're going to say, Maglione, and the answer is the pieces are falling into place."

"Two girls have been sold, Chief, and another one dumped in the trash!"

"And Jim Dudley is getting his takedown team in place. By the way, he wants McCreedy—"

"McCreedy's busy!"

The Chief gave her a hard look, then stood up and began to pace, taking his turn. She watched him, her face a mask of carefully controlled non-expression. He knew she was mad as hell. She didn't need to show or tell him that. As if to further irritate her, he jiggled the coins in his pockets as he paced up and down his spacious office, his black patent shoes reflecting the royal blue of the carpet. "I don't have the budget to give you more bodies, Maglione. I wish I did but I don't." He stopped pacing, went to his desk, picked up the report she'd brought, and waved it at her. "This is why I'm making you a Captain, and goddammit, you don't get to tell me no!"

She ignored the promotion talk as she always did. "We know we've got more hate coming our way, Chief—"

"And every patrol sector knows that if they get a 911 from you they're to roll every possible car your way. Immediately! That's the best I can do, Maglione. I'm sorry."

And she knew he was. "We're going to be spread thin trying to cover all the bases, which means that I'll have to be out in the field some of the time."

"I don't want you out in the field, Maglione, as you very well know!" He was pissed off and, unlike her, he didn't try to hide it. "I want you inside, managing and coordinating and organizing and keeping me informed!"

She knew better than to cross him when he'd delivered an order from a place of anger, which was why she was buried up to her tired red eyeballs in matters related to the covert surveillance of the sex-trafficking warehouse. She was also experiencing and learning a lot about things she'd previously only heard about. The sophistication of the surveillance equipment and techniques rivaled anything she'd seen in police thrillers and spy movies. Cameras now captured every movement into and out of the warehouse. The windows had been boarded up and layered with black paint, but infrared imaging could and did detect movement inside, which gave them some idea of how many people were in there, but not an exact count. That's where the drones came in.

Those stealthy little critters with their infrared, heat-seeking camera mounts hovered and circled and recorded practically at will. It was amazing that, despite the fact people knew drones existed, knew that the military and law enforcement used them routinely, nobody looked up.

Gianna had wanted a monitor screen in the Hate Crimes office but the Chief had nixed that. He wanted the operation near his office so he could monitor it and control it. This was his operation in case anyone had any doubts, and it was housed in a space about twice the size of her Hate Crimes Unit, on a back corridor she hadn't known existed. It was one of the many upside/downside effects of being housed in an old but substantially renovated and remodeled building: There was more space, and more interesting space, than anyone, especially a cash-strapped city government, could afford to construct from the ground up. One of the downsides was the possibility of getting lost where one worked every day.

Gianna stood, stretched, and rubbed her eyes. She had watched the previous night's feed and had been repulsed and sickened by the number of men who'd entered the warehouse, and that was just one night! Those poor girls. It would bring them no comfort to know that the police had recorded the license plate numbers of each of the men and that they'd all be arrested and charged with crimes related to pedophilia. But Gianna found that she didn't care about the legalities of the situation. She wanted those girls—those children—out of that warehouse, and she wanted those men punished in ways that had nothing to do with the criminal justice system. She didn't want or need to watch days or weeks of surveillance videos of hate-filled depravity—because it was hatred of women that led men to rape little girls, and she wanted those girls out now!

"I've got an updated stats report for you, Lieutenant."

Gianna hadn't heard the young officer enter. She gratefully swung her mind away from imagining the horror occurring inside the warehouse to focus on the room, and accepted the sheaf of papers extended to her by the officer whose name tag said he was C.A. JENNINGS. But she didn't know why she was receiving them since she'd neither requested nor expected them. "What exactly is all this?" she asked, looking from the papers to him and back to the papers.

"We think we know exactly how many men are connected to the warehouse, and we have a pretty good idea how many women, give or take a few," he said.

"Why not exactly, Officer Jennings, since you know 'exactly' how many men?" *Don't blame the messenger,* some voice of rational wisdom murmured in her brain.

His face changed from the open, friendly look it had worn to a dark scowl. "It looks like a couple of the girls have been sold—"

"How the hell do you know that?" Gianna demanded.

Jennings didn't flinch at the fury of Gianna's demand. He met her gaze honestly if not eagerly. "Do you recall seeing old-looking cars drive into the warehouse? Twice that happened."

Gianna was nodding. She remembered seeing two old-fashioned hatchbacks drive into the wide door of the warehouse—the door like the one on Dee's warehouse—and she remembered wondering why.

"We think that a girl was in the back of the car each time. Drugged for sure and maybe tied up, but that wouldn't be necessary if she was unconscious."

Rage and disgust made speech for Gianna almost impossible. "How did you conclude they were sold?"

"We counted each time a car drove in and when it drove out. We knew it had to mean something."

Gianna nodded wearily as the rage drained away. "That's good police work, Officer Jennings."

"Thank you, ma'am . . . ah . . . I mean Boss," he stammered.

She gave him a quizzical look. Clearly he'd been told that she didn't like being called *ma'am,* but why was he calling her *Boss*? She wasn't his boss. *You are his boss, Boss.* She almost jumped, she heard Cassie so clearly inside her head.

"Ah . . . Lieutenant? There's one more thing." Jennings looked almost frightened and he backed up half a step. Gianna did, too.

Jennings feared the words he was about to speak. Gianna feared them, too, though she didn't know why until he spoke them. "One of the girls died," he said, and before Gianna could react he explained that the garbage collected from the warehouse was delivered directly to a vacant lot adjacent to the police training academy and thoroughly searched.

"They put her in the trash," Gianna said, bile rising up in her throat.

Jennings nodded.

"How old was she?"

"About twelve, maybe, thirteen at the most."

"How many more children have to be sold or, worse, die, before we shut the goddamn thing down?"

Jennings knew she didn't expect an answer from him. He saluted and turned toward the door, then turned back. "I'll be back in a little while to finish the computer installation." Then he left the room, leaving her to fully—and finally—scrutinize the space she'd come to think of as "Trafficking Central." There were five computer stations. Or there would be when they were set up and operational. There were half a dozen desks with computers and telephones, all waiting to be made operational. There were two long tables with chairs on either side, like the ones in the Hate Crimes Unit. Chalkboards covered two walls; display boards and a wall-mounted video screen shared the third. This room was ready to go operational and house a unit, but it was too large a space for something as targeted as Trafficking Central. So what was it?

"I know that look!"

Gianna turned to see Detective Jim Dudley grinning at her. They exchanged a warm hug. She hadn't seen him since Cassie's funeral two weeks ago. "What are you doing here?"

"Why do you look like you're ready to nuke somebody?"

"Because I am. What are you doing here, Jim?"

"I'm assigned to this thing you've got going," he said, then looked totally confused at the puzzlement that crossed her face. "You don't know that the Chief is putting together a unit to bust this child sex-trafficking thing wide open?"

"I'm not surprised, but the Chief is running it himself," she said, but Dudley was shaking his head back and forth. "Sure he is," Gianna started to say, but stopped at the look on Dudley's face. "Give it up, Jim," she said. "Talk to me."

He glanced toward the door, then leaned toward her. "Here's what I know: He sent for me, asked if I thought I'd like working with you. Hell yeah, I told him! I'd work with you anytime, anywhere. So, he told me to report here."

"But you do drugs and gangs, Jim."

"I do takedowns, Maglione. That's my strong suit and that's my job in this operation: When the order is given to take down the sons of bitches selling those little girls, I'll be leading the charge. And just so you know, I'm bringing Tony Watkins with me. I know you remember Tony."

Gianna looked at him in total amazement and could think of nothing to say. Of course she remembered Tony Watkins. He'd been temporarily assigned to her and Hate Crimes, along with Alice Long, when they were investigating the serial murders of prostitutes. It's when she'd first met Baby Doll. God, that felt like a lifetime ago! But what did any of that have to do with now? Then she remembered Officer Jennings reporting to her and calling her Boss. She felt a headache starting. She was saved by the Chief himself. He came barreling into the room at full speed, as always, hands in his pockets jiggling the change. "Glad you could make it, Dudley," he said—as if Jim Dudley or any other cop would disobey an order of the chief of police to report. "You ever hear how Maglione took down that Irish gun dealer in the New York Avenue tunnel? Freezing rain and ice covered the road, making it slick as an ice hockey rink, but Maglione here ran him down, tackled him, cuffed him, head-butted him—"

"He head-butted me, Chief, and I had a headache for a week afterward."

"Those bastards in that warehouse are gonna hurt longer than that! I know you two will see to it," he said, and sailed out as quickly as he'd entered.

"What the hell is going on, Jim?"

"If I had to guess, I'd say the Chief is setting you up to run a unit."

"I already run a unit!" Something was going on that Gianna didn't know about but apparently other people did. "What don't I know, Jim?"

He raised his hands, palms out, and gave an elaborate shrug. "I don't know nothin' about nothin', Maglione, and that's the truth. I heard that he asked a couple of other people about working with you, the same way he asked me—"

"What other people?"

"I don't know. Honest I don't! But can I tell you what I think, what I feel?"

"I wish you would!" she exclaimed.

"When he asked how I felt about working with you? What he meant was working *for* you. You're about to be a big dog, Maglione, and I gotta tell you, you're definitely looking the part!"

Gianna was wearing what she called her cowboy cop wardrobe: black jeans, starched white shirt, black cowboy boots, and a shoulder holster. She'd adopted the quasi-uniform when the Chief moved her Hate Crimes Unit away from the command of the Intelligence Unit and into the Office of the Chief. There were at least three other units that she knew of that operated with virtual autonomy and which answered only to the Chief. They were not the cowboy cops of TV and movies—they weren't renegades or outlaws who broke the laws they were sworn to uphold. On the other hand, Gianna had been known to twist or bend a law or a regulation in service to the greater good. So would Jim Dudley, now that she thought about it. Who else had the Chief asked about working with her? Or for her? She needed more time with Mimi. What, she wondered, would her journalistic mind make of this situation? And as suddenly as they'd manifested, thoughts of Mimi receded into the background as Gianna switched gears and turned her focus, and her body, toward the Hate Crimes Unit and how they were going to manage to be five places at once with only five bodies.

Then her brain switched focus again and her feet followed. She was headed back to the Chief's office before she could talk herself out of it.

Sunset View Apartments were perched at the top of a small hill and Mimi suspected that it could, indeed, enjoy a very nice view of the sunset. It reminded her a bit of the garden apartment complexes that filled block after block, street after street, of her native Los Angeles: three or four two-level buildings built at right angles to each other and surrounding a central courtyard that almost always contained a swimming pool. However, as this wasn't Los Angeles, there was no pool, but there was a courtyard patio that instead of being lush and pretty was brick-and-concrete sterile, though it was neat and clean. Mimi and Joe had made several visits, day and night, to get a complete picture of what they were investigating. They had driven around to the back of the buildings so they knew that's where the garages were, and the trash bins and the storage cupboards. Each unit also had a back door equipped with a security gate and high-wattage spot-lights above each door and above the garages and the other outbuildings. Mimi and Joe gave the owners points both for proper, if not luxurious, maintenance of the property, and for security.

They also had cruised the neighborhood so they'd be totally familiar with the lay of the land. There were two other apartment buildings at the opposite end of the street from Sunset View, both of them four-story elevator buildings, and small to medium-sized houses lined the adjacent streets, all of them neat and well-kept without the trappings of luxury—like Sunset View and the other apartment buildings. They had driven around the neighborhood on several days and watched dozens of people—men and women—head off to work and their children off to school. The whole area screamed normal. This morning, Mimi and Joe had arrived early and staked out a position opposite Sunset View to watch the women and children leave for work and school, and they were not surprised to see that by 8:30, a

84

woman and her children had exited every back door and had gotten into a car and left. Four older children had walked across the parking lot to the street, to the bus stop at the corner; the mothers drove the younger ones to the elementary school three block away.

"So normal," Joe said. "I wonder if any of the people on the adjacent streets have any idea what's going on at Sunset View?"

"I had the same thought," Mimi said. "Wouldn't you think that at least one of the women at Sunset View would be friends with one of the women in one of these other buildings or in one of the houses? After all, their kids go to the same schools. . . . Hey! Look at this kid! What is he doing?" Mimi had the high-powered binoculars glued to her eyes and was watching a boy walk up the hill to the Sunset View apartments, and with the key that was on a lanyard around his neck, open the front door to one of the units.

"Going back home is what he's doing. He waited for his mom to leave and he doubled back," Zemekis replied, his own eyes not missing a single detail of the boy's entrance into his home. "A day of wild fun ahead, I'd guess."

"He's too young to be holding an orgy," Mimi said.

"Kids these days are pretty advanced."

"Come on! He's no more than ten, eleven at the most."

"What unit did he go in?"

"That's . . . oh hell! That's Sonia Alvarez's place. The woman who got raped. What's the kid doing?" Mimi passed the binoculars to Joe. She now was both worried and, inexplicably, frightened.

"Looks like he's going to bed, Patterson. Holy shit! Whadda you want to bet this kid sits up all night guarding his mom? Trying to protect her? And then is too sleepy to stay awake and pay attention in school."

"As if his little boy self could protect his mom against a grown man with a gun." Now Mimi was mad.

"A grown man who's a cop, for fuck's sake!" Zemekis was, too.

"We've gotta shut this thing down, Zemekis!"

"It's gonna take us three, four weeks before we're ready to

publish . . . uhoh. What's that look? What are you thinking, Patterson? We can't write any faster than that, not and do the job properly."

"I know it," she said with a weary sigh.

"So how else do we shut it down?"

"We don't. We tell the Chief and he shuts it down," Mimi answered, and waited for what she knew was coming. It didn't take long.

"Are you crazy!" Zemekis exploded, and it wasn't a question so she didn't attempt an answer. She let him vent and didn't mind. It was justifiable. No self-respecting reporter would give away a block-busting, ass-kicking story about dirty cops to the chief of police! What the hell was she thinking?! Had she lost her mind?! Was her relationship with Gianna clouding her reportorial good judgment?! She let him go on until he ran out of steam, then she read him into her long-term relationship with the Chief, which had begun years ago when she was a brand-new rookie reporter and he was a homicide detective who took pity on her and took her under his wing. She didn't consider themselves friends, exactly, Mimi told him, but they respected and trusted each other without question.

"You trust him not to burn us if you tell him what's going on here?"

"Did you read the stories I did on McConnell and Burgess?" And when Zemekis nodded, she told him that the Chief knew all the details and that he had asked her to hold publication until he could drop the hammer on the bad cops. "I told him I couldn't make that decision and I passed it on to Tyler, who would agree only if he had the Chief's promise that he wouldn't screw us." Mimi smiled at the memory of her mild-mannered editor going head to head and toe to toe with the bombastic Chief.

"And the Chief agreed and kept his promise?" Zemekis asked, still skeptical.

"Joe, he hates dirty cops worse than he hates perps and lowlifes because, as he says, he expects *them* to be who they are. He does not expect cops—his cops—to behave like perps and lowlifes."

Zemekis was quiet, thinking. "Why don't we take this to your Lieutenant Maglione, Patterson? I think I trust her. I know I like her."

She was shaking her head before he finished his question. "Because there's nothing she can do about it, Joe, except kick it up to the Chief." And he knew she was right.

"OK," he finally said. "But I want to go with you when you tell him."

She bristled. "Don't trust me, Zemekis?"

"Don't trust *him*, Patterson. Not yet."

"What do you want now, Maglione?" the Chief growled at her. "If you're back here to harass me about the same stuff you've been harassing me about, namely needing more bodies, I don't want to hear it."

Stung as well as irritated, Gianna retorted, "I'm very sorry you consider me looking for ways to do my job harassment."

"Thin skin doesn't look good on you," he said with a heavy sigh. He was stopped by a knock on the door, which opened immediately. His aide stepped in, closing the door behind himself.

"This had better be worth interrupting me for, Randolph."

"I think it probably is, sir. Ms. Patterson and Mr. Zemekis are here. They asked if you can give them a few minutes."

The Chief looked as surprised as Gianna did. "The look on your face says you don't know what this is all about, Maglione?" He made it a question.

"I have no idea."

"Then you'd better let 'em in, Randolph," the Chief said, and the door swung wide open to admit Mimi, followed by Joe Zemekis. They stopped short when they saw Gianna.

"Come on in. The more the merrier," the Chief said, sounding anything but merry. He returned to his desk and sat down. "This can't be anything I really want to hear." He looked from Mimi to Joe. "Especially if it takes two of you to tell it." Then he gave Joe a hard look. "Unless of course you don't trust me enough to let Patterson come by herself," and he laughed at the look on

Joe's face. He waved his hand at Mimi. "Start talking, Patterson."

So she did, and when she finished talking the room was quiet for several long seconds. Then the Chief erupted, treating them to one of his profane tirades, the kind in which he cussed loud and long for several minutes, never repeating himself. It was a rare performance, and those who had witnessed it before—in this case everyone but Zemekis—were always amazed. Zemekis was flabbergasted. "How much time do I have before this ends up in that piece of shit newspaper you work for?"

"Two weeks, three at the most," Mimi said, "and it's not a piece of shit."

"Is Carson on board with this?" the Chief asked.

"He will be," Mimi said, "when we tell him whatever it is you're going to tell us since we've put our reputations on the line and told you everything."

The Chief paced in circles for a moment, jiggling the change in his pockets. "Are you certain that one of my cops raped a woman in her own home?"

"Yes, sir," Mimi and Joe said in unison.

"That son of a bitch!" the Chief spat out. "What's his name? And what are the names of the others? And where do they work? East Side Command?"

They told him, and he looked from Randolph to Gianna. "Either of you know these characters?" And when they both shook their heads, he barked an order to his aide that would have the personnel folders of the three cops on his desk before the end of the day. "You two get outta my office," he said to Mimi and Joe, waving them away.

Mimi and Gianna shared a tiny smile before the two reporters exited. Then Gianna's boss gave her a look that she'd come to know all too well. It meant that she wouldn't like what he was about to say. And she didn't. He opened the top drawer of his desk and withdrew a stack of what Gianna knew were personnel folders. He gave them to her. "All of these are at your disposal to use as you see fit, whenever you see fit. I wanted to wait until all the pieces were in place before talking to you about this,

Maglione, but there's no time. So here it is: I'm creating a new unit and you're running it. I don't know yet what it's going to be called but it's an all-purpose thing. Hate Crimes will be part of it. Taking down this sex-trafficking thing will be part of it. Whatever the hell it is that Patterson and Zemekis just dumped all over us will be part of it. You'll have a lot of different kinds of cops answering to you. Some of them you'll choose yourself, some of them—like Jim Dudley—I'll assign to you. You'll operate out of that space down the hall."

Gianna's head was spinning. She couldn't think of anything to say but that didn't matter because the Chief wasn't done talking yet. "Put Alice Long and Linda Lopez undercover at that Sunset View place. Make them relatives of two of the women—the one who called Patterson and the one was raped. I don't want that woman and her child alone for another night."

"Chief." Gianna finally found her voice.

"I know you feel ambushed, Maglione, and I'm sorry, I really am. I wanted to discuss this with you in a more organized way, but so much is happening so fast. You haven't even had time to grieve for young Cassie Ali and I know how much she meant to you."

"They're all important to me, Chief."

"And they deserve better than to hear about such a major change through the grapevine. You're right. Let's go tell 'em." And she followed him out of his office, juggling the armload of personnel folders of the people who soon would be calling her *Boss*.

"I'm not happy about this, Patterson," Zemekis said in the taxi heading to the records department where they'd spend the next several hours researching and copying the documents on all the people and places they'd need to factually support their stories.

"I know, Joe; I'm not thrilled about it, either. But how much of this story is about dirty cops, and how much is about how easy it is for some of our most vulnerable citizens to become prey?"

"Yeah. Especially when the predators are dirty cops," Joe snarled.

"He's not gonna screw us, Joe. Really, he's not."

Zemekis rode in silence and Mimi didn't interrupt it. He had a right to be skeptical. After all, he didn't know her very well and didn't know the Chief at all. She'd be skeptical, too, if placed in the same situation. Besides, the silence allowed her to focus on Gianna. She hadn't looked at all happy seated in the Chief's office like a recalcitrant kid in the principal's office. But there had been that little smile, which she couldn't have managed if she'd been really miserable. Still, Mimi needed to find out, needed to make sure that Gianna was OK, and she didn't want to risk making Zemekis more uneasy than he already was by going off to see Gianna without him.

They were exiting the taxi before Zemekis spoke again. "I know the lieutenant will speak more freely to you without me being present," he said. "Will you ask her what the Chief said when we left? And by the way, did he have to order us out of his office like that? He threw us out like last week's stinking garbage! And it's not a piece of shit!"

Mimi couldn't help but laugh. "I know you've worked in a few major cities in this country and around the world. In how many of them could you have showed up at the office of the Chief of Police and gotten in the door?"

"Well . . . none," he responded grudgingly. "So, you'll call the lieutenant?"

Mimi nodded as she said a silent prayer of thanks. "As soon as we finish in records." It was a task not nearly as grueling and time-consuming as they had imagined. Sunset View apartments had been owned by the same Maryland family for twenty years, during which time they'd paid the taxes in full and usually on time, and had maintained the property in sufficiently good repair so as not to have netted warnings and fines from the housing inspectors too often.

"They should all be so easy!" Joe said.

"No shit, Sherlock!" Mimi responded, remembering too late that it was a favorite expression of Cassie Ali's, then deciding that Cassie wouldn't mind.

The check of the Sunset View residents was equally uneventful. The people were exactly who they appeared to be: hardworking, law-abiding, regular-voting, tax-paying citizens. There were records for the men who had abandoned their families and the ones who were incarcerated, as well as for the ones with records of military service, past and present. "Not a wrong note anywhere," Joe said, sounding both relieved and satisfied.

"Committing a crime is a wrong note, Zemekis."

"Yeah, yeah, I know. What I meant was that they were adjudicated, and even the ones who are out and didn't return to their families, they check in with their parole officers."

"Hmmmm," Mimi murmured. She hadn't really been listening to him and she had only challenged him to let him know that he couldn't get away with making such an inane remark.

"What?" Joe said as relief and satisfaction evaporated.

"What's the woman's name who Virgie said first called in the cops? She was having trouble with her sons and wanted a male influence."

Joe paged through his notebook. "Tompkins, Alfreda."

"Here she is," Mimi said paging through the files they'd just copied. "Married to Tompkins, William Robert. He did a dime at the federal pen down in Virginia for a bank robbery in which he held a teller hostage. They got no money, and he and his partner were apprehended in the parking lot before they could even get in the car, empty money bag in hand."

"So, smart isn't the dude's strong suit," Joe said. "Is he out?"

Mimi nodded. "Out and in the wind. Hasn't been seen or heard from since his release. Is that what you'd call a wrong note?"

Ignoring the comment, Joe said, "Virgie said the sons were exhibiting daddy-like behavior, which is why Mrs. Tompkins called in the cops. She needed help handling the boys. Any woman would, I suppose," Joe said, "if there were no other male figures around."

"Did you see any boys leave the Tompkins apartment this morning," Mimi asked, "either before or after Alfreda left?"

"Well, hell and damn," Joe said. "No I did not. And either she left them at home when she went to work or they don't still live there."

"Those boys aren't old enough to be out on their own," Mimi said. "They're fourteen, fifteen at most."

"So where are they?"

"That goes on the list of follow-up questions for Virgie."

"Maybe that could also go on the list of questions for the lieutenant? Just in case they're in the system?" Joe asked with a sly grin.

"Maybe we should call Virgie right now and ask her," Mimi snapped, no grin in place, sly or otherwise. A feeling burning a hole in her gut told her there was nothing to grin about.

The members of the Hate Crimes Unit looked from their Chief to their Boss, reading their facial expressions. The Boss wore the totally blank look that meant she was controlling her feelings and emotions, letting nothing show. The Chief was pacing, jiggling the change in his pockets, and talking a mile a minute. The team heard everything he said. The look on the Boss's face told them they should listen, too, to what he didn't say. "Your Boss isn't happy with me right now. In fact, she's royally pissed off at me, and she has good reason. But here's the bottom line: She's gonna do her job and she's gonna give it 110 per cent, just like she always does. Some of you aren't gonna like some of what's coming down the pike but, like your Boss, you're gonna do your job and you're gonna give it 110 per cent, just like you always do." And he turned and walked out.

"What aren't we gonna like?" asked Sgt. Eric Ashby, the lieutenant's second in command and the only one who could ask the question and get an answer.

Gianna looked at them and her facial expression relaxed into an almost smile. "I'm really sorry for this, you guys—for such a major change and for the way it was sprung on you."

"When did you find out?" Eric asked, again a question they all wanted the answer to.

"About an hour ago," Gianna said, and gave them the time and space to express their emotions before quieting them. "The part you're not going to like is that some of you will be detailed to the other operations the new unit will be running—"

It took Eric several minutes to quiet the outburst and restore calm and quiet, and Gianna made it clear that she needed and expected their attention and cooperation. Then she told them what was in store. "You're all aware of the sex-trafficking operation in the warehouse on Broad Street. Well, it's on a short leash. A takedown is being planned. Jim Dudley's leading the takedown crew and he's asked to have McCreedy on his team." She gave Tim a nod and watched the emotions travel across his far too handsome face: surprise, concern, and finally pride.

Then she filled them in on the Sunset View situation. "Montgomery Patterson brought this one in the door, and she dropped it in the Chief's lap because of the police presence—"

Bobby Gilliam cut in, all traces of Buddhist peacefulness gone. "Are we supposed to believe that a cop—one of ours—raped a woman in her own home?!"

"That's what it looks like, Bobby, and that's why we're putting Linda and Alice in there, Linda as the cousin of the woman who was raped, Alice as a close friend of the woman who called Ms. Patterson."

"So, are we in there to protect the women, or to rat out the cops?" Alice asked, sounding almost as mean and nasty as Bobby had.

"Job one is to protect the women, but if see you any evidence of illegal behavior by any police officer, you are to contact me immediately. Is that clear?" Gianna looked from Alice to Linda, holding their eyes until she got a "Yes, Boss" from each of them. Then she turned back to Bobby. "I want you backing up Alice and Linda. I don't know exactly how yet, but I do know that whatever is happening at Sunset View has the hair on the back of my neck standing up, and I won't have my people in there looking left and the bear runs in from the right."

"You want me to tackle the bear when he runs in and put

93

him in a choke hold, Boss?" Bobby asked innocently, and the room broke up.

Gianna was still chuckling when she turned to Kenny Chang, their computer whiz. "Everything you can find on that place and the people who live there, Kenny, please."

"Yes, Boss," he said, fingers already dancing across his ever-present and ever-ready keyboard.

She picked up the stack of personnel folders and gave them to Eric. "These belong to us. Sort through and assess. Short term, we need to replace Tim and Alice at Metro GALCO. Long term, we need to evaluate strong suits. And write down the names, Eric, please. Everybody take a look, see if you know any of 'em. And Kenny. There's a computer specialist, tech specialist, IT guy, whatever, in our new unit. Name of Jennings. I want to know if he's as good as you. I already know the equipment is better than ours, but I want you to do your Kenny Chang whatever it is you do!"

"The Kenny Chang thang!" Bobby said, and everybody joined in, making it a chant. Kenny beamed and took a seated bow, his fingers never leaving the keyboard, his eyes never leaving the screen.

"And you all might as well go check out our new digs. I'm going to go call Ms. Patterson and get a plan for getting Alice and Linda in place," she said, and headed for the door.

"Where exactly is the new unit, Boss?" Eric asked, and Gianna stopped walking mid-stride. She wasn't certain enough of its location to direct them to it. She'd have to lead them there. If she could remember where it was, which, thankfully, she did. She left them there and went to call Mimi, who agreed almost too quickly to meet her.

"I'm on my way," Mimi said. They met in the hallway outside Gianna's office, and the sight of each other eased almost all the stress they'd both been carrying. The kiss they shared once inside the office behind the locked door erased the remainder. They stood silently holding each other for a long moment, both reluctant to abandon the peace and contentment they found in each other, both knowing this stolen moment was as good as it was likely to get until very much later that night—and that was if they were lucky. Gianna unlocked the door and went to sit behind her desk, while Mimi sprawled on the couch where Gianna had spent more than a few nights while in the middle of a big case.

"About this Sunset View mess you dropped in our laps," Gianna began.

"It may be a bigger mess than we first thought," Mimi said, interrupting her.

"What could possibly be a bigger mess than cops taking over a woman's home and raping her?"

"The two sons of another woman who haven't been seen in days, not since another of the cops moved in with her."

Gianna looked at her like she'd grown an ear in the middle of her face where her nose should be. "Say what?"

And Mimi explained how Alfreda Tompkins had initiated the contact with the police because she was having problems with her sons, whose behavior was changing from boys-will-be-boys antics to quasi-criminality. "Two officers came initially, Virgie said, and they just kept coming, every day, one hanging out at Alfreda's to help with her sons—"

"Wait a minute," Gianna interrupted. "Who said he was helping with her sons? What did he do to help them? Did anyone see him helping them?"

"Virgie said Alfreda told her that Dexter—that's the cop's name, Dexter Davis—could have arrested the boys for vandalism but didn't because he wanted to help them."

Gianna's face morphed into what Mimi called "Lieutenant Mode." "All right. Then what?"

"Then he became a fixture at Alfreda's, and Virgie said nobody has seen the boys. At the same time, Phil moved in on Sonia. Those were her words, how she described it: that he moved in on her, he chose her because she was Latina and he was Latino—"

"Didn't they complain?" Gianna asked. "Didn't they call the station house and complain?"

Mimi nodded. "That's when the sergeant came and *he* moved in on a couple of the women. He didn't stay with anyone the way Dexter and Phil did. Seems he liked to rotate."

Gianna picked up the tape dispenser and threw it across the room. It bounced off the wall, leaving a deep gash. The roll of tape flew off, hit the file cabinet, and rolled under the chair. She got up to pace but there wasn't enough room so she sat back down. Mimi watched her closely. There was more on Gianna's mind than whatever was happening at Sunset View, but Mimi could only wait to find out what that was. And thankfully Gianna didn't make her wait too long. When she heard what it was, Mimi almost wished Gianna hadn't been so forthcoming so soon. This job already was taking its toll. She could see, could feel, Gianna being pulled in at least two different directions—toward her natural inclination to help women and children at risk, and toward her desire to want all cops to be righteous, and to despise those who weren't and who abused their authority. Then there was a third pull, the one that made the lieutenant in her feel responsible for all the outcomes. Mimi wasn't liking this at all.

"Will you be all right, love?"

"I have no choice in the matter, though I may need a new definition of 'all right.' Work on that for me, will you please?"

"Anything for you, as you know. But . . . I need a couple of favors, too?"

"Of course you do," Gianna said with a grin, and spread her hands.

"Will you see if Alfreda Tompkins' boys are in the system, either as adults or juveniles?"

Gianna nodded. "And Mimi, will you set up a meeting with Virgie and Sonia?"

"Ah, sure," Mimi said. "When?"

"Within the next couple of hours," Gianna said, "so they can meet their new relatives and/or best friends, Alice Long and Linda Lopez, who'll be moving in with them."

Mimi was startled. "Moving in when?"

"This evening," Gianna said, giving her a quick kiss and rushing

96

off to put the finishing touches on her plans for the rest of the day.

They were meeting in the Hate Crimes Unit office until they were told they couldn't, which Gianna expected would be sooner rather than later. Office space was at a premium and she and her new team were expected to use their new, larger space. But for the time being, she, Eric and the new sergeant, Thomasina Bell, had to review the personnel files of the new team members. There were twelve of them, thirteen including Sergeant Bell, who, Eric had told her, was first rate. "You'll like her, Boss. And she's called Tommi."

"Do you know any of these people, Tommi?" Gianna asked as she paged through the files.

Tommi shook her head. "I don't, Lieutenant. I think whoever picked these people wanted to be certain there were no connections, no ties."

Gianna frowned, thinking of Jim Dudley and Tony Watkins, both of whom she knew and had worked with. And she had her original team, which she saw as the core of the new unit. And, she thought, perhaps that was the Chief's point; after all, she was certain that he had hand-picked the new unit, as certain as she was that he wanted her to expand her reach. This was his way of making sure she did. She studied Tommi Bell. Like Eric, she was a few years older than the rest. She might even have a couple of years on Eric. And like him, she exuded efficiency and confidence. Eric had told her that Tommi was a personnel and HR specialist, which Gianna was grateful for since the number of people who answered to her had tripled, literally overnight. "Tell me, Tommi, please, what I need to know about these new people," Gianna said with a smile.

"Shall I begin with myself, Loo?" she asked.

Gianna shook her head. "Eric already told me he's keeping you, so the others."

Tommi smiled and blushed, something Gianna wouldn't have thought possible for a dark-skinned Black woman—and she'd have been mistaken. Sgt. Tommi was back to businesslike in a nanosecond: The other twelve team members were six women and six men, with a detective each. Four of them were gay. "Do you want me to tell you which ones?"

Gianna shook her head. "I don't need to know. At least not right now. But tell Eric and he'll tell me when I need to know."

"OK. We've got three Black, three white, three Spanish-speaking—"

Gianna interrupted. "What's that mean? They're Latino, right?"

Tommi was shaking her head. "They may share a language but they're as culturally different as . . . well, as people from Puerto Rico, Cuba, and Mexico are different. But D.C. natives, all of them."

Now Gianna was frowning. "I thought the largest Spanish-speaking population in D.C. was Salvadoran," she said. Tommi was nodding in agreement. "So why isn't one of these new people Salvadoran?"

The new sergeant gave her a steady look. "I take it you know who put this group together? That would be a question for him."

One I sure as hell will be asking, Gianna thought as she signaled for Tommi to continue with the details of the new Unit: Three were ex-military, and the group as a whole had experience in white-collar crime, vice, gangs and drugs. There was even one from harbor patrol. "And, last but not least, there's our resident techie," she finished with a smile.

"Officer Jennings. Yes, I met him yesterday," Gianna said. "Good, is he?"

"Among the best," Tommi said.

"Then he and Kenny should get along splendidly," Gianna said. "Or not."

"I saw them early this morning," Eric said, "and they looked quite happy."

"And several of them are social media experts, fluent in all the platforms including YouTube and Instagram and . . . and whatever else there is."

"Oh, lord, yes!" Gianna exclaimed with an almost comical

expression. "I don't ever want a repeat of the mistakes I made around the Snatch and the Pink Panther! Eric, make sure—"

"I'm on it, Boss, and I'll fill Tommi in."

Gianna stood up. "Thank you, Tommi, and welcome aboard. I'm looking forward to working with you." She was headed for the door when she stopped, frowned. "You stopped at nine. Who are the other three?"

Tommi laughed out loud. "You're even better than they say, Loo. Middle-Eastern heritage, one of them a Muslim. Pakistan, India, and Israel."

"Then let's go meet 'em."

"Hello, everybody, and welcome to whatever it is we are. A friend suggested we call ourselves the Swoop Unit, since that's kind of what we'll be doing—swooping in to correct or repair or whatever else is necessary to make right a wrong. Sounds simple, I know, but it will be anything but. You know what we're already working on so you know there's nothing simple about any of it. It may also not be to everyone's liking because we may sometimes be standing with our toes on the line, or even over the line, outside the letter of the law. When we take down the doors of that sex-trafficking warehouse, our focus—my focus—will be on putting a stop to the sale and systematic rape of twelve- and thirteen-year-old girls."

"What happens when people—the public—complain that maybe we violated the rights of the people who own the warehouse when we take down their doors?" one of her new team members asked.

The public can screw themselves, Cassie said before she could respond, and Gianna offered a grim grin to recover her equilibrium. "We make certain the public knows the average age of the girls being sold for sex in the warehouse. We make certain the public knows how many times a day the girls are raped. We make certain the public knows the girls are systematically drugged and, if this place operates like others in the rest of the world, they're rarely fed and barely clothed. We make certain the public knows that most of the girls are smuggled into this country illegally, and that the men who buy and sell them more often than not are here illegally as well."

"So you're saying the ends justify the means?" the young officer asked.

Damn straight! Cassie said. Gianna said, "There was a time when I'd have said absolutely not!"

"So what changed?" He followed up his question like a reporter at a press conference.

"The world, and me with it," Gianna replied as she looked down at the piece of paper Tommi Bell had slid before her. *Ofc. Randall Connally. He came from Harbor Patrol.* "I knew that what's happening inside that Broad Street warehouse happened in the rest of the world, but it didn't happen here. Not on my watch. Now it does, and that's not all right with me. Just like what's happening at the Sunset View apartments is not all right with me." She waited for them to shift gears and to grasp what they were being told: The next takedown by the Swoop Unit would be dirty cops.

"How certain are we about the facts at Sunset View?" Sergeant Bell asked, and Gianna knew what she really was asking: *Are those cops really dirty?* Gianna also knew why her new sergeant asked the question: because her new team members weren't yet comfortable enough to ask their Boss the tough questions, but they really wanted to know.

"Ninety-five percent certain, but we'll be 100 percent certain before we move." She stopped and looked around the room, meeting as many pairs of eyes as would meet hers. "Let me say this right now: I realize that a unit like this isn't for everyone, and anyone who's not comfortable can go, no questions asked, no recriminations. You walk away clean, as if you were never assigned here. But if you remain, you'll do the job that's asked of you, and you'll give it everything you've got, every time. Am I clear?" There was no sound in the room. "Am I clear?" Gianna said again, and there was no mistaking the fact that she expected an answer.

A chorus of, yes, ma'ams and yes, Bosses rang out through

the room. "Anybody who's leaving, see one of your sergeants in private. You know who they are: Sgt. Eric Ashby and Sgt. Thomasina Bell, and they're always available to you—to any and all of you for any reason."

"Can I ask one more question, Loo?" This from the one who asked about the rights of the warehouse owners.

"Of course you may, Officer Connally," and she had to work hard to keep a straight face at his reaction to her knowledge of his name. It took him a moment to get himself together, and when he did, he asked, "How is what we're doing at Sunset View different from what IAD does?"

The question truly surprised her but she tried not to show it. "The job of Internal Affairs is to investigate police misconduct. That is not our job. We're not investigating the cops there."

"Then why are we going in there?"

"So that the people who live there, and the people who know them, work with them, and are related to them, aren't left with the impression that calling the cops is a mistake. Yes, we'll remove the dirty cops, but we'll also make sure people see that it's cops who're making it right. I'd really like to see people take cops off the list of people they hate." Gianna stopped for a moment and looked around the room, making it a point to meet the eyes of her erstwhile team. "I may no longer be running the Hate Crimes Unit—there no longer is a Hate Crimes Unit—but I did not stop caring about or worrying about what hatred does to us when my job title changed."

"Boss?"

"Yes, Tim?"

"Are you saying we'll still be able to deal with the assholes who hurt the people they hate?"

"As long as I have breath and a badge, Tim."

Way to go, Boss! Cassie said in Gianna's brain as Tim stood up and broke his six-foot-four-inch weightlifter's body into the queenly stance he used to confuse and confound the unsuspecting—in this case, practically everyone in the room. "That's a real relief, your High Bossness," he crooned. Jim Dudley broke the shocked spell with a loud guffaw, followed by a dash across the room to envelop Tim in a bear hug.

"I've heard about this performance, but it's my first in-person sighting! Believe me, seeing it is so much better than just hearing about it!" he enthused.

"Well thank you, Detective Dudley, sir. Now, if it's all the same to you, let's go get those baby-raping assholes in that warehouse!" Tim growled, looking every bit like the hulking weightlifter and nothing like the mincing queen. Gianna still marveled at the transformation, and she'd been watching it for years. And hearing about the price paid by the macho types foolish enough to disparage Tim's sexuality.

"You lead, McCreedy, and I'll proudly and happily follow!" Jim Dudley said, and Gianna knew he meant it.

"Well, before you two go charging off, I need to meet with you, Jim, and Eric and Tommi, to formulate and plan and assign staffing. My office, fifteen minutes." She surveyed the room again. "A number of you will be assigned to Metro GALCO—Tommi and Eric will make those assignments—and Tim will debrief. He thinks there's a possible threat and I trust his instincts."

Eric, Tommi and Jim Dudley followed her to her office—how much longer will this be my office? she wondered—and closed the door, each of them taking a seat and giving her their complete attention. "Let's get this thing operational, Jim. I don't want another girl to die on our watch."

"On your 'go,' Boss."

"Get necessary medical personnel and any law enforcement support you think you'll need, and use the Phillips warehouse as your staging location. How do you plan to take the door?"

"Gonna blow it, Boss," Dudley said, and hastened to explain at the look on her face. "It's a steel door, and they've got better and tighter security than any bank. We can't knock and announce. We gotta take 'em by surprise."

"Will any of the girls be collateral damage?"

"Negative," Dudley said, shaking his head. "They're too far away from the front door to be harmed."

Gianna stood up. "Give me a written report of your needs and your plan before you leave tonight."

"How late will you be here?" Dudley asked, and he blinked when Gianna laughed—all the answer he needed. He got up and left, and she turned her attention to Tommi and Eric.

"Do we have enough people to do what we need to do?"

"Depends on how many bodies Dudley needs," Tommi said.

"He's talking about blowing doors and staging a major assault," Gianna said. "I'll get the appropriate bodies from the Chief. And Eric, I don't want Tim hurt even though he and Jim think he's some version of the Incredible Hulk."

Eric nodded, then shared a look with Tommi. "We can cover the other stuff as long as no major shit hits the fan."

"From your lips to God's ears," Gianna said.

CHAPTER FIVE

Virgie Barrett had told Mimi more than once that Alfreda
Tompkins probably wouldn't talk to her but now that Mimi
knew for certain, thanks to Gianna, that the Tompkins boys were
not guests of the juvenile justice system, the burning question
was: Where were they? She absolutely had to ask Alfreda and
hear her answer. Virgie was certain that Alfreda didn't know, and
she was deeply suspicious that the cop they knew as DD almost
certainly *did* know where the boys were, and for Mimi the
"where" was less crucial than the "why." Was a dirty D.C. cop
named DD doing to little boys what some Eastern European
shitheads were doing to little girls in a Broad Street warehouse?
And did the boys' mother have the answers? Mimi had to
confront Alfreda Tompkins, but not at home. At work, where
perhaps she'd be a little less fearful and a bit more forthcoming.

"I have to think she'll talk to you," Joe said, "even if she's afraid.
She has to want to know what's happening to her boys! She has
to be more fearful for them than she is for herself, don't you
think?"

"I don't know what to think, Joe, and that's part of the problem
I'm having. If we follow the 'mothers will do any- and everything
for their children' script, then yes," Mimi said.

"Everything we've seen and heard from and about these
women follows that script, Mimi. You do agree, right? Or don't
you?"

"I would if any of this made any sense, but it doesn't. These women did the right thing when faced with trouble: They called the cops. Where do you turn when it's a cop who scares you?"

Joe didn't have an answer and Mimi didn't expect one; she didn't have one, either. Normally, a group of tight-knit women would lean on each other, but each of them had endured such emotional devastation, none of them had the strength to help shoulder another's burden. She'd just have to hope that Alfreda Tompkins was close enough to the breaking point that Mimi's offer of help would be received, even if not with open arms. Alfreda had left home that morning at 7:15 and Joe and Mimi assumed that she was going to work, so at lunchtime, while Joe was on the phone harassing officials of the Pennsylvania Turnpike Authority, that's where Mimi went looking for her.

Alfreda Tompkins was, and had been for ten years, the administrative assistant to the admissions dean at Washington University—no run-of-the-mill secretarial job given the rigorous admissions requirements, coupled with the number of applications received every year. Mimi guessed that the job kept Alfreda busy enough all day so there wasn't time to worry about her home life. Perhaps not even time for a lunch break . . . but Mimi was stationed outside the admissions office at noon anyway. She'd already asked a harried-looking student if Alfreda was in and received a harried-sounding affirmative response. Since Mimi knew what the woman looked like, she could only wait and hope, and at 1:15 she was rewarded. Partially. Alfreda Tompkins and another woman exited the admissions office together, but they parted company at the end of the hall, and Mimi followed Alfreda when she turned right, walked down a flight of stairs, turned right again, and walked down another hallway that led to—*oh hell!* The faculty and staff dining room. Mimi broke into a sprint and caught up with Alfreda before she entered the room where everyone else entering and leaving, Mimi finally noticed, wore an ID badge.

"Ms. Tompkins!"

Alfreda stopped and turned, a pleasantly expectant look on her face. Of course everyone knew who she was, even a stranger. The pleasant part of her expression evaporated, and she backed up a step when Mimi introduced herself. "Why are you here? What do you want? No one here has done anything wrong!" Mimi's reputation as an investigative reporter was well known, as was the fact that frequently the subjects of her investigations suffered the consequences of their often illegal actions.

"I'm not here about your job, Ms. Tompkins. I want to ask you about your sons," Mimi said, and immediately regretted her words.

Shock, then horror, then fear. "What . . . are they . . ." She couldn't complete a thought or a sentence.

"Nothing has happened as far as I know." Mimi took the woman's arm and pointed toward the dining room. "Can I get in there with you? Good," she said when Alfreda nodded. "Let's get some food and maybe some hot tea and I'll explain myself."

Alfreda Tompkins looked a world's worth of better after a bowl of vegetable soup and a grilled cheese sandwich—and Mimi's explanation for her visit—but the worry about her sons had deepened. She was surprisingly relieved at the news that Virgie Barrett had sought outside help, but she also believed that the more people who knew of her situation, the more danger her sons were in, and she seemed to vacillate between concern for her sons and concern for herself. "Will your friend send a police officer to live with me, too?"

Mimi wasn't expecting the question and it threw her off guard. "But I thought—isn't Detective Davis living with you?" How the hell could a cop be safely placed in the woman's home?! Gianna was gonna have a fit!

"But I don't want him there! I want him out but he won't go!" The tears that she had managed to control began to flow and her shoulders heaved. People began to watch them, and that seemed to force Alfreda Tompkins into a rigid self-control, one that Mimi found disconcerting. Something was wrong here, and she wasn't certain what it was. It didn't concern her that the woman swung like a pendulum between concern for her children and concern for herself; in fact, that felt natural to Mimi. A man the woman didn't want in her home was living there against her will while her sons were . . . *where?*

"Where are your boys, Ms. Tompkins?"

The woman's posture became even more rigid, and her eyes darted from side to side, as if she were expecting to be overheard, afraid of being overheard. She lowered her head and whispered, "He has them."

Mimi wasn't certain she'd heard her correctly, even less certain that she'd understood correctly. "You mean Detective Davis?" And when the woman gave a slight head nod in the affirmative, Mimi pressed. "What do you mean he 'has' them? How? Do you know where your children are, Mrs. Tompkins?" And this time the woman moved her head as well as her eyes, looking all around, as if she truly believed that she could be overheard.

Whispering again, she said, "They're selling drugs in Center City Mall."

Mimi felt like she was down the rabbit hole without the benefit of any kind of hallucinogen. "How do you know this?"

"Because he told me," she whispered. "And because I went over there to see and I saw them!" She was crying again, her shoulders heaving again, but there were fewer people to observe her misery now because the room was practically empty. The lunch hour was over. "The baby, Robbie, he looked so little and so scared, but Will looked tall and mean, like he belonged out there with those hoodlums, selling that poison!"

The boys were named after their father—William Robert Tompkins—and thanks to a dirty D.C. cop, were on the way to becoming worse criminals than he ever was. Mimi could barely believe what she was hearing, but her steady appraisal of Alfreda Tompkins verified the truth: The woman was terrified and only sheer force of will kept the hysteria that lived within her at bay. Out of the corner of her eye Mimi saw one of the dining room employees approach their table, and she knew they were about to be tossed out. She stood up and Alfreda Tompkins followed suit. They both apologized for losing track of time and staying too long, and Mimi followed Alfreda back to her office. En route she whispered to Alfreda, asking her to write down and email her every bit of information she knew about DD, to send photos of her sons to her phone immediately, and to go home after work and call when she got there. She left Alfreda Tompkins at her office door and walked away as fast as she could. She wanted to get away, not so much from the woman herself but from what she'd just learned. She wanted to get away from *everything* she'd learned about Sunset Vista and what was happening there. She didn't want to know it, didn't want to know about it, didn't want any of it to be true or even possible. She didn't want to be going where she was headed, but she had to: Center City Mall, to see Robbie and Will Tompkins for herself so that when she told Gianna it wouldn't be hearsay.

And Gianna still didn't believe her. Joe hadn't, either. "This is the most fucked-up shit I've ever heard about!" was his take before he stalked away from her desk, as if it were her fault, and went to talk to the business manager about finalizing arrangements for his trip to Pennsylvania.

"May I see the photos of the boys?" Gianna asked, and then she closed her eyes to the images.

"I'm so sorry, Gianna," Mimi said, and she was. If she'd had any idea the Chief was going to dump Sunset View in Gianna's lap she'd have kept it to herself, but when she expressed that thought out loud, Gianna shook her head.

"You did the right thing, Mimi, and I'd rather have it dumped in my lap than in some other places I can think of. I'm also glad that you're the one Virgie Barrett called."

"I'm still deciding whether I am or not," Mimi groused. This was, without a doubt, one of the shittiest stories she'd embarked upon in a long time, and what really bothered her was that she didn't really know what was bothering her. She didn't believe that any of the women were lying to her but pieces of the story simply weren't hanging together in an orderly pattern. Maybe dirty cops at the center of the thing was what was throwing everything out of balance.

Virgie was crying again but she wasn't hyperventilating this time. She was weeping softly and smiling. She looked from Mimi to

Gianna, back and forth. "I believed that you would help me, Miss Patterson, I trusted that you would, but I had no idea you'd bring a police lieutenant! And you!" She pointed at Gianna. "You brought a police detective to my door! A real police detective! A *woman* police detective!" Virgie's tears fell harder and faster, and her breath caught in her chest.

"Breathe, Virgie!" Mimi admonished, and Virgie inhaled deeply, held it for a few seconds, then exhaled.

"Thank you. I'm all right now. And thank you, Lieutenant! Thank you so very much!"

"Yes," Sonia Alvarez said, speaking for the first time. "Thank you and God bless you. All of you!" She included Mimi, who, after a look from Gianna, was heading for the door. They'd already agreed to meet later, and Mimi understood that whatever happened from this point on was police business. Gianna would share what she could later, when they were alone.

The cops—Gianna, Alice, and Linda—were gathered in Sonia's living room. They'd had the locks changed on her front and back doors because Officer Phil Diaz had a key that he'd refused to return. She had agreed immediately to have Linda Lopez in her home when Virgie explained the proposal. She lived in fear, she said, that once Diaz got over his shame at what he'd done, he'd return. "He keeps calling and calling. I stopped taking his calls because they were all the same," she said, and began to cry at the memory. "He said he was sorry for what he'd done. Then, from the other side of his mouth, he blamed me!"

Linda Lopez embraced the woman and held her tight as the memory of the rape overtook her. The police didn't know it but this was the first time Sonia had told anyone the whole story; she had told her best friend only part of it. "This is not your fault!" Linda whispered. "This is his fault and only his fault!"

"He said looking at me and being near me made him do what he did! He said he couldn't help it, that it was all my fault!" she wailed.

Alice went into the kitchen, rolled off a handful of paper towels, wet them, and brought them to Linda, who helped Sonia dry her face.

"Ms. Alvarez, Sonia. Look at me," Gianna said, and the woman looked into cool, clear, calm—and calming—hazel eyes. The "Maglione Look" was legendary. It could either intimidate and unravel a perp or, as in this case, totally relax a witness and inspire trust. "Listen to me," Gianna said, and Sonia listened. "Phil Diaz is a liar and he is a criminal and he will be punished for what he did to you. I promise you that."

"But you can't be sure of that."

"Oh, yes I can!" Gianna said, and almost smiled. "The Chief of Police sent me here and told me to do whatever was necessary to make things right in Sunset View Apartments, especially where wrongdoing by members of his department was concerned."

Sonia and Virgie both had stopped crying and were sitting up straight, looks of determination and resolve having replaced fear and sadness on their faces. "What do you want us to do?" Virgie asked, and Gianna told them: "Tell the truth—for the most part. Use Alice's and Linda's real names. Linda is a cousin, Alice is a longtime friend. They're here, Sonia and Virgie, because you asked them to come, and you did that because you no longer felt safe in your homes. Under no circumstances, however, should you reveal that Linda and Alice are police officers."

Then Gianna turned her attention to Alfreda Tompkins. "Your brother will show up tonight to pay an unexpected visit. You didn't know he was coming, and he came because you haven't responded to his texts and phone calls."

Alfreda was ready. "What's his name, my brother? And is he a cop?"

"Detective Bobby Gilliam."

Alfreda's head was bobbing up and down, and she seemed oblivious to the tears that were streaming down her face. "Thank you," she whispered. "Thank you so very much." Then, "What if DD knows him, knows Mr. Gilliam?"

"Bobby is certain he doesn't know Dexter Davis, but if Davis knows him, then he'll be arrested sooner rather than later," Gianna said.

"My boys," Alfreda said. "What about my boys?"

"We will secure your sons as soon as Dexter Davis is no longer an issue," Gianna replied, and both Alice and Linda made mental note of the fact that their Boss didn't say 'arrest' when referring to the Tompkins boys or to Davis when that certainly was what she meant, as Alfreda would learn soon enough. Her boys were drug dealers, and DD was . . . the charge list would be long.

"You all have taught me a very important lesson," Sonia Alvarez said. "As much as I appreciate what you all have done for me—a newspaper reporter and cops!—I can't live my life letting other people fight my battles. My husband is dead and I'm on my own, me and my son," she said as she slid her hand down between the sofa cushions. Her next words froze in her throat as the hand holding the gun she'd pulled from between the sofa cushions froze, midair. Her eyes were locked on the two Sig Sauers pointed directly at her.

"Put the weapon on the coffee table," Linda Lopez ordered. "Do it now, Sonia! Do it now!"

Fear and confusion in equal parts played across Sonia's face as she leaned forward and placed the gun on the table in front of her. "I'm . . . I didn't . . ."

"Put your hands behind your head and lock your fingers together," Alice Long ordered, and as Sonia complied, tears streamed down her face.

"I'm sorry. I didn't mean . . ."

"Anyplace else in America you'd be dead now, Sonia," Linda said.

"Anyplace else in D.C. you'd be dead now," Alice said. "What in the world were you thinking, pulling a gun on a room full of cops?"

Gianna leaned forward and picked up the weapon. It was a short-barrel S&W .38 Ladysmith revolver, recently oiled and cleaned. "Where did you get this, Sonia? And why do you have it?"

Sonia had recovered herself and was angry now. "From a friend of mine, my best friend. She saw something was wrong with me and I told her. I didn't tell her what happened, what he did. I just told her that I was afraid all the time and that I was tired of being so alone. Her husband is back from Iraq so she's not scared all the time anymore, and she said I could hold the gun." She was crying again. "But my husband's not coming back and I'll be damned if I'm going to let that . . . that . . ."

Gianna reached out for Sonia and held her, and the woman stopped weeping and pulled away and sat up straight. "I don't think I could have shot him, not really, and I am really thankful that I don't have to find out. But I do know this: I won't ever let anybody take advantage of me again! Never!"

Gianna stood up and so did Linda, Alice, Virgie, and Alfreda. Sonia's eyes followed the S&W that Gianna still held as she headed for the back door, while Virgie and Alice aimed for the front door—as they would if they were friends visiting friends. "Front door for you, too, Alfreda," Gianna said, adding that she was hoping to sneak out of the back and into the waiting rental car driven by Sgt. Tommi.

"When can I have the gun back?" Sonia asked.

"When it's been checked and cleared," Gianna said, opening the back door. The spotlight above the door had been turned off so it was dark as she hurried out and into the car. She was counting on Alice and Linda to make certain the other women followed instructions: to chat out front like friends, for Virgie and Alice to walk upstairs to Virgie's, for Alfreda to go home, for doors to be locked, curtains drawn, for dinner to be cooked and eaten, television watched. "When Davis comes, act normally," Gianna had said to Alfreda, "and when Bobby comes, act surprised and happy to see him, and he'll set the tone for how to deal with Davis." And as Tommi drove them quickly away from Sunset View, Gianna prayed that Dexter Davis wouldn't do or say anything to make Bobby Gilliam angry. That prayer that went unanswered since the very sight of Dexter Davis angered Bobby Gilliam. The condescendingly nasty tone of voice he used when speaking to Alfreda Tompkins was gasoline on the fire.

"Who's he and what's he doing here?" Davis had used a key to enter the back door and he stopped short at the sight of Bobby.

"My brother, Bobby—" Alfreda started to say before Davis cut her off.

"I don't give a damn what his name is! What's he doing here?"

"She doesn't answer to you, whoever you are," Bobby said, stepping in close to Davis, intentionally invading his space. "The question that needs answering is, what are you doing here?"

"Why didn't you tell me he was coming?"

"Let me say it again: She doesn't answer to you." Bobby took a step closer to Davis, requiring him to take a step back or bump chests with Bobby. He picked the smart option and backed up a step. He wasn't as tall as Bobby, or as muscular, but he was younger, which could be a problem if things got physical. But he was also a coward and a bully. Bobby saw that immediately with his attempts to intimidate the woman and ignore the man. Bobby would kick his ass if that became necessary, and that would happen only if Alfreda weakened, but Alfreda was playing her part like an award-winning thespian. She stood close to him, her hand on his arm, but he could feel the tension in her body.

"What's for dinner, Alfreda?" Davis asked.

"I'm taking my sister out to dinner, and you're not invited," Bobby said. "By the way, where are my nephews? Will they still eat anything as long as it's spaghetti?" And Alfreda's hand became a vice-like claw on his arm.

"They're at a friend's," she said. Davis was watching her like a hawk.

"On a school night, Sis? Mom would have a fit!" She increased the pressure on his arm and it became pain. He felt her trying to summon the strength to talk, but whatever Alfreda was about to say was cut off by a sound from Davis that was more a growl than a word, and he pulled open the back door so hard that it crashed against the kitchen wall. He rushed out without a backward glance and they heard him clamber down the steps. Bobby quickly closed and locked the door and whipped out his phone to call Eric. "Davis is on the move, probably headed to wherever the Tompkins boys are. If they're still at Center City, do the roundup and make sure Davis sees it. If they're not, follow Davis because wherever he goes is where those boys will be. Then get that locksmith here on the double." Bobby ended the call and looked at Alfreda, who looked about ready to collapse.

"What's a roundup?"

"They're going to be picked up—"

"Arrested?! My boys are going to be arrested?!"

"Picked up, Alfreda, and taken to a juvenile facility where they'll be held for forty-eight hours. Not arrested or charged—so not in the system—but away from Davis, at least for the time being. They'll be safe and you'll be safe—"

"Until he comes back and finds the locks changed."

Bobby grinned. And after a moment, so did Alfreda.

All day they had looked forward to this—finally a promise to be kept: a whole evening to themselves. First order of business, as always when they were at Mimi's, was champagne in the hot tub. Mimi had converted the potting shed adjacent to her garage into a lush, warm space mostly taken up by a four-seater hot tub surrounded by an Italian tile floor. A small refrigerator took up one corner and provided an endless supply of water, seltzer, and champagne. Humidity-loving plants hung from the ceiling. Music was piped in via speakers connected to the system in the living room. The lighting could be increased or dimmed as required. It was the perfect place to wind down a work-intensive day or week . . . or to fire up a night of intense passion and love-making, and they'd made good use of it over the years, often reminding each other how embarrassing it would be to drown in a hot tub while attempting to make love. Tonight was no exception. Except it was.

Gianna jerked awake when she slipped under the water. She righted herself and looked at Mimi who was fast asleep, her head lowered almost to her chest, the half-drunk plastic flute of champagne still in her hand. Gianna's own flute was floating in the water, being roiled by the bubbles. She took Mimi's glass, which awakened her.

"Was I asleep?"

Gianna giggled. "Ask the drool on your chin."

Mimi grabbed her drool-free chin. "Not funny, Maglione."

Gianna yawned widely. "How long did we sleep?"

"Long enough for me to be starved! Let's go eat," she said, standing up.

"Long enough for you to be wrinkled," Gianna said, tweaking a nipple, then standing and pulling her into a warm, wet embrace. Their kiss further steamed the room. Then Mimi's stomach growled, knocking all of the romance out of the moment. "You and your stomach," Gianna groused, releasing her and stepping out of the hot tub.

"You know you have to feed me on a regular basis," Mimi said, following.

"Yeah. You and the plant in *Little Shop of Horrors*."

"*Feed me*," Mimi said in a deep-voiced imitation of the man-eating plant, and they laughed and cleaned up the area around the hot tub, turned off the jets, pulled the cover over it, and entered the door that led directly to the kitchen and the food from the Indian restaurant in the oven, growing cold. Mimi opened the bags of goodies, and fixed plates and bowls that she sent to the microwave while Gianna opened bottles of seltzer and grabbed placemats and silverware, all of which she took to the dining-room table. "You don't want to eat in here?" Mimi asked, indicating the breakfast nook.

Gianna shook her head. "We're doing our 'just like normal human beings' imitation, remember? Who knows when we'll have another opportunity?" The sadness that suddenly colored her voice kept Mimi quiet until they were seated and eating.

"Isn't this civilized?" Gianna asked through the mouth full of naan bread she was chewing.

"You realize we're practically naked," Mimi said dryly.

"We're wearing towels," Gianna said. "Besides, lots of civilized people eat in the nude."

"Did you hear what you just said?"

It took her a second but Gianna laughed out loud. "Point to Ms. Patterson."

Mimi tried to stand up to take a bow but her towel fell off, and

Gianna laughed some more and said something about the high birthrate in the places where people ate in the nude. Then they ate in silence for a while, enjoying the food and the quiet and each other's company. Until Gianna broke the silence, the sadness back in her voice.

"I don't think I like my new assignment," she said.

"I can see how you'd feel that way," Mimi said, not bothering to moderate the anger she felt. "He dropped you in the deep end of a pool of watery shit, and you're supposed to swim your way out—which, of course, you'll do—but the stink will be all over you! He can really piss me off!"

"And here I was thinking I felt bad enough," Gianna said, trying for levity.

"I wish I'd never taken him that pile of stink called Sunset View."

"You did the right thing, Mimi."

"I know I did. Question is, did he, when he dumped it on you?"

Gianna, who had been wondering the same thing, was quiet and thoughtful for a moment. "What do you think about what's happening over there?"

"I think there's something very rotten in Denmark and it's starting to stink. I'm just not sure of the source." Mimi stopped talking and tried to organize her thoughts, but she hadn't been able to make sense of all that she was thinking and feeling about the situation at Sunset View, to find the logic stream that she could follow to a newsworthy story. "Those women and their children are in a very crappy situation no doubt about it—"

"But you're wondering whether they've done enough to help themselves dig out of the hole," Gianna said, and it wasn't a question.

"That's part of it," Mimi acknowledged, "but the part that really bothers me is Alfreda Tompkins letting that Davis asshole take her children. What kinda mother does that?"

Gianna's lieutenant face was now firmly in place as she said, "Exactly what Bobby said." She stood up. "Let's clean up and go

116

to bed. The thought of more than four hours' sleep—" She didn't finish the sentence because of the wide-mouth yawn that cracked the lieutenant face.

Bed that night meant sleep—they were too exhausted for anything else—but holding each other tight and close, knowing that they were together when sleep claimed them, was its own kind of passionate joy. So when Gianna's phone rang at 3:15, Mimi released her and grabbed a pillow and put it over her head, muffling the sound. She hated the ringing of the phone in the middle of the night more than just about anything. Gianna, on the other hand, always awoke with crystal clarity and sounded awake and alert no matter what time the phone rang or how bone-weary she was.

"Lieutenant Maglione," she said because she didn't recognize the name of the caller on her phone's display: J. PATEL.

"Boss, we got a problem."

One of her new team. She really needed to learn their names. "What kind of problem, where?"

"At the warehouse. The perps are gone."

Gianna jumped to her feet. "How could they be gone? They're under twenty-four-hour surveillance."

"I just came on duty, Boss, and there's a parking lot full of johns trying to get in the door, and we don't track any perp movement inside."

"What about the girls?"

"They're all still there—"

He was talking to air. Gianna was dressing. She'd call Mimi later, at a more reasonable hour. Right now she needed to get downtown. She backed out of the garage, tires screeching, and drove the wrong way up the street, confident that she was the only cop on this tree-lined residential street at this time of the night. Or morning. Once she cleared the residential area she activated lights and siren, the only thought in her head: getting to her unit as fast as possible without endangering any civilians. Somebody's car was in her parking space in the underground municipal garage, and she didn't think twice about blocking it in.

Whoever it was would have to find her in order to get out and they'd have a discussion about what "Reserved" meant.

It was busy in the unit. There was a body at each of the computers, and the images on the wall-mounted screens constantly changed. Gianna entered on an image of the outside of the warehouse. The parking lot was full, cars entering, cars exiting, men pounding on the door when ringing the bell netted no results. She scanned the people in the room, searching for "J. PATEL." Their eyes met and locked as they found each other simultaneously. He stood up and she walked toward him.

"Thanks for the call. Update, please?"

He nodded, sat back down, and his fingers immediately went to work on his keyboard. The image on the screen shifted, showing the inside of the warehouse. Many hours spent watching the surveillance videos had taught her to discern the source of the images—from the drones to the infrared cameras to the rooftop cameras on Dee Phillips's warehouse next door, and what she saw confirmed what he'd told Gianna on the phone: The perps were gone; the girls were alone. Most of them lay inert on their pallets but three appeared to stealthily investigate their apparent new reality. Still, their investigation took them no closer than thirty or forty feet to the door.

"Call the sergeants, please, Officer Patel and Detective Dudley."

"Already done, Boss. They're on the way."

"Good work, Officer Patel, thanks. Now, show me what got you suspicious." She sat down next to him. "But not on the big screen."

He nodded and turned his screen so that she could watch it with him: last night's feed beginning shortly after midnight. It looked like business as usual: a steady stream of cars and men entering and leaving the warehouse, one man visible working the door, two more inside conducting the business of selling the girls and collecting the money. Then something happened. The three men talked among themselves and then began packing boxes and bags. One went to the door and waved all the potential customers away. They seemed to protest until the man brandished an assault weapon. Then the men began loading the boxes and bags into their panel van which was always in the parking lot. Then came the heavy stuff—credit card machines and video equipment and finally, a safe. It took them over an hour to load everything, and all the while prospective clients drove into the parking lot and were run off by the man wielding the assault rifle. Finally, at 2:30 a.m., the men climbed into their van and drove away. Then the clients began to arrive. Gianna recognized some of the same cars that had been warned off by the assault rifle. Had they merely driven a block away and parked, hoping they could safely return? Had they witnessed the departure of the white panel van and assumed it was safe to return?

"You came on shift at three, is that correct, Officer Patel?"

"Yes, Boss."

"And did you follow the change of shift protocol? Who did you relieve?"

Patel suddenly got twitchy and nervous, looking everywhere but at Gianna. She was about to take his head off when he received the momentary reprieve of a distraction in the form of the arrival of Sergeants Eric Ashby and Tommi Bell and Detective Jim Dudley. They hurried across the room to Gianna and she filled them in. "Officer Patel was just about to stand up and explain—in detail—this morning's lapse in protocol."

Patel jumped to his feet, stood at attention, and explained that he received no notes detailing the unusual activity in the warehouse because the duty officer he was to relieve had already left. His use of the term "duty officer" confirmed for Gianna that he was one of the new unit members who was ex-military.

"Hey, Boss! Got it!" Kenny Chang sang out.

"How did he get here?" A surprised Gianna asked Patel. "How did any of them get here?" she asked, finally fully understanding the importance of the presence of all the IT personnel on hand at 3:30 in the morning.

"I called them when I knew for sure we had a problem," he answered, "just after I called you. Then I called the sergeants and Detective Dudley."

Gianna touched his shoulder as she passed by him to reach Kenny, who was pointing to the big screen. They all looked up at it. "This is how it happened, Boss, and when it happened. Watch the john get out of his car and he just happens to look up—watch him!"

When the john got out of his car he was facing the Phillips warehouse, and he just happened to look up—right into the bank of police cameras on top of the building directed at the sex-trafficking warehouse door. "And he thought they were recording their customers," Gianna said, sounding as disgusted as they all felt while they watched the john ring the bell and pound furiously on the door and all but attack Larry. They'd named the three sex traffickers Larry, Curly, and Moe, with apologies to the hapless though harmless Stooge threesome; there was nothing funny about what these three were doing. They watched Larry try to convince his customer that he was not being recorded, and they watched the customer refuse to be convinced. He punched Larry in the chest and stormed back to his car, pulling open the door with such force that it rocked on its hinges. Then he raised the middle fingers of both hands to the cameras, got in his car, and peeled out of the lot.

Larry watched him leave, fear, anger and worry taking turns etching patterns in his face. Finally, just as he closed the door, he stole a glance at the corner of the adjacent warehouse where the irate customer told him the cameras were watching. He blanched and slammed the door.

"Go take that door, Jim," Gianna said to Dudley. "Looks like it'll be a rescue mission now."

He saluted and hurried off. Gianna walked over to Patel. "Who was on shift before you?"

He got shifty and twitchy again, just as he had the first time she asked. "You'll give me a name or you're both out of this unit effective immediately."

"Taylor Johnstone," he replied, shrinking a bit as he said the words.

"That's your roommate," Sgt. Tommi said.

120

"Yes, ma'am," Patel replied, shrinking a bit more.

"Deep background him," Gianna said to Tommi. To Eric: "Send somebody to get him."

"I'll go get him," Patel said.

"No, you won't," Gianna replied.

"Please! I want to bring him in!"

"A minute ago you didn't even want to tell me his name."

"I know. I was . . . I felt betrayed. I don't know why . . . what he was thinking."

"I certainly intend to find out," Gianna snapped. She turned to Eric. "Send somebody to get him and let Patel go along, but they're not to be left alone together." She walked back over to Kenny. "Where's that van, Kenny? What has it done since it left the warehouse?"

"Nothing but drive, Boss. It's on 64. Went straight through Richmond without even slowing down, Charlottesville coming up."

"How far behind are we?"

"Thirty minutes, maybe less the way Connally is driving. The Virginia Staties know we're in pursuit, and they know why, and they're okay with it as long as all we do is follow, even if we break the speed limit a little. And the speed limit on that stretch of 64 is seventy so . . ."

So long as all they did was follow. Shit! "Keep me posted." Then, "Kenny, Patel, everybody, good work. Thanks for coming in and saving our assses on this one."

"Our asses really aren't saved, are they, Boss?" Patel asked, sounding sad.

"We'll get those girls out of that hellhole, and we'll get the scum who put them there, and we'll get a few of the lowlifes who abused them. I'd call that our asses in pretty good shape," she said, heading to the far corner of the room where she'd carved out a mini-office for herself consisting of a desk with a phone and a computer, and three chairs, one behind the desk, two in front. Her two sergeants followed, sat down, and got busy on their notepads, while she woke up the Chief who, in a probably short-lived display of a new behavior pattern, listened quietly to everything Gianna said, asked two questions, thanked her for calling, said he'd see her in half an hour, and disconnected.

"I didn't hear him screaming," Eric said.

"Because he didn't scream," Gianna said.

"Huh," Eric said, and left it there.

"Do you both agree that I should let Patel go pick up his roommate?"

Both sergeants nodded, and Tommi spoke for them. "He did good work this morning, Boss, and he showed a lot of initiative, calling everybody."

"I agree, but why didn't he want to give us Johnstone's name?"

"'Cause they're more than roommates, Boss," Tommi said.

No wonder the kid was twitchy, Gianna thought, feeling sorry for Patel, who no doubt was feeling emotions he probably couldn't even name. Was his lover just a fuck-up, or was he something much, much worse?

"I can go with Patel to grab Johnstone," Eric offered, but Gianna shook her head; she needed him here to be the liaison with the Virginia State Police since they didn't know what Larry, Curly and Moe's end game was. Were they just making a run for it or were they connecting with more like themselves? And if they were part of a larger operation, Gianna wanted to roll up as much of it as possible. She made a note to have the Chief call his counterpart in the Staties.

"Send somebody with Patel who's not pals with them, Tommi, and let's pick up the john who wrecked our op, see if he has anything we can use as leverage to squeeze him. Eric, check in with Dudley, make sure all his pieces are falling into place, especially the medical and translator personnel." They both stood, saluted, and hurried to their tasks. Gianna opened the contacts list on her phone and hesitated only briefly before finding Dee's name and hitting the call icon. It was a crappy time of morning to call somebody, but she knew Dee would not hold that against her.

"Lieutenant?"

"I'm sorry for the early hour, Ms. Phillips, but I wanted to let you know that there will be major activity at the warehouse location within the hour. I do not expect that any harm will come to your property."

"I'm not worried about my property, Lieutenant; it's those girls I care about, you know that."

"Yes, I do, and I'll fill you in, tell you what I can when I can."

"I appreciate it, and I appreciate the call."

"Ah, one more thing, Ms. Phillips . . .? Breakfast?" Gianna could still hear the woman's laughter as she made her way across the room to the action center, and the gleeful looks on the faces of her team as she told them breakfast was on the way would, along with Dee's laugh, help keep her together through what was about to be a truly horrible day.

Gianna took advantage of the momentary lull in activity to gather her thoughts, to order them, to think through things, to be as certain as she could be that she hadn't missed anything or, worse, screwed up anything. This was a big operation and lives were at stake. That kept coming back to being her first and primary concern: getting those girls out of that warehouse alive—in body if not in spirit. Then there were the perps—Larry, Curly, and Moe. She'd already decided to ask the Chief to manage that aspect of the operation since its success would be reliant on the cooperation of law enforcement entities in Virginia, state and local, and local could mean city as well as county, and that meant a very large headache.

But it was exactly the kind of maneuvering and manipulating the Chief enjoyed and that he was so good at, and he arrived loaded for bear. He watched and listened without interrupting as the techs walked him through the videos that led up to the hurried exit of Larry, Moe and Curly and the shutdown of the trafficking operation. He muttered and cursed under his breath when he saw the john observe the cameras on top of the Phillips warehouse. He cursed and muttered some more as he watched the three perps haul the evidence out of the warehouse and load it into the van. He didn't explode until he learned that the duty officer, Taylor Johnstone, hadn't left a written record of the events and that he had failed to alert anyone when it happened, and he went ballistic when he learned that Johnstone apparently hadn't remained until the end of his shift.

"Stupidity, laziness, or something worse?" the Chief asked.

Gianna shrugged. "I don't know him well enough to have an opinion, but I do know that I don't intend to get to know him any better."

He gave her a speculative look, then shifted his gaze back to the video screen. "I'm trying to recall who suggested we take him—ah! I remember now," he said, but he didn't reveal the name to her. He wouldn't, so she'd never know who'd be paying the price for palming this loser off on the Chief and causing a major fuck-up in a major operation. He readily accepted her suggestion that he huddle with the Virginia authorities to guarantee a smooth takedown of the traffickers when that became necessary, leaving her to focus on the rescue operation and on Officer Taylor Johnstone when they brought him in.

Without telling him where she was going, Gianna left the Chief in the unit and headed to the scene. She'd already told him to expect the breakfast delivery at some point, which caused him to smile and pat her on the shoulder. He didn't need to say the dreaded "promotion" word; she knew he was thinking it, that he would continue to think it until she gave in and took the damn test. Dear god she didn't want or need to be a captain! It was stressful enough now.

Dudley and his takedown crew were huddled together in the parking lot, looking intently at the empty space where the door they'd blown off its hinges a short while ago used to be. Gianna had parked at the Phillips warehouse and walked around the corner to the scene, and as soon as Jim Dudley spied her he ran over, his face etched with worry. "I think we got a problem, Boss."

"You think?"

"Can't say for sure—the medics won't let us back in the building—but it seems like the girls don't want to leave. They're refusing to leave, some of 'em, and some of 'em are so strung out they don't know what's happening. They keep asking for 'Jimmy.' We're guessing that's one of the perps, the one who doses 'em. And, Boss? There's at least one fatality, and at least one more is unconscious and unresponsive and the medics can't bring her around. They rushed her to the hospital. That's all they'll tell us."

"Let's see if they'll tell me a little more," Gianna said in the tone of voice Bobby Gilliam called "her chilly self," as she headed for the door in full lieutenant cowboy-cop mode.

"They will," Tony Watkins and Tim McCreedy said in unison. They knew from firsthand experience what to expect when she got this way; the people in the building were about to find out.

"You can't come in here," someone Gianna didn't know said, blocking her entrance with a hand on her arm. Tallish, forty-something, dark blond hair in a ponytail.

"This is my crime scene and I'm coming in and you're getting your hand off me."

"Lieutenant Maglione!" She recognized the EMT who called her name. Her badge said her name was R. Kafkalas. She'd been the one who'd transported Cassie . . .

"You get all the fun calls, huh?"

Kafkalas tried for a sad grin that failed. "It's taking its toll, Lieutenant—"

"You call this fun?" blond ponytail snarled.

"Who the hell is he?" Gianna asked Kafkalas, not looking at the object of her ire. If she looked at him, she'd smack him.

"Arnie Spitzer from the National Center for Missing and Exploited Children."

"The people Jim Dudley called in at your request?" Gianna asked, and when Kafkalas nodded in the affirmative Gianna grabbed her phone and punched in Dudley's number. She heard it ring; he was close by. "With me, please, Jim," she said, and he had pushed Arnie Spitzer aside and was next to her before she'd ended the call to him.

"They've fucked our crime scene all to hell!" he said, glaring at Spitzer.

"This is more than just a crime scene!" Spitzer snarled back.

"Whatever it is, you're standing in the middle of it because this man—Detective Jim Dudley—requested your presence," Gianna said. Then, to Dudley, "Secure what you can."

Dudley, who still held his phone, punched in a number, which apparently answered in the middle of the first ring. "You and McCreedy supervise the crime scene techs, everybody booted, suited and masked. And bring one for me and the Boss."

"While we're waiting," Gianna said, looking from Spitzer to Kafkalas, "tell me about the women, the girls, who are resisting transport—"

"If you'd called us in first, we could have prepped you for the kinds of pathologies to expect—"

"If you don't get your nose out of the air and your ass off your back, I'm evicting you from my crime scene," Gianna said to Spitzer, "and make no mistake, Mr. Spitzer: It *is* my crime scene."

"That may be, Lieutenant, but your department doesn't seem very well prepared to handle this kind of situation," Spitzer said.

"And who would you like to call in, Mr. Spitzer? The president? The attorney general? The secretary of state? The FBI or Homeland Security or some other federal government entity that doesn't give a good goddamn about what happened to these girls?"

Tim and Tony arrived with Tyvek coveralls and helped Gianna and Jim get themselves covered from head to toe. Tim looked at Spitzer. "Him, too, Boss?"

She shook her head. "He's already walked around back there, but do an elimination workup." As she inhaled deeply, she realized that she did not want to venture deeper into the warehouse, that she did not want to see the drugged girls, did not want to see where and how they lived and worked. She knew that Jim and Tim and Tony were watching her. So was R. Kafkalas. And she guessed that all of them—all the cops, anyway—were feeling what she was feeling. This was new territory, and it was bad, ugly territory. And they all knew, without having to discuss it, that they dearly wished it was somebody else's job to investigate this crime scene.

Just past the front door was the office, a space that now held empty file cabinets and desk drawers and a space where a safe once had stood. Not a single piece of paper remained, though there were plenty of stale chips and fries on the dirty carpeted floor. Next to the office was the kitchen. It held a large refrigerator but no stove, a dozen cases of water, and family-size packages of paper plates, cups, napkins, forks, spoons, and chips, and gallon jugs of fruit juice. Jim opened the refrigerator: It was filled with cans and bottles of beer and some store-brand soft drinks. Tim and Tony pulled open the cabinet doors to reveal empty cabinets. Gianna remembered the reports of the trash from this place—a massive and daily accumulation of empty Chinese and Mexican food containers and wrappers, and fried chicken boxes of bones.

The next space was toilets and showers, five of each. There were gallon jugs of liquid soap and packs of disposable razors and toothbrushes. No toothpaste was evident. Gianna was wondering about towels and washcloths when she noticed the half-dozen wall-mounted paper towel dispensers and equal number of hot air blow-dryers. Nothing genteel or elegant about the personal hygiene aspect of things, but it certainly was functional. The same could be said of the sleeping quarters, arranged dorm-like—nine bunk beds, three each on each of the walls.

Then came the work area. Doors lined both sides of the long hallway, all of them open as if they had been checked, which they probably had, a mattress and a chair in each room. Gianna could only hope that nobody had entered any of the rooms, thus compromising any potential evidence. Not that any evidence collected would or could be of major use, given the number of men who had cycled in and out of these in the last seven weeks. She very much doubted that linen was changed daily. She stopped, walked back and counted the rooms: ten. There were more than ten girls, she knew that. How much time did each girl spend with each client? Even though Gianna was sure she didn't want to know the answer, she was also sure that Mr. Spitzer would be able to supply it.

The final area, at the end of the hall, was a large room with mats on the floor, and on each mat a girl wearing a slip-like shift. Gianna counted them: twelve, not including the one who was DOA and the one who'd been transported, which meant that two new girls had been added in the last week. Why hadn't she known that? She made herself enter the room and walk around, looking at the girls. Several obviously were in a drugged stupor and lay unmoving. Others seemed to be emerging from the same stupor, they were tossing and turning and moving about. Three, however, seemed to be awake and were anxious and agitated and they called out for Jimmy, a pitiful, plaintive sound that made her flesh crawl. Then the others began to wail and it sounded more like some kind of animal howling. Gianna checked her watch. It had been exactly four hours since Larry, Moe and Curly had realized they were being surveilled, three since they'd fled the warehouse and the girls.

Gianna looked at EMT Kafkalas, who answered the question she hadn't asked yet. "We'll begin transporting as soon as there's someplace to take them—all of them—and as soon as the translators find somebody who can communicate with them."

"Nobody has talked to them?" She was stunned.

"Nobody has been able to, Lieutenant. They don't understand any of the translators. At least they seem not to. The translators tried several languages and dialects and the women did not seem to understand any of them." The medic looked as miserable as Gianna felt.

"The one who was DOA, what's your best guess?"

"Combination of OD, malnourishment, and being fucked to death, but don't you dare quote me on that! The M.E.'ll have me up on charges. But I'd say the same is true for the one we transported. They're kids, Lieutenant, not much more than babies, and their bodies aren't mature enough for what they're put through day after day."

It was time to ask Arnie Spitzer exactly what that was, and when she did, she wished she hadn't, for he explained in extensive and graphic detail what life was like for sex-trafficked women

128

and children, beginning with the drugs they systematically were introduced and addicted to, to the rapes they learned to accept and endure, and to whatever other forms of sexual depravity the client inflicted. How many sexual partners a day? As many as the trafficker could sell: five, seven, ten, more. Gianna felt the bottom drop out of her stomach, then the bile rose in her throat, and she had to get out into the open, to breathe fresh air. The thought of a twelve-or thirteen-year-old girl or boy being raped ten times a day by a grown man was more than she could stomach.

She hadn't paid attention to their activities but once outside she honed in on the photographers, those with the still cameras as well as the videographers. "Did they get it all, Jim?"

He nodded in grim satisfaction. "Every inch, every corner, every cobweb, every dust bunny."

"Thank you, Jim. This was a lot to ask and you stepped up."

"I just wish we could've gotten those fuckin' baby-rapers before they got away! Who could have predicted that one of the fuckin' johns would see the cameras?!"

Arnie Spitzer was coming her way and she went to meet him, to apologize for walking away, and to tell him, in as much detail as she could, how it happened that she'd gotten involved in a child sex-trafficking operation in the middle of Washington, D.C. "You were absolutely right, Mr. Spitzer: We were in over our heads and playing catch-up from day one."

He extended his hand and she took it. "I hope you don't ever have to do this again, Lieutenant, but I also hope you know that I stand ready to help you in any way that I can if it should happen. I just had one of my staff background you, and you're definitely on the side of the angels."

She managed a dry chuckle. "I wish I'd had some of those angels on my side this morning."

"You did, Lieutenant. How else do you explain that as of this moment, we have a place to take all the girls?"

How else, indeed, Gianna thought, as she prepared to leave. She told Jim she'd find out how to get another steel door installed on the warehouse after the techs had gone over every inch of the place; then she called Delores Phillips and asked to have another breakfast delivered to the techs processing the warehouse adjacent to hers. Then she drove back to her unit, but she needed a few private moments first before facing her team. She locked herself in her office, put her head down on the desk, and wept. She had made a terrible, horrible mistake! She had not known, it had not occurred to her, that the girls would not want to be rescued, to be freed from their bondage, if freedom meant an end to the steady supply of the narcotics that kept them inured to the reality of their existence. That's why all the traffickers all over the world made addiction their first order of business, even before the rapes began. Once addicted and dependent on the drugs, the girls and women—and boys—would do whatever was necessary to keep the drugs coming. And Gianna had thought the traffickers merely evil. Certainly they were that, but they weren't stupid. They knew something else, too. They knew that men who paid to have sex with children didn't care if those children were unusually compliant. In fact, it was better; compliant children didn't care what was done to them or with them.

She had learned an important lesson this morning. A couple of them. It really was necessary to keep a distance between her feelings and the job. If she hadn't been so focused on rescuing children who didn't want to be rescued, she might then have focused on learning what she needed to know about the victims themselves, and that would have meant taking the time to learn from the people whose day-in, day-out job was to pick up the pieces of what was left of the trafficked on the rare occasions they were found alive. She'd also learned to recognize when she was in over her head, and as much as that wasn't something she liked admitting, she knew she'd never again risk somebody's life to protect her own ego. Now . . . if she could only get that wailing, howling sound out of her head!

Quick knocks and the door opened and Sgt. Tommi stuck her head in. "They're back with Taylor Johnstone. Where do you want him, Boss?"

"Let's find an interrogation room."

"Oh, shit!" Tommi said.

"I hope young Officer Johnstone will feel the same way," Gianna said, but he was too stoned to feel much of anything. Tommi said if Patel, the roommate, hadn't had a key, they'd have had to break in to get in, which they couldn't have done because they had no warrant. And once they were in, it took several minutes and a splash of ice water to the face to rouse Johnstone. The variety of illegal substances in his room constituted grounds for dismissal from the job. The fact that he most likely had been stoned on the job was just another nail in his coffin, for which the hole already was dug. Gianna looked at Johnstone and knew it would be a waste of time and energy trying to talk to him. He looked like all the junkies she'd tried to talk to during her days on the drugs squad, and she hoped that's all he was—a junkie, because she didn't think she could stomach another dirty cop. But just in case: "Put him in interrogation and call Internal Affairs. Then, Tommi, do whatever you have to do to drop him from our unit. I'll tell the Chief." And she went to find Patel.

"Boss!" He hurried over to her as soon as she entered the unit.

"What's the *J* stand for?" she asked him before he could speak.

"Jaikirti. Jay. And I swear to you that I did not know how deep Taylor was into drugs."

"How is that possible, Jay? You were lovers—" Gianna began, but Jay Patel was shaking his head back and forth, his hand raised to stop her talking. "You're not lovers?"

"We had casual sex, yes, but we're more friends and room-mates than lovers. We moved in together so we both could quit our part-time jobs; that was six months ago. I knew Taylor smoked a joint now and then, but that's all it was. At least that's all I ever saw, I swear, Lieutenant!"

"Was this the first time he hadn't been present to report at the end of shift?"

"I would have reported it to the sergeants if it had happened before."

Gianna gave him a long, steady look and he held her gaze. She believed him. He had done exemplary work today, and that

131

included volunteering to help take his roommate into custody. "Taylor Johnstone now belongs to Internal Affairs, and they'll certainly want to talk to you, so you know you can no longer live in that apartment."

"I packed my bags when I was there. I'll go back and live with my parents . . . Boss, please don't kick me out of the unit!"

"If IA clears you, I have no reason to drop you, Jay. This unit will support and defend you until or unless we're given a reason not to."

"Thanks, Boss," he said, and he saluted and hurried across the room to Action Central, just as Eric arrived with arms extended, coffee in one hand, juice in the other. She grabbed the cup of juice first and swallowed it in one long, thirsty gulp.

"There's more where that came from," Eric said. "The Phillipses, bless 'em, brought four gallons of the stuff."

"I'd marry them if I weren't already spoken for," Gianna said.

"You'd have to get in line," Eric said with a wide grin. "Behind me!" And in an unusual display of familiarity he slung an arm across her shoulders as they joined the crowd in Action Central. On one screen they watched the activity at the warehouse, which now included the girls being carried out on gurneys and loaded into the kind of ambulances Gianna had seen only on news reports of tragedies in other parts of the world. Gianna was whispering to Eric that they needed to replace the steel door of the warehouse when a cheer went up as on another screen Larry, Curly and Moe were led out of a nondescript ranch house in handcuffs and each put into the back seat of a Virginia State Police squad car. And an even louder cheer erupted as the Virginia Staties sealed the side door of the panel van with crime scene tape and Connally climbed into the driver's seat. Was he on his way home? If so, they'd have the evidence needed to document the evil that had transpired in the Broad Street warehouse.

Gianna approached another screen and pointed to it. "Do we know who he is, where he is?"

"Yes, Boss," several voices answered her.

"Then go get him," she said, grimly satisfied that the baby-raper who had blown their operation and then given them the finger soon would be in her custody. She took out her phone to call the Chief to learn if they could give real names to Larry, Curly, and Moe, and stop insulting three other fellas who made people laugh instead of cry.

CHAPTER SIX

"Well if it isn't JJZ! Where's the Queen B? Somewhere making beautiful music with the lieutenant who can do no wrong, leaving you to do all the work?" Ian had spoken loudly enough that everyone within a ten-foot radius heard him, which, Joe thought, was his intention. To call the man clueless was to grossly understate. Joe stepped around him and headed for his desk. Mimi had stopped in the loo. He hoped Ian would vanish before she appeared, but it didn't seem likely that would happen as Ian continued his high-decibel trash talking.

"That guy is an idiot," said Carolyn Warshawski, one of the weekend editors. "I don't know why they keep him."

"The guy is an asshole," said night editor Henry Smith, "and he's still here only because his probationary period isn't up yet. The Exec'll let him get right up to the edge, let him think he's got it made, then dump his dumb ass."

Carolyn looked at Henry, into rheumy eyes set deeply into sockets rimmed with equally deep wrinkles and bags, and knew that he was correct. He'd been around longer than most, including the Exec, and he knew how the place worked. "The sooner the better, Henry," she said.

"I just wish Patterson had been around to hear what he said, the little fuck. She'd have cleaned his clock and left the pieces on the floor."

Carolyn made a sound and Henry looked at her, then to where

she was looking, to see Mimi headed toward them. Well, not really toward them as much as toward her desk, but they were in her path. So was Ian, but Mimi gave no indication that she saw him. She spoke to and nodded at several people along the way, and she was about to speak to Carolyn and Henry, both of whom she considered friends, when Ian spoke to her.

"Patterson! A little afternoon delight with the lovely lieutenant?" he said, speaking even louder than he had before.

"Oh, shit," somebody muttered as Mimi stopped walking and stood as still as a post in cement.

Ian apparently had no sense of peril because he kept talking. "Give me an hour with her and I'll make her forget all about that wanna-be plastic dick you dykes use. Or is it rubber? I'll slide nine inches of the real thing in her—"

Mimi's fist met his jaw with such speed and power that witnesses weren't sure he'd been hit until he was spiraling backward, yelling at the top of his lungs, arms flailing in a futile attempt to grab and hold something to break his fall. Everyone who could have provided that cushion, that safety net for Ian, quickly moved out of the way, leaving the wall of army-green, old as dirt, metal file cabinets at the back of the room the only option. He hit them hard, and fell to the floor, hitting it just as hard.

The Exec had come out of his office at the sound of Ian's yelling to find the newsroom staff surrounding Mimi Patterson, and cheering her. Nobody but Henry Smith was thinking— worrying—that it was likely that Mimi had broken either her hand or Ian's jaw, and quite possibly both.

"What the hell is going on?" the Exec thundered, and his eyes narrowed to slits as he looked toward the end of the room, where Ian was struggling to his feet. His eyes found the two editors who were present. He looked from one to the other, solid and reliable, the both of them. "Do you two know what happened out here?" And when both nodded in the affirmative, he ordered them into his office. It was a short conversation. He asked them to repeat what they'd heard, confirmed that they agreed about what they heard, asked them to type it up and have it to him within the hour, thanked and dismissed them. By the time Carolyn and Henry emerged from his office, Ian had made his way to the front of the room, rubbing his face and cursing all in his path.

"You fuckers! You could've caught me! Why didn't you?!"

"Because you're such a charming and polite fellow," Joe Zemekis said. He'd come to stand close to Mimi in case Ian had retaliation on his mind, but he need not have worried.

"My office, Wilson!" the Exec bellowed from his office door, and Ian looked almost pleased to answer the summons. He was about to sit down when the Exec snarled, "You are suspended, with pay. Report to HR immediately, which means get your sorry ass out of my office!" The Exec followed him to the door, waving away whatever it was Ian Wilson wanted to say for himself. "Straight to HR, and I mean that, do you understand me, Wilson?"

"Yes, sir," Ian Wilson had the good sense to respond.

"Patterson!" the Exec yelled. "My office," and the smirk almost returned to Ian Wilson's face.

"Hang tough, Patterson," Zemekis whispered to Mimi as she followed the Exec into his office, having the good sense not to attempt to sit down though she very much wanted to. Her hand hurt like hell. She'd take whatever punishment was coming if it meant that she could go run her hand under a stream of cold water. Then she mentally corrected herself: She didn't know what the punishment was for hitting another employee on company property. *Shit, damn, and hellfire.*

"Carolyn and Henry told me what Wilson said to you. Crude little fucker, isn't he? I don't blame you for smacking him. Carolyn and Henry both said they'd have smacked him, too, if you hadn't been so quick off the mark." He looked at the right hand she was cradling in the left. "Hurts like hell, does it?"

"Yes, sir," she answered.

"Go to medical and see the nurse. Find out if you broke anything."

"Yes, sir," she said again, and waited to hear what her punishment was.

"You want anything else, Patterson?"

"Ah, no, sir."

"Then get outta my office and go do some work." He sat down at his desk and picked up the sheets of some reporter's story. Then he looked back at her. "You and Zemekis making any headway on that Sunset View thing?"

"Yes, sir. We are."

He nodded. "Good. I'll take a progress report whenever you have one," he said, and returned his attention to the story he was reading, dismissing her.

The crowd outside his door had not diminished, and it presented one questioning face to her: What was her fate?

She held out her hand. "I'm supposed to go see the nurse, see if I broke anything, then Zemekis and I are supposed to get back to work."

There was a cheer, a chorus of *Atta Girls* and *Way to go Pattersons*, a few claps on the shoulder, one hug, one kiss on the cheek, and several whispers in her ear that Weasel Boy had been suspended. Then they all drifted back to their desks, and Joe draped his arm across her shoulders. "I'll go see the nurse with you."

She nodded her thanks, and they headed for the elevator. "Suppose I have broken my hand, Joe," she started to say, but he cut her off like a meat cleaver through soft butter.

"I don't want to hear it, Patterson! I'm not writing that monster story by myself! You can type one-handed!"

She had no intention of letting him write the story by himself though she did doubt that she could type one-handed. Of course, she'd never tried.

Gianna had agreed that Mimi could talk to Sonia Alvarez, Virgie Barrett and Alfreda Tompkins, and to the cops keeping watch over them—Linda Lopez, Alice Long and Bobby Gilliam. The cops were decidedly less than happy about the arrangement but they were under orders, and Mimi watched their demeanor shift as they saw how their charges responded to Mimi. They met at Virgie's, as much because she was the one who had initiated the original contact as because she had no police officer living with her. When she opened the door, she grabbed Mimi and pulled her into a long, warm embrace, which didn't really surprise her. The fact that Sonia and Alfreda followed suit did, however. She knew that Sonia was grateful for Linda's presence, but she'd had no sense that Alfreda had any strong feelings for her, positively or negatively.

"Come on in, Ms. Patterson! We're so glad to see you!" Virgie enthused, ushering her into the living room and over to the armchair that clearly was the prime seat in the room. "And I hope you brought your appetite 'cause we've got food!"

Mimi stopped halfway down to sitting to take a look into the dining room. If tables really could groan under the weight of copious amounts of food, as she'd read, then this one should be yelling "uncle!" "That's an awful lot of food," she said, hoping she didn't sound as ravenous as the sight of the food-laden table made her.

"You ever seen Bobby Gilliam eat?" Alice Long queried, not at all in jest.

"Hey!" Bobby exclaimed as laughter erupted. Apparently they'd all seen Bobby eat.

"I appreciate you all taking the time to see me," Mimi said. "I wanted to check in with you, to follow up, to see how you're doing, to make sure the cops aren't eating you out of house and home." And she was as relieved to see that the cops joined in the laughter as she was to see that all the women looked so much better than when she'd last seen them. They no longer looked stressed and worried and frightened and fearful. They no longer looked hopeless and helpless, and Mimi hoped that was because they no longer felt that way.

"By the way, Patterson, what happened to your hand?" Everybody no doubt had noticed the lightweight cast she wore, but it was Alice who asked the question.

"She probably punched somebody," Bobby said playfully. Then his expression changed when he looked closely at her. "Shit! You really *did* punch somebody, didn't you? Who?"

Sonia Alvarez looked appalled. "Reporters can punch people?"

"Only if they really need punching," Alice said with a sly grin. "So?"

"I'll bet it was that jerk she works with, the one the Boss threw out of Mrs. Ali's room," Linda offered with way too much insight. "What did he do?"

"He said something I didn't like about somebody I do like."

"Then I hope you broke his jaw," Bobby said. "Good on ya, Patterson. Oohrah."

Sonia Alvarez jumped to her feet. "You a Marine, Detective Gilliam?"

"Yes, ma'am," he said, and he knew in that moment that a cop had raped the wife of a Marine who'd given his life in the service of his country. Two dirty cops in the same place was too much— Mimi could see it all over his face, could see it in his body. She wondered if she should tell Gianna and let her get Gilliam out of there before he killed somebody. He saw her looking at him, reading her thoughts as if they were displayed on a screen on her forehead. He gave her a slight nod. "I'm good," he said, and headed for the table. "I assume we're supposed to eat all this food," he said, and began loading a plate.

Alice came to stand beside her and asked in a low voice, "Does the Boss know?" And when Mimi shook her head, "She won't hear it from us. And I hope you at least left a mark if you didn't break his jaw."

"He'll feel it for a while," Mimi said with a small smile, which netted her an "attagirl" from Alice who she knew, from Gianna, was one tough cop. If Alice had hit Weasel Boy he almost certainly would have a broken jaw as well as a few loose teeth. The thought comforted her.

The food was good and Mimi ate a lot of it, grateful that there either was another vegetarian in the room or that lots of people liked guacamole, beans and rice, and salads with every vegetable on the planet thrown in just to make it interesting. The conversation was spirited and wide-ranging and Mimi found it interesting that when Sonia, Virgie, and Alfreda talked about their lives, it was before the circumstances that had brought Mimi to their door, and when they discussed their husbands, even if the discussion brought tears, it was without the despair Mimi had first heard from them. Was it just because they now felt safe, or was there something else at play? The only topic that was off limits was Alfreda's sons. Even when Sonia and Virgie spoke of their children, nobody mentioned the Tompkins boys. It was as if they no longer or never had existed. Something within Mimi desperately wanted to raise the issue, but some other place within her—her higher self, perhaps?—prevented it. Hoping for encouragement from Bobby Gilliam, she sought his gaze, but he was obviously and intently avoiding the eye contact she sought, which let her know that a one-on-one chat with Detective Gilliam definitely was in order.

"I do have some information to share with you," Mimi said when everybody had finished second helpings and had their eyes on the desserts. "No hard facts right now, but I think that will change soon because my colleague, Joe Zemekis, is on his way to Pennsylvania—"

"The crash!" Virgie Barrett exclaimed. "He's going to find out what happened!"

Mimi was nodding. "We think so," she said.

Virgie was weeping in earnest. "All this time nobody would tell us anything!" Sonia and Alfreda moved in close and put their arm around her and held her close, and that's when another piece fell into place for Mimi. In addition to the fact of feeling safer, these women also felt that they mattered, that somebody cared enough about what was happening to them to do something about it.

"Are you doing interviews this evening, Ms. Patterson?" Linda Lopez asked.

Mimi shook her head. "I didn't come here to write a story. I came for exactly the reason I said, for the reason I gave Lieutenant Maglione. I wanted to see how you all were doing."

Sonia's phone rang then. She answered, listened for about three seconds, hung up, looked at Alfreda and said, "That Dexter is trying to break into your back door."

Bobby Gilliam was on his feet and halfway out the door. "I've got the back!" he said to Alice, who was right behind him and headed, Mimi knew, for Alfreda's front door.

"Watch here," Alice said to Linda as she followed Bobby out. Linda Lopez triple-locked the front door and hurried to check the locks on the back door. She dimmed the lights and ordered everyone away from the windows.

"That son of a bitch!" Alfreda spat the words from her mouth as if they were poison, and rage creased her face. Sonia and Virgie, too, registered only anger at the news of Dexter Davis's violation. No trace was evident of the beaten-down resignation and fear that had marked these women when Mimi first met them.

She stood up. She needed to find out what was happening at Virgie's, but Linda's raised hand and quiet, calm voice stopped her. "Please, Ms. Patterson. We don't know if he's alone," she said. What she didn't say was that DD's arrival at the back door might be a diversion or a setup, which was why they were sitting away from the front door in semi-darkness. Dexter Davis was truly a bad guy who had proven that he'd do anything to get his way. So, would he try to go in the back door and wait for her, or somebody like her, to open the front door? Sure he would. Mimi sat back down. Phil Diaz could be outside, waiting to rush Sonia Alvarez's door. Or perhaps she'd been reading too many mystery novels. Then the "truth is stranger than fiction" reality smacked her upside the head and she remembered why she was there. Dexter Davis was a cop, a dirty cop, and three other cops whom she knew well were at that moment risking their lives to keep her safe, and she was the one who had put them at risk. Round and round. The shit cycle just kept going round and round.

Two slow knocks at the front door, followed by three rapid ones. Linda opened it and Alice, gun in hand, entered. "All clear," she said. "I think Bobby threw Davis down the back stairs. At least that's what it sounded like. It also sounded like a car was waiting for him and it burned rubber on the way out. I got make, model, and partial plate. Nothing unusual in the front parking lot except for your vehicle," Alice finished, looking directly at Mimi. Just in time she stopped herself from asking Alice how she knew what kind of car she drove. She and Gianna co-owned the damn thing.

Mimi stood up. She had to get out of there right now! She'd planned to have private talks with each of the cops to gain some insight into their respective charges, but that would have to wait. "Is it OK if I leave?"

"If you can wait until Bobby returns, that would be great," Alice said, "then I'll walk you to your car." It wasn't a request, so Mimi sat back down as Alice tucked the gun into the back waistband of her slacks and pulled her shirt down over it, but she kept her back to the door while Linda remained across the room within easy reach of Sonia, Virgie, and Alfreda. Mimi hadn't seen Linda's weapon but she knew it was there.

The knock code at the door signaled Bobby's return and Alice opened the door. He was bleeding heavily from a cut above his left eye. Sonia, Virgie, and Alfreda sprang into action as one. Sonia rushed into the bathroom for the first aid kit while Virgie and Alfreda wrapped ice cubes into dish towels. That's when Mimi saw the damage to Bobby's right hand, but the three women, mothers all, saw all the injuries immediately. What Mimi did see was that Bobby whispered something to Alice, then took up the position with his back against the front door while Alice, phone in hand, went into the bedroom. Mimi knew that she was calling Gianna, and she didn't think it was to report that Bobby had thrown DD down a flight of stairs, or even that he had a cut above his eye.

When Bobby was taken care of, a process that he seemed to thoroughly enjoy, coffee was made and dessert was served. Virgie brought Mimi a very healthy serving of blueberry cobbler. "I made it myself and I do hope you like Southern cooking."

"I grew up on it," Mimi said, accepting the cobbler and hoping that having to eat it left-handed didn't mean most of it would end up in her lap.

"Don't believe her," Alice scoffed, the South Carolina Gullah heavy in her voice. "She's from the South all right—Southern California. Los Angeles, to be exact."

"But my people moved west from Louisiana and Texas, and that's the South as far as I'm concerned," Mimi said, her mouth full of blueberry cobbler.

"Only somebody from LA would think Texas is the South," Alice drawled amid hoots of laughter and derision as a good-natured geography lesson took place. Mimi was on her second helping of cobbler when Virgie asked for a report from Bobby on his interaction with Dexter Davis, and the room quieted immediately. Mimi wasn't the only one who wanted those details, and Bobby was happy to provide them. He started with the shock on DD's face when Bobby snuck up the steps behind him as he worked to pick the lock.

"It would have taken him until next week to pick that lock," Bobby said, "and he jumped a foot in the air when I said that. Then he took a swing at me, but I ducked it. Wasn't so lucky the second time. He's fast, I'll give him that much," he said, and returned the ice pack to his face.

"I want to hear the part where you threw him down the steps!" Virgie said.

"That's when I took a page out of Ms. Patterson's playbook," he said raising his right fist in a very powerful-looking jab. No wonder his knuckles were scraped and bleeding, Mimi thought, looking down at her own hand.

"You remember that time the Boss broke a couple of bones in her hand when she fired on that skinhead?" Bobby asked, and Linda nodded; Alice shrugged and shook her head. "That's right, Long Legs, that was before your time. But Ms. Patterson remembers. She was there." He nodded at her and offered her his raised fist.

"I'm not fist bumping with you, Detective Gilliam!" she exclaimed, holding her bandaged hand to her chest. She stood up. "I'm going home before y'all make me hurt myself."

"*Ooooh!* Ms. Patterson said 'y'all', y'all! Now I'm impressed!" Alice was giving full-on Gullah and nobody understood a word she said, but the howls of laughter released all the residual tension.

"Do you want to take some food, Ms. Patterson?" Sonia asked.

"Indeed I do!" Mimi said, knowing that Gianna probably hadn't eaten. "And if there's any of that cobbler left—" And she watched Virgie pile a healthy serving into a bowl before sidling over close to Bobby and whispering, "Call me tomorrow, please." Then she walked over to stand before Alfreda who was sitting alone. "Are you all right?"

She gave Mimi a slender smile and a slight nod and a full shoulder shrug. "I guess I let myself hope that he had gone."

"How can he go, Alfreda, when he has your children?" Mimi asked pointedly, and Alfreda flinched as if she'd been hit. *Something's wrong with this woman! I really gotta talk to Bobby! And soon!*

"Come on, Patterson, I'll walk you to your car," Alice said, holding the bags of food that Mimi was taking with her.

"Thank you all," Mimi said, pausing at the door, "for your hospitality, but mostly for your strength and courage. Lookin' good, like women warriors!"

"Thanks to you, Ms. Patterson!" Virgie said. "You stood up for us." Then she rushed over to Mimi and hugged her and Sonia followed suit. Mimi turned and headed for the door to save Alfreda the embarrassment of having to wrestle with her feelings because it was clear that at that moment, she had no hug for Mimi Patterson.

"Thanks for the assist," Mimi said to Alice when they were outside, walking to her car.

"I envy you," Alice said quietly.

"What, you're jealous of my cast?"

"I wish I had somebody worth hitting somebody for."

Mimi hesitated, then said, "I thought you did."

"You mean Evie?" And when Mimi nodded Alice said, "Evie is a wonderful woman but . . . well . . . she's not the one."

"Oh. I'm sorry. So you all have called it quits?" Mimi asked, trying to recall exactly when she'd encountered Evie at the gym and realizing that she'd lost all track of time. Days had gone by, maybe even weeks.

"Not exactly," Alice said.

Mimi stopped walking. "What's that mean? Either you're a

couple with Evie or you're not, Alice. Either you all have split or you haven't."

"I'm hoping she'll get the message without me having to say the words."

"Well what a cowardly, shitty thing to do, Alice, especially to someone you just described as a wonderful woman!" Mimi was pissed off, mostly because what Alice was doing reminded her too closely and too painfully of her breakup with Beverly. Then she remembered something Evie had said. "Tell me you're not ghosting her, Alice."

"Say what?"

"Ghosting. Pulling a disappearing act. Not talking, not being present."

"I didn't know it had a name but, yeah, I suppose so. I'm hoping that she'll get pissed off and dump me," Alice said. "It's better that way."

"Better for you, maybe, but I'm pretty sure Evie's not feeling so good."

Alice had no response to that so they walked in silence across the Sunset View front courtyard and out to the street. Then Alice stopped suddenly, stiffened, drew her weapon and gave Mimi her own bags to carry. Almost too late she saw what Alice had seen: the car parked next to her car, the person inside taking down the number of her license plate. Alice was taking the plate number of that car, too, only she was speaking it into her phone. "I got all the digits this time," she said. "4-Larry-Thomas-Peter-887. And I swear that's Dexter in the rear passenger seat." But the car sped away before Mimi could get a clear look. "I don't like him scoping your car," Alice said.

Mimi didn't like it, either, but there was nothing she could do about it. She walked around the car to make certain it hadn't been vandalized, then punched the remote, unlocked the doors, and put the food bags on the floor in the front. "You all will be OK, right? I thought that asshole was long gone. What did he do, double back to see if Bobby was still here?"

"Doesn't matter. He gets brought down tomorrow. All of 'em do."

"What's that mean, Alice? They get brought down?"

She was shaking her head. "I've already said too much. But I'm sure you'll find out. Get home safe, okay?"

"Yeah. Alice, what do you think of Alfreda Tompkins?"

"Huh," Alice said with a snort, "you asked the question, you must have the answer."

"I don't; that's why I asked."

"Here's what I know: She didn't kill the motherfucker who took her children and that's all I need to know about who she is." Then, tucking her weapon into the waistband of her slacks, Alice walked back to the Sunset View Apartments and Mimi got in her car and drove home. The ride was anything but pleasant. She tried not to be pissed off at Alice for her treatment of Evie; after all, it was none of her business. But then Evie had made it her business, hadn't she? And there was her ambivalence about the women of Sunset View. Overall they were faring better than when she'd met them but there was some underlying, residual thing that discomfited her, mostly because she couldn't define what it was. Just a feeling in her gut.

She poured a healthy shot of bourbon over some ice cubes and went to sit in her den to think. No TV or music, very little light, just bourbon and brain work.

Phone already in hand, she punched in Alice Long's number. The cop answered in the middle of the second ring.

"Is something wrong?" she asked.

"Just a question," Mimi answered. "What did Bobby say to you when he got back from confronting Dexter Davis?"

There was a long silence and Mimi let it drag out. Finally Alice said, "He said that Davis tried to kill him. That's why he threw him down the steps."

"She won't leave him in there under those circumstances, will she?" Mimi asked, and they both understood that Gianna was the "she" being referenced.

Another silence, this one not as long. "You'll have to ask her yourself. A pillow talk kind of conversation, I'm thinking," Alice said, and disconnected.

CHAPTER SEVEN

Showing up unannounced at morning roll call was something the Chief did. He didn't do it all the time so it couldn't be considered a habit, but he did it often enough that division commanders were not surprised when they saw him roll up in his shiny black Chiefmobile, and the head of the Riverside District, Inspector Gerald Jenkins, who'd gotten a heads up from his duty sergeant, was standing at attention when the Chief walked in the front door that Thursday morning. He saluted and stuck his hand out but it was not until there was no handshake did he realize that something might be wrong. Then he took notice of the number of people who had entered the building in the Chief's wake and he knew this was no routine roll call inspection.

"'Morning, Chief. Is something wrong?"

"Yeah, Gerry, there is, but it gets fixed, starting today," he said, and headed for the shift change room where everyone already knew their Chief was in the building and therefore were expecting him. Before the duty sarge could say the words, "Ten Hut!" all the officers were on their feet, at attention. The Chief strode to the front of the room. Those who'd come with him stood off to the side. "Dexter Davis, front and center!" the Chief said. Loudly and clearly.

DD, looking surprised, even a little smirky, but not fearful, made his way to the front of the room and saluted.

"You're under arrest," the Chief said, grabbing his arms and whipping him around with so much speed and strength that DD was cuffed and facing the Chief, sputtering and stuttering without really speaking. "Will you take his gun and badge, Detective?"

"Yes, sir, Chief," Bobby Gilliam said, fronting DD, who finally found his voice.

"You motherfucker!" DD exclaimed, his eyes widening with recognition. "I should have killed you last night!"

"You say one more word and I'll knock your teeth down your throat," the Chief said, and the former Golden Gloves middleweight boxer definitely could make that more of a promise than a threat. He locked eyes with DD as Bobby stripped the now-criminal of his cop gear. "If I could, I'd walk you out of this building barefoot, in your underwear. You got no business in the uniform of the D.C. police department," the Chief said, and in the next breath, "Phillip Diaz, front and center!"

Diaz looked about to faint as he complied with the order. He tripped several times and only the tight formation of the cops kept him from hitting the floor. He was shaking when he finally faced the Chief and, unlike DD, he knew exactly what was coming. "I'm sorry," he whispered.

"Damn right you are! Officer Lopez, will you take his badge and gun?"

Phil Diaz's knees buckled when Linda Lopez walked before him and he recognized her as the cousin of the woman he had raped. "I didn't mean it," he said. "She knows I didn't mean it! I told her! Ask her! She'll tell you!"

"Stand up straight!" the Chief ordered, and Diaz managed to do that while Linda relieved him of his gun and badge, then turned him around to cuff him. She placed his cop gear in the Chief's outstretched hand and pulled Diaz toward the door where he joined DD in the company of several Internal Affairs inspectors.

The commotion of a struggle in the room captured everyone's attention but only those close to the uniform crabbing along the floor on the tops of the feet of the gathered officers could tell what was happening, which was that Mike Berry was trying to make a run for it. Well, not exactly a run, more like a crawl.

"Sergeant Michael Berry! Front and center!" the Chief ordered, and those nearest Berry hauled him to his feet and propelled him forward with the kind of fervor that suggested that the desk sarge was not a particular favorite among the rank and file. The Chief grabbed him and snatched the stripes off his shirt. "Detective Long!" Alice was beside Berry and had his arms behind his back before his eyes clearly focused on who she was, and when they did he started to babble. She ignored him and took his gun and badge, which she added to the collection in the Chief's waiting hand.

Berry kept trying to make words out of the babble pouring from his mouth, and when he finally did manage coherent speech, it would have been worth listening to on any other day. "He made me do it and I can prove it!" Berry said, trying to shout but mostly croaking.

But DD heard him from across the room. "You shut the fuck up, you little weasel!"

"Tell it to IA," the Chief said. "That's what they're here for," and he waved Alice and Berry toward the door. Then the Chief turned to the room and silence fell. Who else would he call? "As of this moment, Inspector Jenkins is no longer in charge of this station. He is being replaced by Captain Mildred House," and he waved forward the only white-shirted woman in the room, who had most likely been overlooked because, despite the white shirt and the stars and bars and insignia on her collar, she looked exactly like the grandmother she was. However, anyone unfortunate enough to have run afoul of Captain Millie House knew it was a mistake not to be made twice.

She stood in front of the Chief and let everybody get a good look. Then she turned to the duty sergeant. "Call your roll, Sergeant, and make your assignments. Then bring me the roster. I want to know who answered and who didn't, and who's doing what, where."

"Yes, ma'am," the sergeant said, and saluted, as if submitting the daily duty roster to the station house commander was normal procedure—which it most definitely was not, though it most definitely was about to be.

She returned the salute and left the room. The Chief followed her out.

Gerald Jenkins stood as if glued to the floor, uncertain what to do. Two IA inspectors solved his dilemma. One on each side, they guided him out of the room and into the hall where he seemed to come alive. "Let's go talk in my office," he said.

"You don't have an office," one of the IA guys said. "But we can talk in one of the interrogation rooms that's not being used. This early in the morning, gotta be at least one empty one, right?"

Gerry spied the Chief headed for the front door. He broke from his IA minders and ran. "Chief! Chief! I don't know anything about any of this!" he exclaimed when he caught up with the Chief. "Whatever this is, I don't know anything about it, I swear to you I don't!"

"You're either a liar or a fool, Gerry. Either way, you've got no business running one of my station houses," the Chief said, and walked around him and out the front door. Then he stopped suddenly and turned around. He was looking for Bobby Gilliam, Alice Long, and Linda Lopez, and he saw them standing together. He beckoned them forward and they came running, obviously relieved at not being left behind. As happy as they'd been to assist in the takedown of Phil Diaz, Dexter Davis and Mike Berry, they had no wish to be stranded at Riverside HQ with those guys' colleagues and a bunch of Internal Affairs spooks. They wanted to get back downtown, back to their unit, back to their Boss, back to their own colleagues.

And Gianna was glad to have them back—glad and relieved. When Alice had called the previous night to say that Dexter Diaz had pulled a switchblade on Bobby and cut his face, she'd called the Chief and told him—she hadn't asked him, she'd told him—that she was pulling her people out of Sunset View. They weren't trained in the surveillance of other cops, especially one as dangerous as Dexter Davis. Thankfully he had not argued with her. His own research had pointed to myriad and major problems at Riverside and he'd already gotten IA on board. "The Rat Squad," as IA was known among the rank and file, had no problem moving on such short notice, as they definitely were trained in the surveillance, as well as the investigation, of other cops. That, after all, was their job. Between Mildred House and the Internal Affairs investigators, all the laziness, the rottenness, the ugliness in Riverside Station, wherever it existed, would be rooted out and eliminated. And Riverside wasn't the only station in line for a shake-up because the Chief didn't think it could possibly be the only station with problems. There was no time to train a bunch of new commanders, so he'd play station roulette with the ones he had. Everybody would be assigned to a different command, starting Monday. No notice would be given, no choices or options would be offered. He wasn't naive enough to believe that he could prevent the presence of a dirty cop in his department, but he could and would make certain that there would never again be a whole nest of 'em in one station, that there would never again be another Sunset View situation. Not on his watch.

Mimi was surprised that Bobby Gilliam actually called her as requested. She was at her desk contemplating lunch when the phone rang and she immediately invited him to join her. He immediately accepted and asked if Alice and Linda could come along. Of course they could. And how did she feel about the Mexican Cantina on Central? One of her favorites. Good, they'd meet in half an hour.

The cops were there when Mimi arrived and they seemed as genuinely pleased to see her as she was to see them. Hugs all around—then she looked closely at Bobby's eye. "Didn't look like that last night," she said.

He touched it and quickly removed his hand; that had hurt. "Just got a couple of stitches and the drugs must be wearing off. Hurts like a—well, you know what."

She nodded understanding; yeah, she knew. "A fist didn't do that."

"You're right," Alice said, "it was a knife." She said the words and watched Mimi hear and understand them.

"That bastard cut you?! That close to your eye?!" Mimi thought

151

about everything she'd found out about Dexter Davis, and if she'd thought he was a despicable bastard before, this nailed the coffin shut. "I'm glad you tossed him down the steps and I hope he's feeling it this morning."

"What he's feeling this morning is being in jail with cons who know he's a cop," Linda said, and they filled her in on the morning's activities, enjoying the telling, the reliving, as much as watching the reporter's reaction to it. Mimi had known the Chief for a lot of years, long before he became the city's top cop, and she knew his propensity for colorful behavior as well as colorful language. But this—going to roll call and personally arresting three cops—this was new territory even for him. For sure he was sending the message that dirty cops would not be tolerated inside the D.C. Police Department and, Mimi was certain, he wasn't finished with his message-sending activities.

"So, does this mean your job at Sunset View is done?" Mimi asked.

"Pretty much," Bobby said.

"We'll go back this evening and let the women know," Alice said.

"Sonia and Virgie especially will breathe easier," Linda said.

"You think they'll be all right?" Mimi asked.

"Don't you?" Alice asked.

"What do you think, Ms. Patterson?" Bobby asked. "You asked to talk to me about Alfreda, what I thought about her. Why? What do you think?"

"I don't really know what to think," Mimi replied.

"Give it a shot," Alice said, challenging, provocative.

I'd like to give you a shot, Mimi thought, not charitably. "From the very beginning I've wondered how it could happen that an entire apartment complex, even a small one like Sunset View, could lose all of its men, making all of its women vulnerable to predators like DD and his pals. I mean, we all know that women have gotten the crappy end of the stick for so long, and have managed to make it for so long, despite the crap on the stick. So, what made this situation different?"

"And what answer did you come up with?" Linda asked, really wanting to know.

"That every system that should have provided support for them—the large systems—failed them: The military, the police department here in D.C., the police in Pennsylvania, the insurance company, and quite possibly the church, because I can't believe that none of these women belonged to a church, and yet I've never heard one of them mention a church or a minister. And these are women who've done everything right, but nobody—no safety net—was there for them. So they gave up. They gave in. They threw in the towel. But *why?* That's what I'm not getting, that's what I hope you all can help me with. What am I missing?" Mimi looked at the cops and they looked back at her.

"What's the one thing you want to ask all of them?" Bobby asked her. "Just one thing you want to know. What is that one thing?"

"I want to know where their mothers are," Mimi responded. The almost universal support system and backbone for people in trouble: Mom. Mother. Mommy. It's who almost everyone called, or wanted to call, when times got really bad, and except in the cases of the really bad ones, she always showed up, because if anybody knew how to wield a crappy stick it was Mom.

"That's a very good question," Alice said, "and one we happen to have an answer to—at least in the case of the three women we were responsible for. Sonia's mother was deported. She was illegal. Sonia and her siblings got to stay because they were American-born. Virgie's mother died of breast cancer ten years ago. And Alfreda's mother is in prison for prostitution, drug dealing, and murder."

"Well damn," Mimi said, and since there seemed to be nothing else to say, they ate. The black bean burrito and guacamole here were favorites of hers. So was the homemade sangria, and if it hadn't been the middle of the day she would have ordered a pitcher. Her enjoyment of the food, however, could not corral her all-over-the-place thoughts, especially the notion that perhaps she

153

was being unfair to the women, that she was branding them with a women of color stereotype. Black women, Latina women were known for their strength and courage in adversity, for their endurance. Suppose that was just so much bullshit? Suppose women of color were just like everybody else: some were strong and tough and damn near invincible, and some were not.

"One thing I can tell you about Alfreda Tompkins," Bobby Gilliam said, drawing Mimi back into the moment, "is that she is easily controlled and swayed by men."

"Are you saying she just allowed Davis to take her sons and turn them into drug dealers, that she didn't resist?"

"She thought he was going to mentor them, to father them. He was a cop, don't forget. And she thought he was going to be a man to her. By the time she realized who and what he was, and what he had planned for her sons—" Bobby held up his hands in a helpless gesture.

"Tell her the rest of it," Alice said.

"She believed that I came to rescue her, that I was there to replace Davis as the man in her life. I don't know how she's going to react to the news that Davis is in jail and that I'm leaving." Bobby took a deep breath. "And that her sons, at least the older one, probably won't be coming home."

Now it was Mimi's turn for the deep, heavy inhalation. "Oh crap."

"Ain't that the truth," said Alice, who had stepped into Cassie Ali's shoes in more than one way.

Everett Mason was the name of the perp who had spotted their cameras and blown their op and allowed the child sex traffickers to escape. It had taken them a full twenty-four hours to find his sorry ass, and then another hour to get him into custody and to HQ for questioning. They had arrested some badass perps before, but nothing like Everett Mason. First, he kicked and screamed and flailed around like a spoiled brat four-year-old having a tantrum. Then he cried. Then he prayed. Then he cried some more. Finally he fainted, and it wasn't a swoon or a fake; the chump fainted dead away like a distressed damsel in a Renaissance romance. Jim Dudley, Tony Watkins, and Tim McCreedy stood looking down at him, not believing their eyes. They knew what to do with a perp if you had to knock him out to subdue him. But if somebody fainted? They took advantage of the opportunity to cuff his hands behind his back and to join his feet with some plastic cuffs.

"Water," Dudley said, and Tim trotted to the car, grabbed a bottle of water, and tossed it over to Dudley, who quickly opened it and splashed most of it into Everett Mason's face. He came back to consciousness confused and sputtering, but as soon as his eyes focused and he realized who was staring down at him, he began squirming, as if he wanted to return to tantrum mode. The realization that he was immobilized caused a major shift in his demeanor. He went from sniveling and pitiful to furiously mean and nasty. He cursed them and spat at them, coming too close for comfort to Tony, who smacked him upside the head. Then they hauled him to his feet and tossed him into the back of the squad car. With Tony driving and Jim riding shotgun, they headed for the station. Jim called Gianna to let her know they were headed her way with Mason, and he began howling. Jim ended the call, turned around, and smacked Mason. He shut up and they rode in silence for a while.

"I'm going to be sick!" Mason wailed. "I don't feel good and I'm going to be sick!"

"If you puke in here, I will put my fist to your nuts so hard you'll feel 'em in your throat." This from Tim McCreedy who was riding in the back with Mason. Since the back doors in squad cars didn't open from the inside, he knew that if Mason really did throw up he'd never get out of the way in time. But Mason didn't throw up. In fact, he didn't do or say anything else until he sat, handcuffed and shackled and facing Gianna, in an interrogation room.

"I have the right to an attorney," he said.

"Indeed you do," Gianna replied. "We'll have you transported to Central Booking and Holding while we wait for your attorney. Have you already called him? Or her?"

"I called my wife. She knows what to do."

Gianna had done more than call his wife. She'd been to see her, armed with photographs and Everett Mason's laptop and cell phone. Unlike many women, who refused to believe the worst of their husbands, Rachel Mason seemed unsurprised to hear what Gianna had to say. Which is not to say that she wasn't furious. Disgusted and furious. "What should I do?" she asked.

So Gianna listened politely as Everett Mason refused to speak until the lawyer he thought his wife was sending arrived to offer counsel and post his bail. What his wife was doing while Everett waited was emptying their bank accounts and credit cards, liquidating their assets, filing for divorce, and preparing to take the children and leave town. "Take him to Central," she said to Dudley. "And make certain everybody knows why he's there."

"You can't do that!" Mason cried, and Gianna heard the underlying panic.

"I can and I will. I think you need to know how those little girls feel when grown men invade them," Gianna said, and walked out. The words and the images they produced made her ill. She was glad to be away from Everett Mason. Being in the same room with him made her ill, too.

The unit was buzzing with activity despite greatly reduced ranks, though they'd be back to full strength by tomorrow when Bobby, Alice, and Linda would be back. Tim, Tony, and Dudley would return in a couple of hours, after leaving Mason at Central, though she fully expected that they'd have to retrieve him before dinner was served in the cellblock.

"Anybody need me or may I go to my corner and the mountain of paperwork waiting for me?" She walked among them and felt them liking her as much as she liked them. She knew all their names and she was learning their strengths. The veterans among them thought she might be the best Boss they'd ever worked for. The newcomers didn't have any basis for comparison but if what they'd seen so far was what working for Lieutenant Maglione was going to be like, they were in for a hell of a great ride.

"We might need you, Boss."

"We're not really sure. Not yet."

Gianna walked over to stand behind and between Archie Ames and Annie Andersen, known as "The A's." The other similarity they shared was that together they probably didn't weigh 200 pounds— skinny as a twig, both of them. He was as dark as she was fair, he ran marathons (which quickly endeared him to Alice Long), and she was a yogini. And, funnily enough, he was a Buddhist and she a Baptist. Sgt. Tommi had assigned them to be eyes and ears at Metro GALCO because they both were gay—something they hadn't known about each other until the assignment. They'd become fast friends in the two weeks they had worked together, reminding the original HCU team of the bond that had existed between Tim McCreedy and Cassie Ali, but it wasn't something any of them would ever mention to Tim. Besides, he'd been so occupied with the takedown and subsequent events at the sex-trafficking warehouse that he hadn't spent much time in the unit, and therefore would not have noticed the growing relationship between The A's. Gianna hoped—futilely, she knew—to keep it that way. At least for a while, until Tim could begin to heal from losing Cassie.

"What is it you're not sure about?" Gianna asked, and they told her about a group of five people who frequented the center regularly—three men and two women, all apparently in their twenties, all white—and not one of them, The A's were certain, was gay.

"You know what that place is like, especially on weekends," Archie said, and Gianna did know: There were at least a couple dozen organized activities every Friday, Saturday and Sunday— workshops, classes, club and organization meetings, and social gatherings of every kind and description, for every kind and description of group . . . for women, for men, for transgender women, for transgender men, for teen women, for teen men, for transgender teens, for parents of all of the above. Several AA and NA groups held meetings at Metro GALCO, as did a variety of AIDS-related groups. And then there were the people who just came to hang out, who didn't attend anything, who just came to meet friends or lovers or people they hoped would become friends or lovers. People milled about in the hallways inside the building, and on the patios and walkways and grassy areas outside unless it was raining or snowing.

"These five people come at different times," Annie said. "They don't talk to each other. They just watch. One of them will go upstairs and walk around for a while, looking in classrooms but not going in any of them. Then another will go downstairs and do the same thing. One of them will sit on the steps outside and just watch people coming and going. They make eye contact with each other but they never speak. And always, all five are there at the same time."

"Do they carry anything? Backpack, briefcase?"

"Notebooks," Archie said.

"And they write in them," Annie said.

"We don't like it," The A's said in unison.

Gianna didn't like it, either. Not a damn bit. "How do they arrive?"

"We've never seen them arrive," Annie said with a frown.

"Take opposite ends of the block. Get in place early. Get the sergeants to give you surveillance vehicles and a backup with a camera." And she outlined for them a three-night surveillance plan that would have them watch how the subjects arrived, and that would capture any vehicles and/or associates. Once the subjects were inside, The A's would enter as well and continue observing. *I should have insisted on a visible police presence,* Gianna thought. *If I had, whoever these five are, they wouldn't be in play.* Her phone rang. Dudley. "Good work, you two. Really good work," she said to The A's, crossing to the corner of the room that was her office.

"Boss!" Dudley exclaimed as soon as she answered. "Your boy wants to talk! He says he'll tell you whatever you want to know. He'll tell you everything he knows. Just please don't leave him in Central with animals who want to hurt him. His words, Boss."

Gianna disconnected that call and made one to the Chief who, since his return from roll call that morning, had been occupied with the return of the sex traffickers from their trek along I-65 in Virginia, and overseeing the evidence collection process in and on their van. Two of the Virginia State cops who'd assisted in the apprehension had journeyed north to D.C., at the Chief's invitation, to witness the interrogation as well as to find out what the contents of the van revealed. Yes, it was in part a thank-you for their assistance, but more than that, it was concern—fear, even—that a group of international sex traffickers had a bolt-hole in Virginia. Did that mean they also had an operation there, as well? So far, however, the traffickers had refused to speak. Not a word. The Chief didn't even know if they understood English. His mood improved greatly after speaking with Gianna.

"Are you certain that Everett Mason character can name these bastards?"

"I'm fairly certain that he can tell you how he knew when and where the Broad Street warehouse went into operation. These people have networks of people like themselves. Of course, it all may be dependent on leaving him in the care of Dudley, McCreedy and Watkins, with the return to Central an ever-looming possibility," Gianna said. The last thing she heard was the Chief laughing.

That got a laugh from Mimi. They were stretched out on the benches in the steam room of the gym, which they had to them-selves that evening, though Mimi was worried that wouldn't last. She had told Gianna about Evie's fears and concerns—and her pain—about the deterioration of her relationship with Alice Long. What if Evie, a regular to the gym and the steam room, saw them and wanted to ask Gianna about Alice? "I'll tell her the same thing you did. Now relax."

She'd also told Gianna about her conversation with Alice and wished she hadn't in the wake of the wiseass response she received: "That's very good advice you gave her, sweetheart. Gaining some wisdom in your old age?"

Mimi let the old-age crack pass and instead congratulated Gianna on the successful completion of two major operations, and sang the praises of Alice Long, Linda Lopez, and Bobby Gilliam. "Not only are they first-rate cops, they are truly fine human beings. I feel better knowing they're out in the city fighting on the side of the angels," Mimi said, and meant it.

Gianna thanked her, with reservations. "I keep hearing what you said and realizing how right you were. I was thrown into the deep end of a pool of watery shit and I'm damn lucky nobody drowned, especially me. I'm also damn lucky that I have a few really good additions to the new team and that the one screw-up revealed himself early on." And she filled Mimi in on the hapless Officer Johnstone. "I turned him over to IA, but after this morning, he won't be at the top of their to-do list."

They lay in companionable silence for several long moments, both remembering but not at all regretting the time they spent keeping the details of their work lives separate for fear that one or the other of them would be compromised. Cops and reporters were notorious adversaries, and in the early days of their association they had almost killed the relationship before it became one, trying way too hard to maintain what they believed should be the proper distance between their lives and their jobs. Both had come to realize, though neither had articulated it, that despite how important their jobs were to them, they cared more about each other than they did about their jobs.

"How's your story coming? Has Joe uncovered the truth in Pennsylvania?"

"Joe is kicking ass and taking names! Pennsylvania may never be the same!" Mimi had spent an hour on the phone with him after her return from lunch with the cops, and what he'd uncovered was sure to rock the Pennsylvania state law enforcement community: It was the drunk-driving brother of a state trooper who'd caused the accident that killed the husbands of the Sunset Vista women, and the cops had covered it up to protect one of their own. But that was Joe's story, Mimi said. She wasn't sure what her story was, or if she even had one.

Gianna sat up quickly to look at her, losing the towel that was loosely draped over her and exposing breasts that always made it difficult for Mimi to think about anything but them. "This was your story! What happened, Mimi?"

Mimi sighed, sat up and told her. All of it. All of her doubts and concerns, including how she was guilty of stereotyping the women and then unfairly blaming them for failures that weren't theirs. "I'm as guilty as any right-wing fool who blames the victim for her misfortune!"

"No you're not! Stop whipping yourself."

"And I've got lots of ambivalent feelings about Alfreda Tompkins."

"You're not the only one. She called and cussed me up one side and down the other for 'taking Bobby Gilliam away from' her!"

"'Taking him from her?' Like you're, what, a rival instead of his boss?"

"Exactly like that. What was she supposed to do now? she asked. I told her to hire a lawyer. She wanted to know why. To keep her sons out of jail, I told her. Then she really got pissed off and that's when I hung up."

"Let's get out of town," Mimi said.

"What?"

"A long weekend—Thursday, Friday, Saturday, Sunday. Let's go up to the lake on Wednesday, come back Sunday night. What do you think?"

"If you'll let me sleep for four days, I'm in."

"You definitely can spend four days in bed but you'll have to do more than sleep, love of my life."

"I'll put in for the days off tomorrow."

"Me, too."

"Shall we go home and practice for those four days?"

Mimi's answer was to pull Gianna up and into an embrace that dramatically increased the temp in the steam room. "You know you're wet," she said into Gianna's mouth.

"Imagine that," was the breathless reply.

Gianna's debrief of Alice, Linda, and Bobby didn't take long; she already knew most of what they had to report because she'd been in such close contact with each of them for the duration of their covert stay at Sunset Vista. She just needed their written reports so she could complete hers. And despite the fact that she'd promised herself she wouldn't comment on the damage to Bobby's face, she couldn't help herself. "I'm glad you threw the son of a bitch down those steps! He came way too close to putting your eye out!" She wasn't expecting the grin she received in response.

"That's almost exactly what Ms. Patterson said."

She allowed the smile that lifted her lips. "Smart woman, Ms. Patterson," she said, waving them away and pointing to her desk. "Paperwork calls!"

Linda and Alice saluted and left. Bobby stood standing at the corner of her desk, facing her, so his words wouldn't be overheard. "I'm kinda worried about Alfreda Tompkins, Boss. She's—"

"She's mad as hell that you left. I know. She called me."

"I tried to explain—"

"But she didn't want to hear it. I know. Don't beat yourself up, Bobby. You did your job, more than your job if I know you—and I do."

"She kept wanting me to tell her what she should do, Boss: Should she keep her job, should she leave town, what should she do about her boys? And the worst thing is, she'd have done anything I said!"

"I told her to get a lawyer to help with her sons."

"I told her to go see Beverly Connors to help with herself," Bobby said. "The woman needs all the help she can get!"

"You're a good man, Bobby Gilliam, and a damn fine cop. I'm honored to work with you."

This time he saluted and left. She watched him make his way across the room to sit at the table with Alice and Linda, and she watched some of the others watch the three of them—the new guard taking the measure of the old guard. The HCU team would always be close, no getting around that, and the glue that was Cassie Ali would never erode. But next assignment she'd mix-and-match. Same thing with Jim, Tony, and Tim. Then her eyes and her thoughts returned to Bobby Gilliam. How on earth would he know to refer Alfreda Tompkins to Dr. Beverly

Connors? Bev was Gianna's best friend, Mimi's ex-lover, and a clinical psychologist in private practice who specialized in the treatment of families but who, thanks to Cassie Ali, also saw a fair number of cops who didn't want to be seen by the department shrink. Was Bobby a patient? She thought it a real possibility and hoped that Alfreda would take his suggestion to see Bev. She also hoped that he'd suggest the same to Alice Long. She was wound way too tight, and given how Mimi said she was handling things with Evie, not doing much to help herself. Alice really needed to see Bev. *Don't count on it,* Cassie said in her head. What they all needed was a vacation—she picked up the phone to call upstairs to her old office. She'd turned the space over to Eric and Tommi since much of the work her sergeants did involved personnel and HR matters, which couldn't be handled in a room full of people. When Tommi answered, Gianna asked her to fill out whatever paperwork Gianna needed to request days off, and to please get it signed by the proper person.

"That would be the Chief," Tommi said, "and you have to do that yourself. I'll get it ready and bring it to you." Gianna thanked her and hung up, imagining four days in bed with Mimi.

Tyler signed off on Mimi's vacation request without even reading it. "You going to hang out with the girls?" Kate and Sue were friends of his that he'd introduced Mimi and Gianna to. They had a house in Dunedin, on Florida's West Coast, on the Gulf of Mexico, that was close enough to a villa to be called that. Government employees both, they'd made a killing in tech stocks, had taken early retirement, left D.C., and never looked back. Mimi wished they were going to hang out with the girls, which would have felt like a real vacation. "Up to Freddie's cabin," she said. "Getting Gianna to take four days—might as well ask her to take four weeks."

"So you'll take what you can get and be happy about it," Tyler said, his eyes never leaving his computer screen and the story he was editing.

163

"You know me too well. Thanks," Mimi said, and returned to her desk and a ringing telephone.

"This is Sancho Panza," she heard when she answered it. He was a source inside the Corrections Department, so-called because he called Mimi Don Quixote for all the windmills she attacked—with varying degrees of success. "I'm calling about a juvenile whose name I never confirmed and who I never acknowledged was in our system," he said, and Mimi knew he meant Will Tompkins, Alfreda's oldest son.

"I wish I knew what you were talking about," she said.

"Then you won't care that the little fucker and a pal escaped early this morning and put two of ours in the hospital—one in serious condition. The little fucker sliced his face with a knife."

"Why should I care what somebody I don't know has done?"

"'Cause it looks like his daddy set the whole thing up. That's daddy with a capital *D*." And the call went dead.

Mimi sat still and quiet, turning over in her mind what she'd just heard. But before she could reach any decision about what to do the phone rang, and before she could speak Alfreda Tompkins was a shrill presence in her ear, demanding a phone number for Bobby Gilliam.

"First, I need for you to stop screaming in my ear, Ms. Tomp-kins, and calm down and tell me what's going on."

"What's going on is I need to talk to Detective Gilliam!"

"Then you're talking to the wrong person. You need to call his boss. Good-bye, Ms. Tompkins."

"Don't hang up! You helped me before! I need you to help me now!"

"Help you with what, Ms. Tompkins?"

There was silence on the other end of the phone and Mimi let it play out. She knew why the woman wanted to talk to Bobby Gilliam, and Mimi needed to hear her say it. Finally she did but she was no longer screaming and yelling. "My son escaped from that detention facility this morning and all these people have been calling me looking for him but I don't know where he is."

"What does this have to do with Detective Gilliam?"

"I don't know what to do, Ms. Patterson!" she wailed. "What should I do?"

"Do about what? Help me understand, Ms. Tompkins. Do you know where your son is?"

"No! I haven't heard from him."

"What have you heard? What happened this morning?"

"They say he escaped, that's all I know."

"So why do you have to do anything?"

Another long silence during which Mimi's patience went into retreat. She was about to hang up when Alfreda, with a heavy sigh, finally came clean. "He hurt a guard when he escaped, Will did. He was with another boy, and the two of them, they attacked the guards, put one of them in the hospital. They're calling it attempted murder, Ms. Patterson!" She was crying now. "He cut the man with a knife. The guard. And he said it was Will who cut him, not the other boy." Sobs choked off her words and Mimi waited for her to regain her composure, but she ended the call. Mimi gave her ten minutes to call back, and when she didn't, it was time to go to work. She spent the next two hours on the phone, calling friends and sources, checking, double-checking, triple-checking the facts surrounding William Tompkins's escape from the Mid-Atlantic Juvenile Correctional Center, and she had all the confirmations she needed—except the big one: that Will Tompkins's escape had been orchestrated by Dexter Davis. Mimi certainly believed it was possible; the cutting of the guard's face was too eerily similar to DD's knife attack on Bobby Gilliam. But she needed to get it independently confirmed.

She pulled her cell phone out of her pocket to call Bobby when a truly nasty thought ran through her brain: Was it possible that Dexter Davis was out? She called the Chief instead. He wasn't in and Randolph, his aide-de-camp, didn't know when he would be. "I don't really need to talk to him, Captain, I just need a question answered, please: Is Dexter Davis still locked up?"

Mimi knew that Randolph tolerated her because the Chief did, but she also knew that addressing him by his rank scored her points in her own right. However, lest she forget even for a second

165

that he was a cop first, he wanted to know why she asked the question, and when she told him, she heard his muttered curse. "I don't think he knows this," Randolph said. "I need to tell him."

"Will you answer my question first, please, Captain?"

"Dexter Davis is still locked up, Ms. Patterson, and he will be until the Internal Affairs Bureau completes its investigation. And it's my understanding that will take a while."

I'll just bet it will, Mimi thought as she punched in Bobby's number, then had to be content with a message asking her to leave one. She did, and then she called Gianna. If the Chief didn't know about Will Tompkins, then Gianna probably didn't, either.

"Oh fuck a duck!" was Gianna's less than professional response to hearing the news, and when Mimi shared all the information she had, Gianna's only response was, "I'm just glad we don't have to catch the little bastard. I've got enough to worry about."

Oh, shit. "Like what?"

"Like maybe some homegrown terrorists wanting to blow up Metro GALCO. I gotta go, babe. Love you."

"Love you, too," Mimi said to dead space. Homegrown terrorists. Did it ever stop? Would it ever stop? At least this one was in Gianna's wheelhouse. Blowing up the gay and lesbian center certainly was a hate crime, unlike the sex trafficking and Sunset View operations, which were—whatever they were. She still was pissed at the Chief for treating Gianna like some kind of recycling bin: Put lots of nasty stuff in and get back sanitized order. She supposed she should feel gratified at the level of trust he had in Gianna but she didn't; she felt resentful. She also thought she should feel excited at the prospect of so many potential stories on the back burner doing a slow simmer, just waiting to erupt, but she didn't. Any other time she'd have been standing in front of Tyler's desk, hopping from foot to foot, rattling off the details of first one story, then another, then another. No doubt the news of the escape from the juvenile detention facility already was on the wires, the attack on the guard being a centerpiece of the story, but there would be nothing about Dexter Davis and why he was important to the story . . .

Ah shit! She knew where young Will Tompkins was. At least, she had a pretty good idea. Wherever DD was housing and hiding the kids he had slinging his drugs was most likely where Will would go, though, as far as Mimi knew, the cops didn't know where that was; they hadn't had time to find out. So, who should she tell? Gianna had already made it clear that finding the boy wasn't her job, and if that was the case, then it wouldn't be Bobby Gilliam's job, either. The Chief? *It's not your job, either,* she told herself. You're a reporter, not a cop, so act like a reporter. She typed up all her notes from the last several hours, blending what she already knew with what she'd learned, and the truth was that while she had at least three potential stories, she didn't have one fully resourced, ready to go to publication story. Not yet.

CHAPTER EIGHT

It took them four days but The A's finally connected the five persons of interest who'd been a presence at Metro GALCO to a vehicle and a residence. It was a tedious and painstaking process: waiting and watching until they had photos of all five; then more waiting, watching, and following until they were tracked to the vehicle; then more of the same until they were able to follow them to a townhouse development in suburban Prince William County, Virginia. In addition to The A's, Eric and Tommi had assigned four other unit members, including the other two gay ones and four of the white ones, a decision made by Gianna after the vehicle, a four-wheel drive with Idaho license plates, turned out to be registered to a well-known member of an ultraright extremist group. C.A. had done a very thorough internet search and printed out pages of info on the group, which called itself, Why We Put the Constitution First. "Just reading about these freaks makes me want to take a shower," he said. "They hate pretty much everybody and they've wrapped all that hatred in the Constitution and tied it with a Bill of Rights bow."

"Which is good for us," Gianna said. "Those big footprints leave an easy trail for us to follow."

"So why do they think they're so damn smart?" Tommi groused.

"White privilege," Jim Dudley answered, and when he got

half a dozen "what the hell are you talking about?" looks, he expounded. "Everybody knows white people are smarter than everybody else, right? I mean, look how elaborately they set up their Metro GALCO operation. Whatever it is they're planning, when it happens, nobody will be able to trace it back to them. So damn smart they sent people in there who couldn't pass for gay in a room full of ninety-year-old straight church ladies with cataracts." Laughter exploded and continued for a while, but Jim wasn't finished. "One thing they do just right, though, is trust that the people they hate don't hate them back. That little fucker who massacred all those people in that church in South Carolina? They invited him in to pray with them. And I'll bet you my paycheck that your—what do you call 'em—A's? They're not the only ones to notice that those five shits aren't gay, but the others just aren't cops and don't think like we do."

"Yeah," Tommi said. "They're not devious, which could very well get them slaughtered, just like those good people in that South Carolina church."

"Which pisses me off all over again that Metro GALCO wouldn't let us in there—"

"Let's not go there, Eric," Gianna said calmly. "Dead horse. Besides, if we were a presence there, whatever those little shit-fucks are planning, wouldn't be happening—at least not there. So—"

"Hey, Boss! Come look at this!" Kenny Chang was on his feet, waving her over with both arms like an air traffic controller landing a plane, and they all hurried across the room to him where he thrust a handful of paper at Gianna. "That townhouse in Prince William they live—"

"The shitfucks," Tommi said.

"The—yeah, that's a pretty good name for 'em," Kenny said with a frown, then a nod. "Anyway, Boss, the house is leased to an outfit called WeNet4U, based in—you guessed it—Idaho, with an address listed as the same P.O. Box listed on the vehicle registration."

"I'm liking this a lot," Jim Dudley said. "Good work, you guys," he said to the A's. "And what are your names? I can't keep calling you A's."

"Archie Ames," Archie said.

"Annie Andersen," Annie said.

"Geez," Jim said. "Couldn't call you B's, could we?"

"I sure wish we could see inside that car and that townhouse," Eric said.

"They've been very careful not to give us the probable cause we need to look," Gianna replied, then added, "but I think it's just a matter of time before they do. So let's get the warrants ready."

"Warrants!" Eric exclaimed. "We don't even know their names!"

"Warrants for the vehicle and the residence," Gianna said, "based on their connection to known race hatred and terrorist activities. We'll start there. And involve Captain Randolph. He writes such good warrants the U.S. attorney tried to get him to teach a class."

The A's looked at each other, then at Gianna. "Ah, who's Captain Randolph?" Archie asked.

"Work with your sergeants on the warrants. I don't expect you to handle them, I know you're not ready, but you need to know and understand the process. Many an arrest has tanked because the language in the search warrant wasn't sufficient to cover the search." She turned to head back to her corner, then turned back. "And get him thinking about arrest warrants. Tell him everything we know about those five people. When they do whatever it is they're going to do, I don't want us wasting time waiting for warrants."

"You seem pretty sure they're going to do something," Tommi said.

"Just a matter of what and when," she said, and turned back to her corner. "Jim, with me, please, and by all means bring your colorful shitfuck vocabulary." She waved him into the chair beside her desk. "You guys all recovered from that warehouse thing?"

He shrugged. "As recovered as you can get from something

170

like that. Tony has seen some pretty ugly shit in his career, but McCreedy—?" He shook his head. "The good thing was that it took his mind off losing his friend. At least for a little while."

"Yeah. Now they're all back with plenty of time to miss Cassie. Which is what I want to talk to you about, Jim. I want to integrate the two units, Hate Crimes and this new thing that we still don't have a name for. What I'm thinking to do, at least initially, is have two operational teams within the larger unit: You'll run one and I'm thinking to have Bobby Gilliam run the other, with a mix of old and new people in each. You can keep Tim and Tony if you want, and then get with the sergeants to make some other picks."

"How about those A's? Sharp kids."

"Anybody but them," Gianna said. Jim nodded his understanding. "But it'll affect Gilliam the same way, won't it?"

"He'll be too focused on the responsibility of running a team to let that get in his way," she said, and she knew that was the truth. "I want everybody to be able to do any and every assignment, Jim, but if you notice that somebody has a particular talent, develop it. Okay? And if you spot a weakness, do whatever it takes to fix it."

He stood up. "Yes, Boss, and thanks."

She stood, too, and spied Bobby across the room just coming on shift. She waved him over, sat him down, and told him the same thing she'd just told Jim Dudley. First he stared at her in total and complete disbelief. Then he saw that she was totally and completely serious. "I don't know what to say. Except . . . are you sure?"

She gave him a hard look. "What's going on, Bobby?" And he laid out his concern for Alfreda Tompkins's mental stability and her unhealthy focus on him. "She called me half a dozen times and I never called her back," Gianna said. "I'll do that today and make it clear that she is not to attempt any further contact with you or I'll have her arrested."

"What about her son?"

"Not our problem, Bobby. Our job at Sunset View is done. Now, I need your head in the game. In *this* game. All the way in, is that clear?"

"Yes, Boss!"

"Good. Two of your new team will be Archie Ames and Annie Andersen—"

"The A's! I've heard about them. I hear they're pretty damn good."

"They are. You and Dudley get with Tommi and Eric and choose the rest of your team. Do it now. I want you guys operational if we need to move. And Bobby? I'm 100 percent sure." She got up from her desk and went to stand over him, looking down. "That cut beside your eye is healing."

He touched it and nodded. "Stitches come out tomorrow."

"You know that little shitfuck cut a guard in the face during his escape."

"I heard. From Ms. Patterson, as a matter of fact. Guess Davis taught him how to do more than sling drugs." He shook his head sadly. "Kid deserved better than that." He stood, saluted, and crossed the room to join Dudley and the sergeants, and the four of them left, going, Gianna knew, upstairs to the office. She pulled out the stack of message sheets she'd been ignoring and called Alfreda Tompkins, only to hang up when she realized the woman wouldn't be home from work yet. She'd call her later. Then she returned a call to Delores Phillips and spent a very pleasant few minutes talking with her and telling her what she could of what happened in the warehouse. Delores didn't mind that she couldn't know everything, she was just grateful to have what she called "the nightmare next door" over. But Gianna knew the nightmare wasn't entirely over—not for the victims. The one upside was that Everett Mason had proved to be an excellent snitch. Not only did he give up information on the local traffickers, he provided access to an international network of what, thanks to Jim Dudley and Tim McCreedy, they now all referred to as baby-rapers. Virginia authorities were grateful because they were able to shut down an operation before it got

172

up and running; Arnie Spitzer and his National Center for Missing and Exploited Children got information they needed to close several open cases; and even the federal agencies still interested in pursuing sex traffickers were happy to take over the case when the Chief offered it to them gift-wrapped. But nobody wanted to take responsibility for twelve girls who'd been brought into the country illegally, hooked on heroin, and raped repeatedly. Nobody wanted to be responsible for seeing them through detox and restored to health, to say nothing of trying to find out who they were and where they were from and returning them home—if, indeed, they had homes to return to. And Gianna couldn't get the sound of their wailing and howling and whimpering for drugs out of her head. The noise woke her at night.

She forced herself to focus on the piles and stacks of paper on her desk, most of which could be easily handled. As soon as she got reports from Dudley and the warehouse takedown crew, and from the Sunset View people, she could write her own reports of those operations. She looked at the pile the Chief had left with his hand-scribbled note on top: *DEAL WITH IT MAGLIONE! NOW!* and she knew he meant it, because on top of that was her signed vacation request form. Yes, he was saying—you got what you want; this is what I want. She sighed and opened the top folder and wished she could be with her sergeants and team leaders as they built their teams instead of digesting the paperwork for promotion to Captain.

As she sat and worked with Eric, Jim and Bobby, Tommi thought, and not for the first time, how unusual and different Gianna Maglione was as a boss, and how lucky and grateful she felt to be one of her sergeants. Here was a boss who wasn't a control freak, who actually trusted her subordinates to do their jobs and do them well, who was so secure in her own abilities that she didn't spend a lot of time looking over her shoulder or sticking knives in the backs of others. And the people who worked for her were the same way. There was no conflict or competition between Jim Dudley and Bobby Gilliam as they studied the roster and selected their teams. It was easily agreed that since Bobby had The A's on his team, Jim should have the other two gay members. "But since I already have McCreedy, doesn't that create an imbalance?" Jim asked.

"Then how about I take the Patel kid? Boss likes him, right?" Bobby asked the sergeants. "Thinks he's got lots of smarts? Then that'll make us even in the gay department. Now. How about women?"

And so it went until both teams were complete. "One thing bothers me, though," Bobby said, and he looked at each of the other three, one at a time, eye to eye: "Alice Long should be heading up one of these teams. Why isn't she?"

Eric and Tommi looked at each other. No way Gilliam could have overheard their discussion with Gianna on that very topic! And no way were they going to say why it was decided that Alice wasn't being given a team. They knew that Bobby knew that discrimination wasn't part of the picture: Alice was a lesbian, the Boss was a lesbian. Alice was Black and both Jim and Bobby were Black, so whatever the reason was, it was about something else, and because they all trusted the Boss 100 percent, they accepted her decision. But Eric and Tommi could see that they wondered. Nobody else did, though—nothing but excitement reigned at the unit meeting that afternoon when the teams were announced. Whoops and hollers, followed by hugs, high fives, fist bumps, and back slaps, followed by the self-designation of themselves as Team D and Team G, followed by separating into their designated teams, surrounding their team leader.

"I'm so glad you're all so happy," Gianna said, and got a standing ovation. She shared looks with Jim and Bobby and they restored order. "A few orders of business," she said, and updated them on the warehouse sex-trafficking and Sunset View operations. "Although neither one is totally wrapped and tied with a bow, our involvement in both is finished—unless there's a dramatic change and we're back on the case. And before anyone asks, the Chief would make that decision." She let that sink in. Then, "To put all the rumors to rest, Taylor Johnstone was dismissed from this unit and from the Police Department. I do not know the final results of the IA investigation and I don't care—unless somebody in this unit is involved. So, if anybody here had anything to do with his behavior, tell your team leader." The blank faces staring at her was answer enough. "OK, I like the Team D and Team G designations, but understand that you are *not* in competition with each other. We're all in this together— whatever 'this' might be at any given time. I want everybody trained and qualified to do everything, and I want all of you physically fit. If anybody doesn't understand what that means ask your team leader." She paced a few steps. "You all know that very often, information drives police work and investigations, and we happen to have three of the best information gatherers in the business: Vik Patel, Kenny Chang, and C.A. Jennings, and yes, they're assigned to teams, but their first job always is to provide the info we need to do our jobs."

"Um, Boss?" Kenny Chang's hand was in the air.

"Kenny?"

"Does that physically fit thing apply to the information gatherers, too?"

"I'm in training for my first Iron Woman competition, Kenny," Alice Long drawled. "You're welcome to train with me." She didn't crack a smile, but Kenny looked about to faint and the room broke up, Gianna included. She finally got herself under control.

"I'd be afraid to train with Alice, too, Kenny, so you can take a pass on training for the Ironman, but not on the physical fitness requirement." Still chuckling to herself she adjourned the meeting and watched as the team leaders took their charges to opposite corners of the room. She walked over to Eric and Tommi. "Good job, you two—thank you."

"Jim and Bobby did all the work, Boss. We just listened and took notes," Eric said, and Tommi agreed.

"Make sure Jim and Bobby know not to take their eyes and ears off Metro GALCO."

Gianna headed back to her corner feeling guilty for the sense of relief she felt. She knew that it most likely would be short-lived, but something was better than nothing, and having the heavy weight of the responsibility of the unit off her shoulders, even for a little while, was rejuvenating after the ugliness of the warehouse and Sunset View. Knowing that the people who shared the weight and the responsibility were among the most reliable and trustworthy people she knew was soothing. Her reward before settling down to the paperwork would be a quick check-in conversation with Mimi. They both were exhausted in mind, body, and spirit. They ate, sometimes together, sometimes not. They didn't talk very much when they were together, both finding the right words hard to come by, something that really worried Gianna because Mimi always had the right words. It was she, Gianna, who usually found it difficult, if sometimes not downright painful, to put her thoughts and feelings into words. They didn't sleep so much as they passed out from fatigue. But they made sure they talked to each other several times a day, if only to say, *I love you*. And when Gianna said those words to Mimi and heard them back from her, she was ready to get to work, as was Mimi.

"I don't know that I agree, Patterson, that the Sunset View thing isn't ready to be a whole story," Tyler said. He had pulled over a chair from the reporter-less adjacent desk and was seated next to her desk. The sight was unusual enough that more than a few people wandered by to take a look. Tyler, as usual, was oblivious. He concentrated only on what he was concentrating on, to the extent that Mimi often wondered how he managed to be an award-winning reporter when reporters had to notice everything and everyone all the time. But then again, it no doubt was his ability to single-focus that made him such a good editor. A great editor. "You've got three huge pieces to work with: the original situation that Virgie called you about, that shitstorm that Zemekis has managed to uncover in Pennsylvania—"

"That's Joe's story, not mine."

"And he'll be back tomorrow to write it. Then there's the Chief showing up at roll call to fire three dirty cops, and there's the

Tompkins boy's escape from prison, his attack on the guard, and the fact that the cops can't find him. Those are stories, Patterson."

"Yeah, all right, Tyler. If you say so."

Tyler rolled the chair closer and stared at her. "What's wrong with you? And what's that look that just crossed your face? Something just came to you."

"Get outta my brain, Tyler," she snarled at him, because what had just come to her was to wonder if the cops had figured out where to look for Robbie Tompkins. His arrest definitely would be a great jumping-off point for a story, but before she could share the thought, their names were called.

"Carson! Patterson!"

They looked toward the sound and saw the Exec beckoning. Tyler muttered something Mimi didn't hear and stood up. She followed suit and followed him across the room to the Exec's office, but the Exec kept walking and turned into the conference room, the one without windows and with a door that closed. Mimi saw why. The Weasel and one of the company attorneys were seated at the table—the two people Mimi despised most on the planet. "What is this shit, Tyler?" she muttered. He shrugged and shook his head and she followed him into the room. The Exec brought up the rear and closed the door. Not a comforting sign.

"Have a seat, folks," the lawyer said expansively, as if it were a social gathering. Mimi looked hard at him and his grin wavered, which was all she needed to see to know that whatever was on the agenda involved her. Tyler and the Exec sat. She didn't. She stood watching him—and trying to remember his name. She couldn't. "I said sit down, Miss Patterson," he said, grin wiped now.

"I hear better when I'm standing," she said.

"Then hear this: You are hereby suspended without pay for two weeks, effective immediately, for the assault on Ian Wilson, and you will apologize to him, in writing, said apology submitted to the executive editor being a requirement for your reinstatement."

"How about you hear this: I quit." She turned and walked out, missing the facial expressions left in her wake: fury on the Exec's, shock on Tyler's, surprise on the Weasel's, joy on the lawyer's, who said, "That went better than I expected! No more of her fake news! From now on, Todd, let's have Ian report to Stu."

The Exec stood up so hard and fast his chair rolled back and hit the wall behind him. "You don't make assignments in this newsroom. Ian Wilson will continue to report to me until I say otherwise." Tyler followed him when he stalked out and headed directly for Mimi. She was cleaning out her desk drawers when Tyler reached her.

"Please don't do this, Mimi! You don't have to do this!"

"Yes, I do, Tyler. I don't mind the suspension. To tell you the truth, I was surprised that I wasn't suspended that day. After all, you can't go around smacking an asshole in the workplace no matter how much he might deserve it—I get that—but I will not apologize to him, Tyler. Not ever."

"I think if we make that point to Todd—"

"I'm done talking, Tyler. And we both know that Todd isn't the final word on this." Cleaning out her desk meant putting lots of stuff in the trash because important things lived in her briefcase and left with her at the end of the day, and since she routinely backed up her files on an external hard drive, eliminating her presence on the office computer's hard drive was a matter of selecting all, and then deleting. She was ready to leave in a matter of minutes.

"Please, Mimi. Please don't."

"I'll call Joe and prepare him," she said, walking toward the elevator. He followed, silently. He stood there while she waited for the elevator, watched as she got on, watched her until the door closed on not only one of the best reporters he'd ever known, but on one of the best friends he'd ever had.

Her first inclination was to go to the gym for a strenuous workout, and while her body no doubt needed it, she didn't think her brain could withstand it, so she went home. She'd never been able to figure out what to do at home in the middle of the day. On the rare occasions she'd found herself in that situation she'd been sick or injured and therefore inclined to sleep the hours away. She was not so inclined this day. She changed clothes—she always was happiest in sweats or shorts and a tee shirt—then popped and buttered a huge bowl of corn, grabbed a cold seltzer, settled into her favorite chair in the den, and turned on the TV. She had so much stuff stored in the DVR she could watch for hours and not be caught up. She'd start with the British mysteries, her favorite, but she found she couldn't focus. Unlike so many of the American shows, you really had to pay attention to the British ones and her brain wouldn't settle down. It demanded that she deal with the reality at hand: She had quit her job. She was unemployed. That's when she exchanged seltzer for vodka, and pretty soon it didn't matter what was on television. Buttered popcorn was as good with vodka on the rocks as it was with ice-cold seltzer.

Gianna was surprised as well as pleased to see Mimi's car in the garage as the door slid up. Since she hadn't called to say she was on her way home, and she hadn't responded to Gianna's text that she was headed home, Gianna assumed that she was tied up at work. Surprise quickly became worry when Gianna opened the door and heard the TV blaring from the den and spied the almost empty vodka bottle on the kitchen counter. She hurried down the hall to the den—no Mimi. She crossed the hall to the bedroom and there was Mimi, in shorts and a tee shirt, sprawled across the bed, on top of the covers. And drunk! Gianna did a quick examination: She wasn't injured in any way. At least not physically. But something definitely was wrong.

"Mimi? Sweetheart? Wake up for just a second, please."

Mimi pulled a pillow over her head. Gianna pulled it away. "No, go 'way," Mimi mumbled, pulling the pillow back over her head.

Gianna wrestled with her to get her under the covers and knew she'd have to wait for morning to get an explanation. She undressed and, in bra and panties, went into the kitchen for one of her all-time-favorite dinners: a huge bowl of raisin bran with extra raisins. She took it to the den to watch at least two episodes of *The West Wing*, a program she hadn't seen when it aired, primarily because of her work schedule, but also because watching TV hadn't been one of her things to do. Mimi had watched it, though, and it remained one of her all-time-favorite shows despite the fact that, in her words, it made politics and politicians look a lot cleaner than they really were. Gianna had come to like it just as much, especially in the current climate. Yes, it was escapist television, but there really had been a time when being the president of the United States was a position of honor and respect, even if it wasn't who you voted for. Now? It didn't warrant a discussion. She ate her raisin bran, then got a glass of chardonnay, and fell asleep in the middle of the second episode. Mimi didn't budge when Gianna crawled into bed beside her. How drunk was she, Gianna wondered. She squeezed a nipple and Mimi still didn't budge. Pretty damn drunk, and an explanation definitely was called for.

Mimi grabbed her head and groaned when Gianna's phone rang at 7:15 the next morning even though Gianna answered it in the middle of the second ring, as she always did, as if it were noon instead of before daybreak.

"Good morning, Eric," Gianna said, sitting up and swinging her legs over the side of the bed. It was time to get up anyway.

"Sorry, Boss, but we've got a problem."

"Of course we do," Gianna said, taking the phone into the bathroom when Mimi groaned again, a sign she was in for a huge hangover, made worse by the fact that she rarely drank to excess. And as much as Gianna wanted to know why, she was working to stifle her own groan as Eric explained that the local TV news programs were full of reaction by local politicians to a BBC America story on how the D.C. police department took down an international sex trafficking ring, arresting three Eastern European men and rescuing a dozen underage Asian-appearing girls. The congressional committees with D.C. oversight powers were apoplectic but some local officials, including some from Virginia, were grateful to the D.C. police chief for putting a big dent in what could have been a very large operation. No, she told Eric, she had not known about the story; she was certain that no one inside the department had known about it. But everybody would know about it now.

And when she got to the unit, it seemed that everyone did. At least everyone who worked for her. They were all there and the BBC story was playing on the big screen on the back wall—all the images of the girls being rescued from the warehouse, the images from inside the warehouse, and the arrest in Virginia of the traffickers, their faces visible for everyone to see, as visible as those of the girls had been obscured, because while the identities of rape victims were protected by law, the identities of their rapists were not. And the only police officers speaking in the story were the D.C. chief and a Virginia state police official who was so visibly relieved at having a trafficking operation in his jurisdiction stopped before it had a chance to get started that he almost cried. Both cops decried the lack of federal involvement in what clearly was a federal crime.

"Well, we're in for it now," Eric muttered.

No shit, Sherlock, Cassie intoned, and Gianna jumped, then looked around to see if anyone had witnessed her reaction to the voice only she heard. Cassie had been so quiet of late that Gianna thought perhaps she had decided to be at peace. *No justice, no peace,* Cassie said, putting that theory to rest.

Bobby and Jim walked over to her. "What do you need us to do, Boss?" Jim asked.

"Nothing you can do," she replied. Nothing any of them could do unless requested by the Chief, and so far, she'd heard nothing from him. "No reason for you to be here this early."

"We had planned an early start to the day," Bobby said. "First the track, then the gym." And they were all dressed for it, Gianna realized.

"No need to change your plans," she said. "Just make sure you can be reached. And leave me at least one of the internet people and one of the social media people. I don't care who—one from each team, maybe?" Whatever the fallout from the BBC story was going to be, they needed to keep track of it. And she needed a cup of coffee. And the unit needed a coffee pot and a refrigerator and a TV, she thought. And at that moment a live news program appeared on one of the screens on the wall, and Tommi was coming her way with a carrier containing four large cups of coffee in one hand and a bag that was screaming raisin bran muffins in the other. The lousy start to the day had just improved with the ability of her staff to read her mind.

Mimi, however, felt like warmed-over death on a rusty plate. That was one of her old friend Freddie's favorite sayings to describe his worst hangovers. Mimi didn't have such a saying of her own because she seldom had hangovers, but she had one now and it was a doozy. She squeezed her head between the palms of her hands, hoping to mitigate the pounding as she sought to remember drinking enough of whatever she'd been drinking to result in a head the size of California. She wandered into the kitchen in search of clues. There were none; the kitchen was spotless. She opened the dishwasher—the popcorn bowl, the largest soup bowl, her favorite rocks glass. Gianna had been here and had cleaned up and she had slept through it. She opened the refrigerator—no extra food. That fact, along with the big soup bowl, meant Gianna had eaten raisin bran for dinner. She opened the freezer and the sight of the almost empty vodka bottle did the trick. She remembered everything, and it was enough to return her to the bedroom and to bed. She had opened that vodka and downed almost all of it because she was unemployed. Because she had quit her job. Because the stupid-ass company lawyer wanted her to apologize to stupid-ass Weasel Boy. Oh god! She was unemployed. She had quit the only job she'd ever had, the only job she'd ever wanted. Well, at least she now knew that getting drunk wouldn't make her feel any better.

She had crawled under the covers when she remembered that Freddie always took lots of aspirin when he was hungover, so she got up and found the aspirin in the bathroom cabinet. She shook four into her hand and guzzled the bottle of water on the bedside table. Then she downed the bottle on Gianna's side as well. She was back in bed when her phone rang, and she was surprised to see that she'd missed four calls. The current one was from Tyler, her no-longer editor. "What, Tyler?"

"Are you watching the Chief? What is he doing?" The low-emoting editor sounded almost frantic, which, had she been in a better mood, would have amused Mimi.

"No, I'm not watching the Chief, and I'm not going to. I'm going back to sleep."

"You gotta watch him, Mimi, and explain this BBC thing to me! What is he doing? You know him better than just about anybody, and if anybody understands what's going on, it's you."

"What BBC thing? What are you talking about, Tyler?"

"Just turn on the TV and tune into any news program. I'll call you back."

She grabbed the remote and turned on the TV and there was the Chief. She upped the volume to hear him explain how an observant citizen had alerted the police to the possibility of a child sex-trafficking ring operating in the middle of D.C., not five miles from Congress and the White House. He was, he said, shocked but not surprised. "After all, this is a worldwide problem but here in the U.S., because we don't see it, except on television, we think it doesn't affect or involve us. But it does." Then the local newscaster overrode the volume on the BBC report to share that federal authorities were calling for the Chief's head for over-stepping his authority, not only in surveilling and eventually shutting down the child sex ring in the Broad Street warehouse, but in pursuing its operators across state lines into Virginia. Then the BBC audio of the Chief returned, and he said, "I contacted every federal law enforcement official that I know—and I know a lot of them—in every agency and department of the federal government that might have any responsibility for enforcing the laws against the trafficking of women and children for sex, and there was no interest, *none*, in stepping in to take over my investigation, or to assist me and my department. So yes, I made the decision not to allow another child to be raped in that ware-house in my city and I shut it down."

Mimi muted the sound when the local newscaster's voice took

over. She was sitting upright in the bed, hangover and headache reduced to background noise. "Wow," she said. "You crafty son of a bitch!" Tyler was right. She knew exactly what he was doing. It was a brilliant tactic, and she was surprised that Tyler didn't get it. Did Gianna, she wondered? *Gianna!* "Ah, fuck!" she said as her new normal grabbed her by the throat, returning both headache and hangover to the fore. She picked up the phone to call Gianna, and it rang. *Tyler.*

"We got it! He is one savvy, sharp customer."

"Better late than never," Mimi said. "I gotta go, Tyler—"

"Wait, Mimi! Listen, we really need you on this story."

"No, you don't, not if you know what he's doing. All you need to do is sit back and wait for it." *It* being the shitstorm that the Chief had set in motion when he announced to the world, courtesy of the BBC, what anybody who'd been paying attention to the malfunctioning, misfunctioning, pitiful excuse of a federal government—or what was passing for a "federal government" these days—could see. All of the vacant, unfilled jobs in the State Department, the Justice Department, the Attorney General's office, the Department of Homeland Security, the U.S. Agency for International Development, even the CIA, were positions responsible for investigating and enforcing the laws that protected women and children from being stolen and sold into sexual slavery worldwide, including within the U.S. Not filling those jobs had nothing to do with streamlining the government and balancing the budget and everything to do with deliberately ignoring the dangers faced by women and children around the world. And the D.C. Police Chief had just told the world that the emperor was naked, while at the same time taking the heat off himself and, by extension, the D.C. government, for overstepping his authority. And, showing a very canny understanding of how the media works, he had done it on a Friday, guaranteeing that the story would have legs throughout the weekend: front page on all the major newspapers on both coasts and lead topics of conversation on the weekend TV talking-head news programs. "You crafty son of a bitch," she said again.

"That's why we need you, Mimi. He won't talk to anyone else. All calls are going straight to his public affairs office, which is handing out statements but not making him available in person."

"I can't help you, Tyler. I don't work for you, remember?"

"I only wish I could forget, like I wish it wasn't true."

"I gotta go, Tyler. Go have fun. This is a great story that should be enjoyed!" And it was, and if she were still a working reporter she'd be enjoying the hell out of it. But she wasn't, and that very important fact still was unknown by the woman she shared her life with. She called Gianna and got voicemail so fast she knew the phone was off, and there could only be one reason for that.

She hoped that Gianna wouldn't suffer any blowback from the Chief's actions and, leaving both text and voice messages, decided that she could tolerate coffee now. In fact, needed it now that the fog of the hangover had begun to dissipate. If she hadn't promised it to herself in her drunken state, she was promising it now: Drunk was not the state for her. Aside from being able to sleep until well after ten o'clock, which was when her feet finally hit the floor, drunk had nothing to recommend it. A drink or two was enough, though under the circumstances the momentary lapse in her usually good judgement was understandable. She had no experience being unemployed, but she'd get used to it. Much more difficult, though, would be adjusting to the absence of the feeling, the belief, the certainty, that what she did mattered. It had mattered for so many years because the notion and nature of a free press had mattered. Then, almost overnight it seemed, a loudmouthed, thin-skinned, narcissistic bully who didn't like the truth that was reported about him began to whine loudly and often about the fake news attacks on him, and the locust swarm of his supporters took up the whine until the bleat got so loud that news organizations like hers took to defending themselves and their output, while the real fake news outlets continued producing the fakery and outright lies. That made doing her job difficult enough, without the kinds of stories she found herself reporting: The murder of Cassandra Ali half a block from her mosque; the international sex-trafficking operation not five miles from Capitol Hill; the

185

group of women, willing victims in their own homes because the systems they trusted had failed them and they believed they had no recourse—she just couldn't do it anymore. Didn't want to, day after day, the need to understand hatred and depravity so she could write about it. Unemployment would be a welcome change. *Never figured you for the kind to cut and run.* Mimi sloshed coffee all over the counter and herself. The voice was so clear in her head. Who the hell was that?! *And the systems didn't fail them. You were there every time. The real news. And so were the real cops.* Shit. Cassie Ali. Why the hell was Cassie Ali in her head?

"Are you listening to me, Maglione?"

No, Chief, but I hear you, Gianna wanted to say. "Of course I'm listening to you, Chief." She couldn't tell him that she was trying to silence Cassie Ali in her brain. "It was brilliant, Chief. I just hope you haven't left yourself too exposed. You know the long knives on the Hill, not to mention those on the City Council, are kept sharp just for you."

He gave an evil grin. "The ones on the Hill will be slitting their own throats by Monday morning, and I have a little surprise in store for my friends on the council. Don't you worry. I just wanted to be sure you know that you and your people were protected on this thing, and that if anything goes south, it's all on me." He was up and pacing and jiggling the change in his pockets—a habit Gianna had come to dislike intensely. "How're things going with the new people?"

She told him in detail about Team G and Team D and he clapped his hands, then clapped her on the back. "We're scheduling appointments to qualify them all at the range and then some basic classes—arrest procedures, evidence collection—things they've already had but I want to satisfy myself that they're up to speed. Then I'm going to turn the undercover specialists loose on them: Alice Long and Tony Watkins. They should be ready for whatever comes down the pike."

"That's good stuff, Maglione. Now, get back to work. I don't want to keep you from it," and he waved her away.

Captain Randolph was waiting for her in the Chief's outer office. "Your warrants are ready, Loo," he said with a satisfied nod. "You'll be able to get whatever there is to be had from that townhouse and the car. And I took the liberty of notifying Fairfax County that we might be in their neck of the woods sometime soon and they almost threw me a party. Apparently, somebody down there likes you. A lot," he said, and made no secret of the fact that he was waiting to learn why. She told him what the case was and he remembered it. "That was some ugly shit," he said.

"Yes, it was," she agreed, recalling the serial murders of prostitutes in D.C., committed by boys from suburban Maryland and Virginia. "Thanks for your help, Captain," she said, and left.

Back in the unit, the Team G members were on computers, taking instruction of some kind from Eric while Bobby looked on. Team D and Tommi were nowhere to be seen, leaving Gianna to think that they were somewhere having a lesson of their own. She went to her desk and checked her phone, gratified to see that she had several messages from Mimi. The last one was a text, saying that she was going to dinner with Joe Zemekis who was back from Pennsylvania with really good news for the women of Sunset View whose husbands were killed in that Turnpike crash. Gianna was glad of the news, especially since it would be Zemekis and the insurance company delivering it and not her people. She was still both pissed off and unsettled by her conversation with Alfreda Tompkins, who had lashed out, looking for someone to blame for the fact that her eldest son was on his way to prison, not jail this time, for his assault on the prison guard. Whenever they found him.

Team D made a noisy arrival, then received a welcoming cheer when they raised hands that held bags from everybody's favorite deli. Dinner was served! Gianna joined them at the long tables in the center of the room and wolfed down the turkey and swiss Tommi had brought for her, eating every chip and both pickles. "Guess I was hungry," she said, and instead of giving away the cookie that came with the sandwich as she normally would have done, she ate it, too. Every bite. She looked up at the wall of

187

clocks. "Whoever is working tonight should head out to your assignment. Everybody else go home. Is tomorrow night's assignment made?" And when she got a "yes, Boss," from both Jim and Bobby, she stood up. "Good work, everybody, and that includes team leaders and sergeants. It's very good work and I very much appreciate it."

The A's and the other team members assigned to Metro GALCO went to work. Tim drove them in his new SUV, and everybody else cleaned up, but nobody left. Gianna knew that Eric, Tommy, Jim, and Bobby would stay until the team left. The team members were still learning about each other and learning to enjoy each other and, given her experience with the HCU, Gianna knew they'd hang around for a while. She didn't mind. She could do her work at her corner desk and keep an ear on what they were talking and laughing about. She enjoyed it, and she was comforted by the fact that they were comfortable enough with her to relax and be themselves. She heard the cadence of Alice's low, slow drawl, the one that meant she was putting on the South Carolina Southern with a spatula, and laughter erupted. Alice was one of their team leaders, and they didn't even know it. And Alice was all right with that.

Gianna had met with Alice privately and explained the formation of the two teams. "By rights, you should be heading one of the teams, Alice, but I need you to do something else. I need you to be a role model for all the young women in the unit. I never had a role model when I was starting out, and I'll bet you didn't, either. Not somebody who was close at hand all day, every day. Somebody you could see and hear and talk to, somebody who was an equal. If you don't want to, Alice, say so, and you'll be one of the team leaders." But Alice had readily agreed and Gianna could already see how the younger women from both teams gravitated to her. Gianna would see to it that she had her sergeant's stripes within the next year, even if it meant losing her, which it probably would.

She sent Mimi a text, then turned her attention back to her work, tuning out the activity and conversation across the room and losing track of time until shouts of *Boss! Boss!* had her on her feet, sprinting across the room. "What is it?"

"The Idaho 5 showed up together tonight, with a backpack," Jim said.

"Eyes on them and that backpack at all times," Gianna said, "but from a distance for now. Put the bomb squad on standby. If they leave the backpack and try to leave the building, get the bomb squad in and arrest them, but separately. Separately, understood? Keep them apart, handcuffed, and take everything away from them: Phone, keys, pens, anything in a pocket. Do a thorough pat-down. Leave nothing on them, is that clear? Get going, everybody! Don't let their vehicle leave the parking lot; make sure there's nobody in it! Alert PD in Fairfax that we're coming to the townhouse. Everybody deployed except a computer person and a social media person. Go! Go! Teams, deploy!"

The room emptied in seconds. Computer guru Kenny Chang and social media maven Justine Turnbull plied their crafts. If any mention of any action at Metro GALCO appeared anywhere they'd know it. Gianna went to her corner, strapped on her shoulder holster, disconnected her phone from the charger, slipped on her jacket, and headed for the door. "Wait, Boss!" Eric exclaimed. "You're not going to Metro GALCO!"

"I am," Gianna said, "and you're taking me."

Eric activated lights and sirens and sped out of the underground garage. Because they were at police headquarters, people were used to moving out of the way, and even on a Friday night in downtown D.C. they had clear passage. For a while. Then the stupids took over and Eric had to ride some bumpers and blare the horn to get them to move. Gianna knew him to be a good driver so she ignored the traffic and concentrated on getting real-time updates on the phone. All five suspects were in custody—shocked and angry and demanding their constitutional rights! They were, as Gianna had ordered, handcuffed and isolated. They had visuals on the backpack: It was in the middle of the third-floor hallway, leaning against the railing and, yes, the bomb squad was en route. "Then notify the management and begin evacuating the building. We'll be with you shortly."

The scene at Metro GALCO looked like the set of a doomsday movie. Eric added to it when he pulled the unmarked onto the first available spot on the sidewalk and left the lights flashing as they bailed and ran toward the building. Eric ran toward Bobby Gilliam and Jim Dudley; Gianna headed for the Metro GALCO co-executive director, shouting as she got close, "Is everyone out of the building?"

"Is there really a bomb?"

"Is everyone out!"

"I thought so but—"

"But what?" Gianna demanded.

The woman looked all around, even turning around in a circle. "I don't see anyone signing. A group of deaf gays has a class twice a week—"

"Where's that class and how many in it?"

"Second floor, the room at the top of the stairs. There are about fifteen of them." Gianna cursed and took off running at full speed toward the building. Running was something she did often and she did it well. She was inside and up the stairs before it registered with observers what she was doing. She flung open the door to the classroom, and the energy of that motion caused most of the heads to turn and look at her. She ran to the front of the room, grabbed a piece of chalk, and wrote BOMB on the board, then ran back to the door, beckoning them to follow. She held up her badge but they had guessed she was a cop and they were following, but much too slowly. She grabbed a couple of them by the arm and propelled them forward; then the others followed. She waited until the room was empty before running to the stairs herself. She had to do a little pushing and shoving to get them to run, not walk, down the stairs.

Eric, Bobby, and Jim had seen her dash into the building at the same time. Bobby pursued her while Eric and Jim aimed for the Metro GALCO exec. "What's that all about?" Eric asked.

"The deaf class. It doesn't look like they made it out."

"There are people still in there? Deaf people?!" Eric yelled, but nobody heard him over the sound of the blast. It literally was deafening. The blast force knocked Bobby back out of the building even as he was holding the door open for the first of the deaf students to make it down the stairs, and it knocked everyone else to the ground where they lay in stunned silence for a moment. Then all hell broke loose. Half of those assembled ran away from the crumbled structure, while the other half ran toward it. They had seen one of their own enter just moments ago, one who was liked and respected by all who knew her or knew of her. Paramedics began to tend to the obviously injured, and firefighters began to move everybody back—everybody except the bomb squad members who were already picking through the smoking rubble, looking for clues.

Eric, Jim, and Alice surrounded Bobby and kept him down until paramedics could examine him. He wasn't happy about it but he was outnumbered. The blast had reopened the knife cut on his face and it was bleeding. He allowed treatment for about two minutes before pushing the medics aside. "We gotta get the Boss outta there!" he wailed.

Then the Chief was standing over them. "Tell me she's not in there," he demanded, and when all he got back was pain-filled looks, he paced and cursed for several seconds. Then, "I understand you have the fuckers who did this?"

"Yes, sir," Eric said, and led the Chief to them, while Bobby, Jim, and Alice started to climb the rubble mountain.

"Did you have eyes on her, Bobby?" Alice asked.

He shook his head. "But the deaf kids were coming down the staircase, which was right there," and he pointed to the pile of rubble where the door once was, the pile where Alice began her climb.

"Boss! Gianna! Can you hear us? Can you make any noise?" she called out, and the others joined her in calling Gianna's name. They kept it up until one of the bomb squad techs joined them, a device of some kind in his hand.

"A heat sensor," he said, and he began moving it inch by inch

191

over the area where they'd been calling Gianna's name. Then Jim's phone rang. He answered, listened, disconnected.

"The Chief wants us—all of us—right now. We're to leave search and rescue to these guys."

"We know it's your boss, and we know who she is and none of us will leave here tonight until we get her out. That's a promise," the S&R guy said. He looked into the three pairs of eyes staring back at him and he knew it was a promise he'd better keep . . . or die trying.

The five suspects were lined up facing the bomb-squad truck, hands cuffed behind them, feet spread wide, separated from each other by two team members between them. Every time one of them tried to speak the Chief slapped him or her upside the head until they finally got the message and shut up. "I don't need you to speak. I don't care what you have to say. We have the vehicle you like to park at the Metro lot, and we're inside the Falls Church townhouse. We'll be in your computers and your phones in the next couple of hours. We've had warrants ready for a few days. We were waiting for you to pull your stupid little stunt. That's why the building was empty when your bomb detonated. Now stand there and keep quiet."

Eric had been watching their faces while the Chief talked. "We got the reaction we wanted," he said. "Total shock."

They walked several paces away to stand with Tim McCreedy, who told the Chief what he'd already told his team leader: The suspects bragged that the cops could do nothing to prevent the bomb from detonating. "They said, 'the bomb is smarter than you cops, it knows what to do and when to do it,'" Tim said.

"So even if one of them didn't detonate it, it was on a timer and would self-detonate," the Chief said, disgust heavy in his voice.

Tim looked from Jim to the Chief, not sure who he should address. Alice knew what he wanted to ask. "The bomb squad guys are all over it, Tim. They'll get her out. They will."

He nodded and walked away. He wanted to believe her. He had to believe her. They couldn't lose the Boss, too. They just couldn't.

"I want to meet these A's I keep hearing about," the Chief said, and Jim waved them over, introduced them and explained how they had concluded that the five suspects were up to no good. The Chief beamed at them, shook their hands, told them he was honored to serve with them, then went back to the bomb site.

Annie Andersen grabbed Alice's arm. Tears were streaming down the girl's face. Alice pushed her own tears back up where they belonged and wrapped the girl in a tight hug. "They're going to get her out, and she's going to be fine."

"How do you know that? A whole building just fell on her!"

"In the first place, it wasn't the whole building. And in the second place, that's not who she is, Annie. She might bend—just a little, and only on special occasions—but she doesn't break. Not ever. She never has and she never will." Three other women from both teams joined them and it became a group hug. Then several of the guys joined in, then Bobby and Jim added their long, strong arms, and Alice just knew that it was a hug that Gianna felt.

"We know where she is, Chief!" the search and rescue guy yelled as soon as he saw the Chief, who broke into a run. "She's right about here," he said pointing to a pile of rubble. "She made it to the bottom of the stairs, and she's in a pocket."

"What the hell does that mean?"

"It means there's nothing directly on top of her, that the heavy stuff all around her is what's protecting her."

"And do you plan to dig her out anytime soon?" the Chief snapped, and the digging commenced. It was, of necessity, a slow process, a brick by brick process, but many pairs of hands were involved. The Chief gave them all shoulder pats and announced to all that he was on his way to lock up the hate-filled little bastards responsible. He got a cheer. Then he walked back to the pile of rubble. "Maglione!" he yelled. "I know you can hear me! I'm putting your ass on report as soon as they get all these damn bricks off of you!" And he stalked off, the grin on his face his secret.

He was about to organize the transportation of the five suspects to booking when a loud, "Get your hands off me, goddammit!" permeated the air.

"That would be Patterson," the Chief said. "Somebody go get her before she assaults a cop and we have to lock her up, too."

Alice took off at a run. "She's with me!" she yelled at the uniforms holding Mimi. They happily released her, and she ran in the direction Alice had come from. She saw everybody—the Chief, Bobby, Jim, Tim—everybody but Gianna. She looked from one to the other, then the bottom dropped out of her stomach and she ran toward Metro GALCO, Zemekis close on her heels trying to slow her down. They knew about the bomb, but the sight of the totally collapsed building that had once been an elementary school stopped them cold. Alice grabbed Mimi. "She's all right; they're working to get her out."

Mimi pointed to the building; then she looked at Alice and began shaking her head. "She's . . . no, she can't be . . . not in there . . ." and her knees buckled. Alice had an arm around her waist and Jim, Bobby and Tim were there, too, holding her up. Alice beckoned to the search and rescue guy and he trotted over. "Tell her what you told us, about where Lieutenant Maglione is."

He looked at Mimi, who was seconds and inches away from a faint. "She's in a pocket. There is no debris on top of her so she's all right; she's not injured. But we do have to be very careful about removing the rubble off her. It has to be brick by brick and it's going to take a while."

"And you all were going to leave her here?" Mimi was coming back to herself.

"We were going to process the perps—"

"You know who did this? You have them in custody?"

"We do," said Eric, who had joined them.

"But it doesn't take all of you to process them. Surely some of you could stay here, surely some of you would *want* to stay here until she's safe!"

"We all want to, Mimi," Alice said, "but the Chief wants us downtown."

"The Chief is an asshole and you can tell him I said so!"

"I heard you," the Chief said. "One team with me, one team here. Can't have the Fourth Estate thinking I'm an asshole," he said dryly, and turned away, leaving Bobby and Jim to decide who got to stay and help dig Gianna out of the rubble.

"Half and half?" Jim asked, and Bobby nodded. "In fact," Jim said, "everybody who was Hate Crimes stay here with Bobby, everybody else come with me."

"That's not fair!" Annie Andersen wailed. She loved her new boss!

"No, it's not," Jim said, "and I'm sorry. But it is the easiest way to do it. So let's go."

The HCU team was ready to start digging, but the S&R guy held up a hand to stop them. "You all take the handoffs," he said, referring to the debris removed from the pile and handed off down a long line, out of the way, a line that Mimi became a part of, too. She watched the HCU team, their thoughts written all over their faces. They'd lost Cassie; no way were they losing their Boss. The pile steadily grew as the pile on top of Gianna was just as steadily diminishing. Every few minutes the S&R guy called out, "Give me three taps if you still can, Lieutenant," and three taps would sound from within the debris mound. They were faint but they were there. It took four long, dirty hours, but finally the S&R guy held up his hand, then motioned for the paramedics and their stretcher. "Lift her straight up, and be careful!"

A great cheer went up when Gianna was lifted from the debris pocket. She was dirty—she was filthy, truth be told—and she looked exhausted, but aside from a few cuts and scratches, she looked fine. She smiled and extended her hand when she saw Mimi. Then she saluted when she saw her HCU team, all of whom were crying, and they returned the salute, which brought tears to Gianna's eyes. "You guys need to move away now, so we can keep digging," and that's when the realization hit all of them that Gianna wasn't the only one buried in that rubble; she was just the only one who could hear the rescuers calling out and respond to them.

Bobby called the Chief and Tim called Jim Dudley, his team leader. Then they called Tommi and Eric. Mimi hugged them all, reserving an especially tight one for Alice, then climbed into the back of the ambulance for the siren-shrieking, rapid ride to University Medical Center. Mimi hoped the emergency trauma surgeon that she'd become way too familiar with was not on duty, and she was relieved to see that her wish was granted, but the procedure was too painfully familiar. Gianna was whisked through the swinging doors into the trauma surgery suite. Even though she didn't need surgery, she was the victim of a bomb blast, and she'd been buried beneath what probably was tons of rubble for several hours, so they were taking no chances. She'd be examined, x-rayed, MRI-ed, and whatever else was deemed necessary while Mimi sat on the bench in the hallway and waited. She somehow still had her wallet and phone in her pockets, so she stepped outside to check in with Zemekis who still was watching the excavation at Metro GALCO. Two more bodies had been removed, one alive, one not. "Hate crime murder," he said. "They're going away for life."

"Good," Mimi said, and she meant it.

"Any chance the lieutenant will talk to me?"

"Not tonight," Mimi said, "but she likes you, so see how she feels tomorrow."

"Thanks, Patterson," he said. Then, "Are you sure you want to stay quit?"

"So sure I don't have all the words I need to tell you. Good-bye, Zemekis," she said, and ended the call. Then she headed for the cafeteria. She was hungry and thirsty, and she kept wondering why she was getting odd looks from people until she looked down at herself and saw that she was also filthy. She should go home and shower and change, she thought, and she would—as soon as she found out that Gianna was all right.

"She's fine, Ms. Patterson," the doctor told her two and a half hours later, "and she'll sleep for the next several hours. We gave her a sedative when we were certain she didn't have a concussion or any kind of head injury."

"No broken bones or—"

"Nothing but a few scrapes and scratches," the doctor said. "She's dehydrated; she inhaled quite a bit of dust and probably some mold spores. That's an old building. Was an old building. We're monitoring her breathing and her lungs and her heart—"

"Her heart?!"

"Breathing dirty air makes the heart work extra hard, but that's usually over a prolonged time. We don't think you have anything to worry about in that regard. Honest. Go home, get some rest."

Mimi stood up and looked down on Gianna. She seemed to be resting peacefully. She'd been cleaned up, her hair washed, something the color of Betadine applied to her cuts and scrapes. Mimi touched her face. *Cool.* She leaned down, kissed her, whispered words of love in her ear, thanked the doctor and left, surprised to see that the sun was fully up. Surprised also to remember that she didn't have her car, but given the sudden fatigue that overcame her, she probably had no business driving. She hailed the taxi that was dropping off a fare at the ER door, climbed in, gave her address, and didn't wake up until the driver told her she was home.

A long, hot shower revived her mind and a big bowl of microwaved spinach lasagna did the same for her body, so she dressed, grabbed her phone charger, almost grabbed her laptop but put it down when she remembered that she wouldn't need to be writing, and headed for the hospital. She could sleep just as well there as at home, and besides, she wanted to be there when Gianna woke up. And she was. She had bought a newspaper because she knew that Gianna would want to see the story as well as check the latest details. Should've brought the laptop after all, she thought, as she watched Gianna scroll the the images and info on the phone's small screen.

Gianna was heartbroken that four of the people from the deaf class hadn't got out in time, but Mimi reminded her that they all could have perished if she hadn't rushed in to get them out. "If anybody gets blamed for that loss of life, it's the Metro GALCO staff," Mimi said. "They all rushed out, and nobody checked to see if the people who couldn't hear the alarm and the loudspeaker announcement got out. Don't blame yourself, Gianna."

Then Gianna's unit started to arrive, one at a time at first, then in groups, and Mimi got up to leave. "You don't have to go," Eric said.

"Sure I do," Mimi said, laughing. "You all can't talk your cop talk with me here. Besides, one thing I know for sure: She's in good hands! Lots of them!" She gave him the bag containing Gianna's weapon and police credentials, which the nursing staff had given her, and he hugged her tightly. "Please clean the gun and polish the holster," she whispered to him. "You know how she is about her cop stuff." And he did know—better and for longer than Mimi had. And Mimi knew that.

Alice followed her out. "I wanted to thank you for the good advice. About speaking honestly to Evie. It really made a difference."

"Is she all right?"

"She is now, but she was really hurt at first, and my silence just made it worse. She deserved better."

"She's a good woman, Evie is."

Alice nodded. "She definitely is, and I'm lucky that she's willing to be my friend."

"I hope you'll both be all right, Alice. You're both good women."

Alice chuckled. "Know a lot about good women, do you?"

"I hurt one once and swore I'd never do it again. That's what I know."

Alice was silent for a moment, then, "Do you think the people who hate us know we hate them?"

"Wow!" Mimi said. "I didn't expect that."

"Those dipshits who murdered Cassie, and the ones who bombed Metro GALCO and killed four people: Do they know how much we hate them?"

"Hmmm, probably not," Mimi said. "It requires a special kind of self-centered arrogance to do what they do. They think they're right and everybody else is wrong so, no, they probably don't think their hatred is reciprocal. Besides, a lot of those who are the most hated often believe in forgiveness and loving their enemies."

"Huh," Alice said. "You're right. For the most part. But some of us have gotten tired of turning the same two cheeks. I'm from South Carolina, so the massacre in that church in Charleston hit home for me. If they had killed the Boss yesterday, right after killing Cassie, I'd have been done with this job and I'd be out there with getting even on my mind."

Mimi pointed to the room where Gianna lay. "It would be good if you never let her hear you talk like that, even though I don't think you really mean it."

"I definitely mean it, but you're right. I'd never say it to her. It would disappoint her, and what she thinks matters too much to me." Alice gave her a sad look. "See ya, Patterson."

"Alice? She's out there, and when you stop looking for her, she'll find you." And Mimi walked down the hall and out the door and went home. She'd call Gianna later, but the day should belong to those people who loved Lieutenant Maglione as much as she did. She'd take Gianna home tomorrow and have her all to herself, and she'd explain her new status as unemployed journalist.

Sunday morning an almost rested Mimi walked in just as a nurse removed a mask from Gianna's face, pulled her upright, and put a bowl in her lap. Was she nauseated, about to throw up? Then, Gianna was coughing so hard Mimi was afraid she was about to expel a lung instead of some of the dirt and debris she'd inhaled yesterday, and it was painful. Mimi knew that because of how tightly Gianna was squeezing her hand. Her breathing trouble had begun during the night, and when oxygen alone didn't resolve the problem, a pulmonary specialist was called in to begin the process Mimi now was watching: Gianna was inhaling something that caused her to cough and expel the mucous-y buildup in her lungs. An expectorant it would have been called in the drugstore, though she was pretty certain that whatever Gianna was inhaling couldn't be bought over the counter. She was just as certain that what Gianna was expelling wasn't just the common-cold variety of phlegm or mucous.

The coughing stopped and Gianna fell back onto the pillows, still gripping Mimi's hand. She was sweating and her breathing was labored. Just as Mimi was about to ask for it, the nurse wet a cloth and wiped Gianna's face and neck; then the pulmonary tech put a mask on her nose and mouth and turned on a machine. Mimi could hear the hiss that indicated Gianna was inhaling something via the mask. "What's in that?" Mimi asked, pointing to it.

"You'll have to ask the doctor," the tech responded.

"I'm asking you," Mimi retorted, and the nurse intervened before things got ugly.

"The doctor is on her way right now," the nurse said, wiping Gianna's brow, "and she'll be able to explain what's happening and why, okay?"

Mimi nodded but she wasn't placated. "Why wasn't I called?"

"She didn't want us to call you," the nurse said, "since it wasn't a life-threatening situation. Her words, by the way. She said you didn't need to watch her breathe and cough and spit."

But I do need to watch her still be alive, Mimi thought. "Thank you," she said to the nurse, then, "The doctor's coming, right?"

"The doctor's here," said a Madeleine Albright look-alike who bustled in, emanating efficiency. She extended a hand, which Mimi shook, then, after a squirt of hand sanitizer from the pump on the wall, she put on her stethoscope and, with the help of the nurse, adjusted Gianna's gown so that she could listen to her lungs from the front and the back. "Much, much better," she said, stuffing the stethoscope into the pocket of her white coat and turning her attention to the hissing machine next to the bed. "You know that she inhaled quite a lot of toxic particulate matter yesterday, and in a prone position. That's the bad news—the only bad news. The good news is that the lieutenant has lovely lungs! She has never smoked and her regular exercise has kept her lungs operating at peak capacity and performance." The doctor was now reading a tape spit out by the hissing machine while writing in the chart—obviously an expert at multitasking, though she probably didn't call it that, probably just called it doing her job. If she called it anything. She told Mimi that Gianna was inhaling a mixture designed to help her breathe, make her cough, manage the pain, and sedate her.

"Why does she need all that, especially the sedative?"

"Her body was severely traumatized even though she suffered no broken bones, and what we're doing to clear her lungs is also traumatic. Rest is how the body heals itself. Making sure she sleeps is how we make sure she rests."

Mimi nodded, inhaled, exhaled, nodded again. "Thank you," she said.

"You're welcome," the doctor said.

"When can she go home?"

"Tomorrow. Probably," the doctor said, and left. The nurse and the tech followed.

Mimi focused on how the doctor had said "probably." As in maybe . . . maybe not. As in, "we'll see." She stood beside the bed holding Gianna's hand. She did look peaceful now that she no longer was coughing up her lungs and sweating. *I can live with "probably"* Mimi thought.

"Hi," she heard from the doorway.

"You would be Sgt. Tommi," Mimi said to Thomasina Bell, who came to greet her with a smile and an outstretched hand.

"It's a pleasure, Ms. Patterson. You are admired, respected— and loved—by the HCU. I hope us new guys get the chance to get to know you that well."

"I don't see how you'll be able to escape," Mimi said and, pointing to a chair, "Have a seat."

Tommi sat. "Glad to see she's resting." Then, pointing to the hissing machine, "What's that?" Tommi listened intently as Mimi explained, nodding her head in understanding. The look on her face, however, said that she didn't much like what she heard. "So, she's not getting out of here today?"

"The doctor says tomorrow. Probably."

Tommi sighed, then held up a thick folder. "I brought some light reading for her to take home."

"I can give it to her tomorrow. Probably," Mimi said.

Tommi shook her head. "It'll be outdated by then." She pulled out her phone. "I better call Eric." Then she pulled out a card and gave it to Mimi. "I'd appreciate it if you'd add my number to your call list, Ms. Patterson, and put me in the ranks of those who'd go to hell and back for her," she said pointing to Gianna. "Take care of her."

"I will," Mimi said, and holding up Tommi's card, "on both counts."

Mimi followed Tommi out, her own phone at hand. She really should be the one to call the Chief. She knew he'd hold it against her for a while, calling him an asshole, but to hear of a change in Gianna's condition from somebody else—he'd really hold that against her. Probably forever.

Maybe this wasn't a bad way to spend Sunday. The doctor had said Gianna's body had received a severe trauma and the body needed rest to recover. Reading the reports Sgt. Tommi had brought would not be restful and knowing Gianna, no way she'd go home, get in bed, stay there. Not to rest anyway. Sitting here watching her sleep—watching her rest and recover—was rather restful itself. She could watch the news reports of the futile attempts of the Capitol Hill bullies to try to get the best of the Chief: He was winning that one. Zemekis had written really good stories on the events at Metro GALCO. He'd even focused on the fact that it was the head of the Hate Crimes Unit, Lt. Giovanna Maglione, who'd saved the lives of the deaf students in the second-floor class-room after she discovered that the Metro GALCO staff had left them in the building, rushing in to lead them out. Because she was hospitalized recovering from injuries suffered in a bomb blast, the Chief was happy to speak for the lieutenant, and about her. She and Joe would meet in the hospital cafeteria for a late lunch and she'd update him on Gianna's condition. The national and international media were blaming the administration for allowing the trafficking of women and children for sex, and the administration was responding by calling those reports fake news. And it still hadn't been possible to identify all the girls taken from the warehouse or to determine where they came from or how they got there.

Mimi turned off the television, closed her laptop, put the newspapers on the floor, and settled in for a nap, the last thoughts on her mind before drifting off being that on Wednesday afternoon she and Gianna would leave town for a four-day mini-vacation at a luxury cabin in the Catoctin Mountains four hours north of D.C., and that she never would have believed it possible that she could miss George Bush.

CHAPTER NINE

Packing was the easiest part of preparing to go to Freddie's mountain cabin: It was a casual clothes to no clothes kind of trip. The "cabin" was, in reality, a chalet carved into the side of a mountain in Garrett County in western Maryland, overlooking Deep Creek Lake, and, unlike the image usually conjured up at the thought of a cabin in the woods, the place exuded the luxury of, well, a chalet. Because Freddie was a retired football linebacker, everything in the place was sized to fit him, which meant that Mimi and Gianna could lie side by side on the sofa and watch TV and movies on a screen that took up one wall; the fireplace took up the adjacent wall. This part of the state was pleasantly warm in the summer, frighteningly frigid in the winter, and deliciously cool in the fall and spring. Mimi was finished packing in the time it took to think about packing. Because Freddie and Cedric always maintained an overabundant supply of food and drink, including Mimi and Gianna's favorite popcorn and raisin bran, there was no need to take food, and the satellite hookup guaranteed that every film and television offering known to personkind, foreign and domestic, was available at the touch of a button. She was due to pick up Gianna within the hour and they'd be off! Though there was no chance of snow or freezing rain on the roads this time of the year, they always preferred arriving before dark.

"I just finished packing," Mimi said, answering her phone. "I'm ready to go when you are." Then she heard the garage door rumble up, and she hurried into the kitchen to open the door that led to the garage and there was Gianna. "Did I misunderstand? I thought I was picking you up."

"No misunderstanding," Gianna said, kissing her as she entered the kitchen. "At least not on your part."

Mimi looked closely at her. She was still a little wan following her four-hour, buried alive ordeal less than four days ago, but the look on her face bespoke something else. "Gianna? What is it?"

"I can't go today. Can we leave early in the morning?"

"What has happened, Gianna? Are you all right?"

"I'm fine. The problem is that the Chief scheduled a meeting with—"

Mimi exploded. "That selfish, self-centered son of a bitch! I'm really sick of him and how he takes you for granted!"

"He doesn't take me for granted—"

"The hell he doesn't! He knows you scheduled this time off. He approved it!"

"He probably forgot—"

"And by all means cover for him."

"I'm not covering . . . why can't we leave in the morning?"

"Because we planned to leave today and because we lose a day of our extravagant holiday." Mimi was really pissed off—at the Chief, not at Gianna—and she was trying to rein it in, but she knew that she was failing because she could see that Gianna was getting pissed off, too.

"I'm sorry, Mimi. I don't know what else I can say or do."

"Nothing. Don't worry about it."

"So, we'll leave in the morning?"

"Unless your boss calls another meeting."

"Why don't you just go ahead?" Now Gianna was really pissed off. "Since it's so important that you go today, go! I hope you and your shitty attitude have a great time!" Mimi started to retort but thought keeping her mouth shut would be a better idea, so she just stood there watching Gianna, waiting for whatever was coming next, hoping whatever it was would allow her to say something that would dial down the heat of the moment, but Gianna was on a roll.

"I know you're the newsroom star and can probably take vacation whenever you want, but I'm not so lucky. I have to suck it up and salute whenever the boss says so! And I have to go back to work!"

Mimi deflated like a pin-pricked balloon. What was so important about this evening was her plan to talk to Gianna about her plans—the ones she was being forced to make as a result of needing a new job. An argument in the middle of the kitchen when Gianna had to hurry back to work wasn't the time or the place for heart-to-heart revelations. "Then I suppose you're the one who should go."

"I suppose you're right," Gianna said, and left.

A suddenly furious Mimi ran into the bedroom, grabbed the overnight bag and her purse, and headed for the kitchen, only to find Gianna standing there. Her expression changed from contrite to pissed off again. "I decided to follow your advice and take my shitty attitude and leave. Join us tomorrow if you can," she said, and she brushed past Gianna and into the garage. She threw the bag into the back seat, climbed behind the wheel, and burned rubber backing out of the garage.

"Shit! Shit! Shit!" Mimi pounded the steering wheel as she yelled, then realized that pain sliced up her arm with every pound: It was the hand that had punched Ian Wilson's jaw. That his weasely ass was still causing her pain added to her fury, an interesting realization since she wasn't totally certain who the object of her fury was. It wasn't Gianna. She had never been furious with Gianna. In fact, this was their very first serious argument. Maybe, she thought, that's why she was furious: She'd stormed out of the house and now was driving without a destination. It was the Chief—that's who she was furious with! Sure, he had a tough, thankless job, but the people he relied on to help him manage that job had lives away from that tough, thankless job. There was no guarantee that Gianna would be free to travel tomorrow, either. So . . . to the cabin. That's where she'd go.

Will she really go without me? Gianna wondered, despite the fact that she'd all but dared her to go. She drove slowly back to Police HQ, in no hurry to return to the task facing her, yet

206

needing to hurry back so she could complete it as the Chief had ordered. So that she could attend the late afternoon meeting he'd scheduled—the mandatory meeting. Had he really forgotten that she had the afternoon and the next three days off? Or, as Mimi said, did he really not care? Did he really take her for granted? Mimi so often was right about so much. Was she right about this?

She pulled into the underground garage and parked on the bumper of the car that was parked in her reserved space. She was glad to see that it wasn't the same car that had blocked her before; that one—an inspector—had learned that it wasn't possible to outrank a reserved parking space. She was at the building entrance when a surly suit-and-tie in the doorway said, "Can you move your car so I can get out?"

"Excuse me?"

"You parked behind me, blocking me in."

Gianna turned and looked toward where she'd parked. She could not see her car. "You blessed with x-ray vision?" she snapped at the suit-and-tie, who now was blocking her entrance into the building. "And you need to move out of my way."

"When you unblock my car," he snapped back.

"What makes you think I'm blocking your car, especially since you can't see it from here?"

"Because I'm in your parking space," suit-and-tie snarled at her, and she laughed at him, pushed him backward out of her way, and entered the building.

"You need to call security about that," Gianna said, leaving him standing there fuming. She didn't look back. He knew who she was, and he thought he could get away with taking her space.

"Bitch!" He said it loud enough for her to hear. He wanted her to hear. Who was this jerk?

She called security when she got to her desk and reported that she had parked behind the car in her reserved space. The guy thanked her for the heads up and she put that incident out of her mind, creating the space she needed to deal with the situation with Mimi—whatever that was. Their first real disagreement was what it was, and it made her feel sick. How on earth did people do this on a regular basis? She called her again . . . immediately to voicemail again. Mimi was refusing to talk to her. This was awful. This was worse than awful. She made herself tune in and focus on the work she had to complete in the next two hours.

Bedlam at the other end of the room marked the return of Teams G and D. Everything they did excited them, and that excited Gianna. Mimi, too, for she had mentioned, more than once, how impressed she was with what she'd seen of Gianna's new unit. "I really like your Sgt. Tommi, " she had told Gianna, and "Bobby and Alice seem to have blossomed and matured overnight. " Yes, they had. "And they worship the ground you walk on, " Mimi told her. And I'm grateful to have them, Gianna thought, not for the first time, as she watched them tumble into the room like litters of baby kittens or puppies— boundless energy! And it wasn't just the team members, she realized, as Bobby and Jim bounded toward her, as excited as adolescents. Responsibility frightens some people, and they withdraw. Others, like the two grown men standing before her, grinning—well, some blossom.

"Kenny Chang got the highest score at the shooting range!" Bobby enthused.

"Yeah, then he fell off the treadmill," Jim said with a smirk. "And he was just walking! All the internet and computer brainiacs, Boss? Combined they couldn't lift a twenty-pound weight bar." He gave his midsection a slap. "My wife, by the way, thanks you for insisting on the physical fitness training and a more conscious eating plan for the team."

"They can all shoot and they ride the exercise bikes real good," Bobby said, "and yeah, they're smart, but they're not cut out for field work, Boss."

"Well, the good news is that whenever we go operational, we most likely will need the brainiacs doing what they do best— unless we need to shoot somebody!" Gianna appreciated sharing the light moment with Bobby and Jim; she needed it. "But make certain they can do a minimum of thirty minutes on the bike at top speed. And, here's a thought: See how Annie Andersen feels about teaching a yoga class a couple of times a week. You can't fall off a yoga mat."

"Yeah, but you can fall on it!" Bobby said with feeling, and Gianna laughed through her pain, but she sobered in a hurry when she saw the look Sgt. Tommi was wearing as she hurried toward her.

"Thanks, Bobby," Gianna said, turning her attention to the sergeant. "Tommi?"

The sergeant waved an envelope at her boss. "Some asshole trying to get into your office ordered me to give this to you, and demanded that you come see him immediately." She got control of herself. "What he said was, if you know what's good for you, you'll get your ass down there."

Gianna took the envelope, opened it, read the heading, and picked up the phone. So *that's* who the suit-and-tie asshole was. She punched four buttons and almost immediately said, "Captain. Dexter Davis's union rep is at my office making threatening noises to my staff, which I don't like. He also parked in my garage space and called me a bitch when I blocked him in, which I like even less." She listened for a moment, then, "Yes, sir, he's there now. Sergeant Ashby is in the office, Sergeant Bell is here in the unit with me; she delivered his message. Thank you, sir." She hung up the phone with a grin for Tommi. "You might want to hurry back to the office so Eric doesn't have all the fun."

"Who was that, Boss?" Tommi asked, "And did that jerk really call you a bitch?"

"Captain Randolph and yes, he did," Gianna answered, and she laughed as Tommi sprinted across the room and out the door. She'd get there in time to see the Chief's encounter with a drug-dealing dirty cop's union rep. Gianna wouldn't mind seeing that herself—but she'd first have to care what happened to DD to make the effort, and she didn't. She only cared what Mimi was doing.

Mimi wiped her eyes—again. It was practically impossible to drive and cry at the same time, and it seemed equally impossible that she'd stop crying anytime soon. She'd gone to the gym when she rushed out of the house, Gianna's "GO!" ringing in her ears. She'd run on the treadmill for an hour, then lay in the steam room until she felt dizzy and knew she had to eat, so she'd gone to her favorite Chinese fast food carryout and ordered her favorite sauteed (really fried) tofu and broccoli with spicy red peppers. The dish, a guilty pleasure, always made her feel good when she ate it. Not today. So she had driven to police headquarters just in time to witness the two SUVs that served as the temporary transportation for Gianna's Teams G and D drive into the underground garage. Whatever Gianna had been doing, she now would be engaged. No matter how much Mimi might wish it, there was no way Gianna was leaving work in time to make the drive up the mountain before darkness fell. She might as well dry her eyes and hit the road. As long as she'd been visiting Freddie at the cabin, driving up there on that winding mountain road in the dark still spooked her.

Gianna was surprised to find half a dozen other people in the Chief's office for the late afternoon meeting. She knew two of them well and considered them friends: Inspector Eddie Davis, who had been her boss until the Chief moved Hate Crimes into his office under his control, and Capt. Mildred House, just recently moved from HQ to oversee the overhaul of Riverside Station, formerly home to Dexter Davis. Capt. Dick Randolph, the Chief's aide de camp, hurried over to her before she could sit down. "Thanks for alerting us to that union guy's attempted end run. He had no business trying to talk to you about Davis," he whispered.

"I'm assuming he knew that?" Gianna whispered back.

"Damn right he did!"

"Then what was the point?" Gianna asked, genuinely confused.

"He just wanted to rattle your cage, find out exactly what happened at Sunset View, find out how the Chief got on to Davis, find out how Gilliam got put in there."

"Then he ended up talking to the right person," Gianna said calmly as the Chief entered.

He wasn't a small-talk kind of guy and he got right to the point: They were there because each of them was being promoted. Right now. The public ceremony for family, friends and cops would come later, but right now—Eddie Davis and Ellen DeLongpre from inspector to commander. Mildred House and Richard Randolph from captain to inspector. Giovanna Maglione and Thomas Mintz from lieutenant to captain. The promotions, he said, were part of an ongoing reorganization of the department designed to increase productivity and eliminate waste and corruption. "Some of you already have assumed responsibility for installations where corruption was a problem." He looked at Millie House. "I can already hear the hum of a well-oiled machine in the Riverside precinct," he said, and applause rippled around the room. "What some of you may not know is that the takedown of that sex trafficking warehouse on Broad, the arrest of those hate-mongers who blew up the gay and lesbian center, which prevented a true disaster, and the exposure of the dirty cops in the Riverside precinct—all that is down to Capt. Maglione and a newly formed unit under her command." He let the cheer go on for a little while, to Gianna's discomfort. "And I know you all know how much I don't want to relinquish Randolph—" and the good natured chuckle that followed that was directed at both of them. "But if you think he did a good job of keeping me in line, wait until you see what he's going to do for Internal Affairs. And if you thought Randolph could be a pain in the ass, wait until you have to figure out how to get in Tommy Mintz's good graces."

As he mentioned each new promotion, he gave the designee his or her new stars, bars and insignia, and nobody failed to notice that the new assignments for new Commanders Eddie Davis and Ellen DeLongpre were not publicly announced. They'd have to wait and see, but whatever their new jobs would be, everybody in the room no doubt would answer to one of them directly or indirectly.

Gianna exchanged congratulatory hugs with Eddie Davis and Millie House and promised to spend time with each of them, and handshakes with all the others, even as she accepted their congratulations on her recent accomplishments—including "getting her ass almost blown to bits."

"How long does your good friend hold a grudge?" the Chief said in her ear.

She turned to face him, surprise all over her face. "Sir?"

"I've put in three calls to Patterson in the last couple of hours and she hasn't called back. I know she was pissed off at me Friday night. She called me an asshole. Did you know that?"

Hoo boy! "No, sir, I didn't," Gianna said, remembering vividly, however, what Mimi had called him several hours ago.

"Is she mad at me? Is that why she won't return my call?"

"Ah, she's out of town, sir . . ."

"Without you? Where would she go without you—uh oh. Oh, no! Maglione, I am so sorry!" She saw him remember that, according to the vacation request form she had submitted and he had approved, she should be wherever Mimi Patterson was at that moment. "I forgot! I am so very sorry. Where is she? Where are you supposed to be?"

"In the mountains, up near Deep Creek Lake—"

He bellowed for Randolph and hurried into his office, giving her a head beckon over his shoulder. She followed in time to hear him tell Randolph to get somebody named Al Garibaldi on the phone. "Baldy! I need a favor! If I chopper one of my captains up there, can you have somebody meet her and take her to Fred Schuyler's place?" He listened for a moment, then, "She'll be there within the hour. Thanks, Baldy. I owe you." He listened again, then said, "I've got a new adjutant starting Monday, name of Tom Mintz. Same phone number. Call and set it up and we'll do it. Thanks again."

"Chief—"

"Just go get on the chopper, Maglione. A Maryland Statie'll take you to the cabin. I'm sorry I forgot. So much has been going on—and so much of it involving you. I can't tell you how grateful I am for all you've done, but I'll be sure to do that when you get back. And tell Patterson I'm sorry she thinks I'm an asshole. I'll make it up to her. And don't come back to work until Tuesday. We can survive a day without you, can't we, Randolph?" To his credit, Randolph remained silent.

Mimi was more out of sorts than she recalled being in a very long time, including her recent foray into drunkenness, and that realization depressed her as much as it angered her. In fact, the more she allowed herself to fully feel what was happening inside her, the more depressed and angry she became. What the hell had happened?! Here she'd been looking forward to spending a quiet, private four days alone with Gianna at Freddie's mountain cabin, and now here she was at Freddie's mountain cabin, angry, depressed—and alone. Well, it certainly would be quiet and private. Freddie and Cedric were in Europe on a real vacation, and the summertime hikers and bikers and boaters and swimmers who thronged to western Maryland hadn't yet arrived, but give 'em a week or two and the drive up here would have taken twice as long, even in the middle of the week. Up here in the Allegheny Mountains the leaves were returning to trees that had been stripped naked by winter, the green so bright only nature could produce the color, and Deep Creek Lake shimmered dark aquamarine, deceptively and dangerously placid. This was Mimi's vista from every window in the A-frame hillside chalet.

Inside, a fire blazed on the hearth. Better than turning on the heat in the chilly cabin, Keith Jarrett simmered on the CD player, and Mimi seethed as she paced up and down. A lousy four days. It was not too much to ask, especially considering that two of the days were Saturday and Sunday, and Gianna had enough accumulated vacation that she could take off until next year this time. Could take off but never would. She had returned more vacation time to the city than many people earned in a year. Mimi, on the other hand, used every second of her earned vacation every year. She worked as hard as Gianna did, often going two or three months without taking a day off when working on a major story. She understood dedication and commitment to work as well as

Gianna. She just refused to allow the job to own her. Although now, that no longer was an issue for her since she no longer had a job. The morning's argument replayed itself in her head as it had been doing all day. "The job doesn't own me, Mimi," Gianna had said, sounding both weary and angry. Mimi could tell she was tired of their argument and she was getting annoyed. Mimi, already angry, had shot back, "Bullshit, Gianna! We've had these plans for almost a month but your boss, selfish bastard that he is, snaps his fingers and nothing else matters to you."

"What's bullshit, Mimi, is what just came out of your mouth," Gianna had said as she walked out the door, which she closed gently and quietly behind her instead of slamming it, as Mimi knew she would have done. And here she was. And there Gianna was . . . at work.

Mimi had made the three and a half hour drive alone, not enjoying the scenery or the workout her new Audi convertible was getting on the mountain roads. She switched off the CD and switched on the TV. Something stupid and mindless to watch instead of listening to Keith Jarrett's moody, provocative chords that made her think and feel too much, too deeply. And watching TV at Freddie's always was fun because it was like being at a movie theater: The screen occupied an entire wall, and the rooftop satellite dish would pick up a signal from Mars. But for now: What was on television on a Wednesday afternoon? Freddie had every available channel in the universe, and Mimi flicked through them until she saw Morgan Freeman and Denzel Washington on the screen. "Glory." She'd seen the film half a dozen times and never tired of it.

She awakened to darkness and momentary disorientation. Then it all came back to her, where she was and why. She shivered, sat up, yawned, and almost choked to death. She jumped to her feet, not believing in ghosts but not believing her eyes, either. "What are you doing here? How did you get here?"

Gianna hesitated briefly before answering, clearly weighing her words. "Would you rather I went back to Washington?"

"Don't be a jerk," Mimi snapped.

"Then don't ask me a question like that," Gianna snapped right back. "You know very well what I'm doing here."

Mimi turned from her, crossed the room to close the draperies and turn on a light, and then to add more logs to the fire, which had burned down to embers. Then she turned back to Gianna. "What changed your mind?"

"You could have told me you were coming up here," Gianna said, her calm, reasoned tone of voice belying the anger she felt.

As usual, Mimi let hers hang out. "I shouldn't have had to tell you anything, Gianna. We planned for almost a month to come up here today. Then you change your mind and I'm supposed to, what? Sit home and sulk?"

"So instead you come up here and sulk," Gianna said, picking up the half empty wine bottle. "And get drunk."

"I am not drunk!" she shouted, remembering all too well what drunk felt like.

Giana gave a slight smile, then quickly stood and strode over to Mimi, reaching her in a couple of steps. Mimi turned away to face the fire. Gianna spun her back around, grabbed her arms, and pulled her in close. She started twice to say something, and twice stopped herself. Instead, she kissed Mimi, hard and fierce and demanding. Her hands dug into Mimi's arms, her tongue probed Mimi's mouth. Shock froze Mimi momentarily, then passion ignited her. She returned the kiss with equal ferocity. She plunged her hands into Gianna's hair, seeking leverage and control of the kiss. Gianna wouldn't give it. Her hands moved from Mimi's arms to her breasts and, a nipple in each hand, she began to squeeze and massage, at first gently and then not, and the sound Mimi made deep in her throat startled them both. They took their mouths from each other but kept their faces close, their eyes locked. They had never been really angry with each other before and therefore didn't have a protocol for being really and truly pissed off. So they did the next best thing. Since passion fuels anger and they knew a lot about passion, they gave in to it. Together they sank to the floor, eyes still locked together. Gianna took control of Mimi's arms again as they eased into a reclining position, and she pushed them above her head as simultaneously she pushed Mimi flat on the floor and positioned herself above, knees on either side of Mimi's body. "You," she started to say, but couldn't finish because Mimi raised her head and restarted the kiss.

Gianna stretched out full length on Mimi, pinning her to the floor. Then she slid one leg forward and, knee bent, pried open Mimi's legs. She released one of Mimi's arms and a hand followed the knee. She could feel Mimi get hard through the material of her pants and, as she reacted, Mimi took advantage of the situation. She quickly flipped Gianna over, pinning her the same way she'd been immobilized just a moment earlier. "Don't ever walk out on me again," Mimi whispered, leaning over Gianna and holding her gaze in a piercing eye-lock.

"Don't ever give me a reason to," Gianna whispered back defiantly. Mimi held the eye-lock for a long moment before releasing it and dropping her head to Gianna's breast. She took an erect and hardened nipple in her mouth, first nuzzling it with her lips before taking it between her teeth. Gianna was more than ready for what she knew was coming. She couldn't have been more wrong, for what came from Mimi was a strangled sob followed by a flood of tears. Gianna sat up straight, pulling Mimi up with her. "What is it? What's wrong, Mimi? Tell me, sweetheart, please."

"I quit my job."

Gianna was momentarily speechless. "When? Why? What happened, Mimi?" Because something huge and awful had to have happened to cause Mimi to quit a job she loved as much as she loved being a reporter. Gianna held her tightly until she stopped crying and could talk.

"It was the day you came home and I was really drunk." She shivered at the memory and told Gianna everything, every ugly, horrible detail of the events that led to the confrontation in the Exec's office that led her to quit. "And here's what's really so odd, so strange: I don't think I care. I haven't missed having to write about those girls and what was happening to them in that warehouse. I haven't missed having to write about those sick bastards who blew up Metro GALCO and killed those deaf kids and almost killed you. I haven't missed having to write about some depraved cops who victimized some demoralized women in their own homes. I'm sick of depravity and evil and ugly, and I'm tired of trying to explain how and why it happens that some people do the depraved, evil and ugly things they do, 'cause most of it can't be explained. Like those idiots who killed Cassie!" Mimi was shaking so hard Gianna feared that she would hurt her if she held her any tighter. "I'm not allowed to write that three women are dead due to racist stupidity so I have to try to find some other words. I don't want to do that anymore, Gianna. I can't do it anymore!" Tears she had been holding in for weeks, for months, perhaps even for years, poured out, and Gianna held her until they abated.

"Why didn't you tell me?"

"With all you've had to deal with, Gianna? I couldn't drop another morsel on your plate. You've had more than enough to think and worry about without me in the mix."

Gianna pushed her a little away so they'd be face to face, eye to eye, and said, "Nothing I do is more important than you."

Mimi kissed her. "And I'm grateful you feel that way, but I would do nothing to get in the way of the lives that depend on how well you do your job, not to mention those two dozen or so foot soldiers who go into battle on your command. Anyway, after I told you I quit, there wasn't much else to say."

"Oh, yes there was! Everything you just said about what you feel about the work you do. The work you've always loved doing."

"And what about how you feel about the work you do? You haven't talked about Cassie, or about the girls in that warehouse, or about the women at Sunset View or the cops who preyed on them, or about the deaf kids killed in the bomb blast. And I know why you haven't talked about any of it, Gianna—because you haven't had time to think about it, to say nothing of feel anything about it! It just kept happening, one after the other. Have you had time to feel Cassie's loss at all? I worry that you haven't talked about her."

Gianna gave a wry chuckle. "That's because she keeps talking *to* me. I hear her in my head all the time!" She pushed herself up from the sofa; only Freddie and Cedric had legs long enough to stand up from being seated all the way back. "I need a drink and something to eat. Other than you."

Mimi joined her in the kitchen. "You're not just avoiding the topic of discussion, are you? Because if you're not ready to talk, I won't press you."

Gianna kissed her again. "I actually am ready to talk. I *need* to talk. But I need to eat more. Is there anything already cooked?"

"Meat lasagna for you, spinach lasagna for me, ready for the microwave, and bags of salad. Vodka in the freezer, or I can open more wine."

And they ate and drank and made love in front of the fireplace until several large logs were reduced to embers. Then they went to bed and fell immediately and deeply asleep. It was full daylight when Mimi awoke, and she almost fell out of bed trying not to wake Gianna, forgetting it was Freddie's several feet taller, king-size bed, and not their own normal queen-size bed. She heard Gianna in the shower and was ready with coffee and scones in bed when she emerged. And along with breakfast came conversation.

"Cassie's last words—literally the last words she spoke—were 'I love you, Gianna.' I had nightmares for days afterward."

"I remember," Mimi said. "'No Cassie No Cassie No Cassie' you cried out in your sleep a few times, and I thought you meant no, don't die. You meant—"

"I meant don't say that to me, and more importantly, don't mean that!"

"You really didn't know how she felt?"

"Are you saying you did?"

Mimi grinned at her. "It was all over her face whenever she looked at you. But truth be told, I think it was mostly a case of hero worship. Now Alice, on the other hand—"

"It's *you* Alice has the hots for, Ms. Patterson! I swear she was mad at me for a while because you weren't available to share her bed, and she tried, didn't she?"

Mimi avoided and evaded by changing the subject. "I know it sounds way too weird, but I've been hearing Cassie in my brain, too!"

"Maybe not so weird," Gianna said, sounding pensive. "Cassie liked you, respected you. She was always amazed by the amount of information you put in your stories." Gianna gave a wry grin. "Especially when you had info we didn't have."

Mimi gave her own wry grin. "Guess that won't be an issue in the future."

"Speaking of work-related matters," Gianna said, and hurried to the front door to the briefcase she'd dropped on the floor there. She grabbed some items from it and hurried back to Mimi and dropped the items into her lap. It took her a moment to realize what she was looking at, and when finally she did, she grabbed Gianna and wrapped her in a bone-bruising hug. "Congratulations my beautiful Captain!"

"This was the reason for yesterday's mandatory late-afternoon meeting: A private promotion ceremony for just those who were promoted."

"When, how did you possibly have time to study?"

"When Eric and Tommi and Bobby and Jim were shouldering most of the load. Those four people are more wonderful than I have words for."

"You know they feel the same way about you."

Gianna first bowed her head, then shook it, as if to banish thoughts contained there. "I never wanted this. I never sought it. You know that, right?"

"I know," Mimi said, "which is why you're going to be so damn good at it! It's what your bastard of a boss knows so well."

"Speaking of which, he wants to know how long you're going to be pissed off at him. He tried to call you a few times but you didn't call him back."

"That's because I have more important things to do with my time."

They didn't spend the entire four days in bed. The weather was perfect and they went for walks, they drove down to the lake and rented a boat and rowed around until their arms were about to fall off. The cure for that was a long soak in a Jacuzzi the size of a small swimming pool. They cooked and ate and watched movies and talked and laughed and cried. And made love slowly and carefully. All too soon it was Sunday afternoon, and Gianna surprised Mimi with the news that they could stay another whole day because she wasn't due back at work until Tuesday. "Oh dear, whatever shall we do for another whole day?" Mimi said. Gianna showed her.

Mimi drove and Gianna slept all the way back home. She still was healing; Mimi remembered the doctor saying that rest, sleep was how the body healed itself from the effects of trauma, and Gianna still was traumatized, not only from being buried in the rubble of the bomb blast for four hours, but from everything she had experienced beginning with Cassie's murder. She had finally been able to talk and cry it out, and that in itself was exhausting. And she had slept, at first fitfully and restlessly, then deeply, and finally peacefully. By the time they were headed home Monday afternoon, they both felt calmer and clearer, and while Mimi still refused to return to work as long as apologizing to Weasel Boy was a requirement, she was back to believing that her profession not only had a necessary place in the scheme of things, but that these days it was a vital and crucial place, especially when the people in power believed in alternative facts. Question was, where would she ply her craft? Gianna didn't think she'd have any trouble finding a job.

She was debating whether to wake her when Gianna sat up, wide awake and fully alert. "Home already?"

"Yes, and I obeyed the speed limit. Pretty much."

Gianna gave her a sideways look. "You have never obeyed the speed limit. We can stay at your place tonight if you'd rather."

"I'm just going to grab my journalism file and the PEN America journal and then we're going to your place like we planned. And is there a reason the garage door won't open?"

He did a square block drive-around, just like Daddy D. taught him, so he was familiar with the Patterson woman's neighborhood, the block she lived on, the street she lived on, and the approaches to her house. It was the kind of area where the houses had driveways and garages and people used them, so there was plenty of street parking. It also meant, though, that a strange car parked there for too long would be noticed, so he moved around, not staying parked too long in one place. And like Daddy D. told him to do, he was driving the Chevy, not the Jaguar. People noticed Jaguars but they didn't pay attention to Chevys. Daddy D. also told him that the Patterson woman didn't keep regular hours, that the kind of job she had at the newspaper wasn't a normal 9-to-5 kinda job so there was no telling what time she'd get home. He just had to wait. He'd already jammed the garage door so she'd have to get out of her car and walk to the front door when she got home. He could take her out and be back in the Chevy and out of the area before anyone knew what was happening. The fact that she lived on a one-way street helped. Then he'd ditch the Chevy, just in case someone had noticed it—another reason for driving it and not the Jag: He didn't mind having to ditch the Chevy but he liked the Jag too much to have to abandon and torch it.

He was parked three houses up and across the street from where she lived, which meant she had to drive right by him to get home. White Audi convertible. He spotted the car from a block away. Not as cool as a Jag but still, a ride he wouldn't mind having. He had time for a quick text. She had slowed down and was holding her hand out the window, pointing to her house . . . oh! He knew what she was doing! She was aiming the garage door opener at the garage door that refused to open because he had jammed it. He grinned as she pulled into her driveway and opened her door. He was about to open his when the Audi's passenger door opened. "*White bitch with her*" he texted before dropping the phone into the passenger seat and getting out. He held his weapon—a Sig Mosquito with a silencer—down close to his leg as he jogged across the street. She was still looking at the garage, and she was talking to the white bitch who wasn't looking at or talking to her, because she was looking directly at him as she ran around the rear of the white Audi. She, too, held a Sig—larger than his and not held down at her side but up and straight out and aimed directly at him, even as she ran fast as hell toward the Patterson woman and knocked her down before his shot hit her. But he did hit the white bitch. Once. She hit him half a dozen times before she went down. He heard the Patterson woman screaming the white bitch's name. At least he thought it was her name. It was the last thing he heard because he certainly did not hear his phone ringing or the constant pinging of the arriving text messages telling him to get the hell out now because the white bitch was a cop!

"Gianna! Gianna!" Mimi stopped calling Gianna's name to talk to the 911 operator. "Officer down! Officer needs assistance!" she yelled, and gave her address. Then she disconnected from 911 and called Eric Ashby.

"Miss Patterson? Mimi?" His voice was full of concern bordering on fear. There was only one reason she'd call him.

"Gianna's down. My house. I already called 911 with an officer down but I need you here, Eric. Please. Hurry."

He had disconnected after "house" so she called the Chief next. "Is she alive?" was all he said, and he disconnected when she answered yes. Then she looked at Gianna. Her face was white and bloodless because all her blood was pooling beneath her in Mimi's driveway. *Gotta stop the blood!* She'd watched enough cop and hospital shows to know that. How long had it been? No more than several seconds, surely, but more than enough time to bleed out. Where was the blood coming from? *Oh shit! Her thigh. Femoral artery? Oh shit!* She was undoing her belt when one appeared, along with hands and arms belonging to a woman and a man—her across-the-street neighbors. A nurse and a retired Marine.

The nurse not-so-gently got the belt beneath Gianna's leg, threaded it, and told the Marine to tighten it. He did, and Gianna groaned and opened her eyes. She was trying to speak when screaming sirens, drawing ever closer, made conversation impossible. EMTs and their stretcher cleared a path to Gianna, Sgt. Eric Ashby in their wake.

"Who's the dead guy?" Eric demanded to know, certain that Mimi would have an answer.

"The older Tompkins boy," Mimi answered, watching the paramedics.

"Shit!" Ashby exclaimed.

"The Chief's on his way," she told him, still watching the paramedics working on Gianna, getting ready to lift her on to the stretcher.

"Can you tell me what happened, Mimi?" he asked as he helped her stand. She told him everything she'd seen and everything she remembered as she followed the stretcher to the ambulance. She pointed to the gray Chevy across the street, told him she thought it belonged to Tompkins and he ran toward it, summoning several cops to follow him as she followed the gurney rolling Gianna to the ambulance. Then the energy shifted and the Chief was there, as were a couple dozen more cops.

"Ashby!" he bellowed, unnecessarily, as Eric was already standing beside him, filling him in.

Gianna was in the ambulance now, and Mimi had climbed in behind the gurney. The Chief materialized just before the doors were slammed shut and the EMTs gave him a dirty look, which he ignored. "I need you here, filling in the blanks, Patterson," he said.

"And I need to be with Gianna in case she needs me," she said to him. "I told Eric Ashby everything I know." Then to the EMTs she said, "Let's go!" And the doors slammed and the ambulance screeched off, and the Chief of Police stood watching it disappear; then he went looking for Eric Ashby.

"Don't let her die," Mimi said to the paramedic riding in back with them. "Please don't let her die."

"She's lost a lot of blood," the paramedic said. "She's stable for now but she needs blood right away, and a lot of it."

"How much longer to the hospital?" Mimi could tell where they were even if there were no windows to see through. She knew that she lived twelve to fifteen minutes from the trauma center in regular traffic, driving a regular car, and obeying the speed limit. In a screaming, speeding ambulance?

"Five, maybe six minutes."

"Can you do it any faster?"

The paramedic hit the side of the truck three times hard, and the engine revved and roared and the big rig picked up speed. Mimi took Gianna's hand, which seemed colder than it had just a moment ago. She leaned over and began to whisper in her ear—words of love and pleas for her life. Mimi saw Gianna's eyes move behind lids that remained closed, and she felt what she swore was a faint pressure on her hand—Gianna had squeezed her hand! Then the EMT yelled, "Her pressure's dropping!" and they burned rubber into the ambulance bay at the trauma center. Mimi jumped down out of the way as a half-dozen trauma doctors and nurses met the gurney. She recognized the doctor who'd operated on her a year or so earlier, who had tried to save Cassie Ali a couple of months ago, and the doctor recognized her. She also recognized Gianna. Everybody was running, including Mimi, but she had to stop when they reached the swinging doors.

"I'll find you," the doctor said to Mimi, and they took Gianna from her. She collapsed onto a chair and was treated to a view of her lower extremities. Her pant legs were soaked with Gianna's blood where she'd knelt beside her. She'd been debating whether to call any of their friends to tell them what had happened, but one look at herself answered the question. But who: Freddie and Cedric or Beverly and Sylvia? Both couples had keys to her house, and both couples would come immediately without question. Out of habit, and out of respect for the fact that Freddie and Cedric had arrived back in the country at dawn following an overnight trans-Atlantic flight, she called Bev first. She listened, asked no questions, said she'd call Freddie and Cedric, and would get clean clothes and be at the hospital within the hour. Mimi immediately felt calmer. A therapist by profession and her ex-lover, Bev knew her better than anyone, even Freddie, and she'd known him longer; they'd gone to university together. She could tell Bev what she was thinking and feeling, thoughts and feelings that she could tell no one else. For the second time she had watched a murderous young man die in her front yard, but this time she didn't care. She felt no pain and no sorrow.

"Patterson." She looked up. The Chief and Eric.

"They just took her. I don't know anything yet—"

"You were the target, Mimi," Eric said, overriding the Chief.

It took her a moment to process what they were telling her and another to accept it. She had naturally assumed that Gianna was the target. "Me? Why?"

"Dexter Davis blames you for everything that has happened to him, and he sent Will Tompkins to make you pay," Eric said, explaining that they had the boy's phone, which he'd left in the car and from which he'd apparently never deleted any text or email he'd ever received. "You were targeted the day you had lunch with Alfreda Tompkins and she sent you the boy's photo. That's when Bobby showed up in her life."

"So she almost gets killed saving me. Why doesn't that give me the warm fuzzies?"

"Get your head out of your ass, Patterson!" the Chief snapped at her, to no effect. She sat still as a statue, her eyes contemplating Gianna's blood on her pant legs, now turning a rusty red-brown color and becoming stiff and hard. "She was doing exactly what she was trained to do. She protected you and she neutralized the threat," the Chief said. "Same thing she did at Metro GALCO."

"But if she hadn't pushed me out of the way—"

"You'd both be dead," the Chief snapped again, then turned and began to stalk away, not getting very far before returning. "Who're they sending to cover this?" he asked.

"What?" Mimi asked, looking momentarily confused before responding. "I don't know," she said, unaware of the looks the cops were giving her. She was still looking at Gianna's blood, at how much of it there was. *She's lost a lot of blood*, the paramedic had said. Maybe too much?

"Haven't you called Carson?" the Chief asked, and when she shook her head his look turned to concern and he sat down next to her. "Why not?"

"Because I don't work there anymore."

"Why not?" he asked again, and she told him. All of it.

"Does Gianna know this stuff?" Eric asked.

Mimi nodded. "I told her over the weekend. I didn't know when I told her that she might be about to die," Mimi said, choking back the sob that had been building in the back of her throat ever since Gianna had been wheeled through those swinging double doors into surgery.

The Chief slammed his palm against the wall. "She's not dying, goddammit!" And this time when he stalked off, he kept going.

Eric stayed with her, not talking, his eyes following hers, from the swinging doors leading to the trauma surgical suite, back to rest on her blood-drenched legs. Then he did something he'd never done before: He took her hand and held it between both of his, so surprising her that she didn't resist.

"He was right, you know—about Gianna doing the right thing in protecting you. That's what we're trained to do. And he was right about the other thing, too—the dying thing. She won't die, Mimi."

"You can't know that, Eric, and he can't, either, despite the fact that he thinks he knows everything."

"I've known Gianna a long time."

"Since the Academy. Yes, I know. So?"

"She waited a long time for you. She's not about to die and leave you!" And with that he stood up and headed for the door, but walking, not stalking.

"Eric!" He stopped and turned when she called his name. "Thank you." He smiled, saluted, and went to find the Chief, who could be heard raising hell as soon as the ER door swooshed open. Everybody in the parking lot could hear him

"The whole damn town will know before breakfast that your lawyer is a wife beater! And don't tell me to calm down!" But he calmed down and listened for a long minute, walking back and forth, his head down, one hand in his pocket, jiggling coins. Then he nodded his head several times and disconnected the call. "Patterson shouldn't be alone, Ashby, so if you want to stay here—"

He stopped talking and looked where Eric was looking—at Beverly and Sylvia and Freddie and Cedric, running across the parking lot toward the ER.

"She won't be alone, Chief," he said, "and she'll call us as soon as she has news."

The Chief nodded and the two cops went back to work—the Chief to his office to manage the firestorm that was coming, and the sergeant to the scene where his boss and good friend had, not quite two hours ago, shot and killed a fifteen-year-old boy in the front yard of her lover's home. Good thing, he thought, that Mimi Patterson had quit her job and therefore had not called her editor to send reporters to the scene. Or to the hospital where the head of—they'd have to give this new unit a name soon—was in surgery fighting for her life because another cop had ordered the fifteen-year-old to assassinate her. Who would believe this shit? He could barely believe it himself.

"I don't believe it!" Freddie Schuyler said.

"This can't be true!" Beverly Connors said, a horrified look contorting her lovely face. "It's not believable!"

"It's true. Believe it," Mimi Patterson said to her best friends.

"Go change your clothes, Mimi," Bev said, pushing the travel bag she'd brought from her own home with fresh clothes and a towel, washcloth, and soap. Mimi gave the bag a strange look: It wasn't hers. She transferred the look to Bev. "Your house is a crime scene, Mimi. They wouldn't let me in the front yard, to say nothing of the front door."

"Oh fuck them!" Mimi grabbed the bag's handle and pulled it behind her down the hall to the bathroom, feeling relief with every step that she'd soon be free of the blood-soaked clothes. That Gianna's blood no longer would be soaking into her own skin.

Her dearest friends watched her retreat; then they looked at each other, worry undisguised in their eyes. "She's not right," Freddie said.

"Of course she's not right, Fred!" Cedric chided. "Her clothes are drenched in Gianna's blood and she watched it happen!"

Freddie shook his head. "It's more than that. There's something else."

Beverly nodded. "You're right. She's changed."

"Oh, Bevie, don't shrink her!" Sylvia said gently. "They've had a rough time lately, both of them."

"I can't shrink her unless she talks to me, which she has steadfastly refused to do."

"I don't blame her," Sylvia said. "I wouldn't want to talk about all that ugliness, either—not even to you, my sweet love, because no amount of talking will make it any less ugly."

They were a glum-looking group. United as they were in their love for Mimi and Gianna, and in their desire to see them both through the crises they were facing, the reality was that they were powerless to help and they knew it. Beverly and Freddie gave each other hopeless, helpless looks. They'd known Mimi the longest, and they agreed that something had shifted and changed deep within her in the last couple of months. She had, without feeling the need to explain, declined invitations to see both of them and had stopped returning their calls. As her ex-lover, Beverly had, unfortunately, experienced Mimi not at her most charming. As UCLA classmates, Freddie had only known her as his "girlfriend" as they blithely double-dated with their respective lovers, hiding their secret in plain sight. As Beverly's current lover, Sylvia knew that Mimi had hurt her deeply; she also knew that Mimi had worked hard to repair the damage and that Bev had forgiven her and welcomed her back into her life and her heart. Cedric only knew Mimi and Gianna as Fred's dear, wonderful friends who had quickly welcomed him into their lives and who loved him because Freddie did. "We must do something! We must help her! We can't just sit here looking morose!"

Cedric, "pronounced Cee-drick," was British and a professor of poetry, and usually took a good-natured ribbing about his speech patterns. But not today. Nobody was in the mood.

"We can't help her unless she allows it, Cedric," Bev said.

"People don't always know what they need," he responded, and got to his feet. He saw Mimi's return before the others. She and

Bev didn't share wardrobe sensibilities, and Mimi was a couple of inches taller and less well-endowed of butt and bust, but they both were fond of starched white shirts and well-worn Levis, which is what Mimi now wore. She gave Bev a wan smile and a brief hug and thanked her for the clothes, a thank-you hug that included Sylvia, whom she had come to love almost as much as she loved Bev.

"I know you'll want to stay here with Gianna tonight, Mimi, but if they're still treating your place as a crime scene, you know you can stay with us," Freddie said.

"Or with us," Sylvia said.

"They can keep the damn house! I won't live there ever again! All that death in my front yard! I'm moving in with Gianna. If she'll have me," Mimi said, giving voice to thoughts and feelings that became a decision the moment the words left her mouth, but it was the right one and she knew it. She could no longer live in a place where two young men had died in the front yard—men who had come to kill her for the same reason: Stories she wrote exposing the evil they did would cost them their freedom forever.

"We think Gianna will have you," Sylvia said with a wide grin, "with open arms!"

Then everybody stood up as a doctor wearing bloody scrubs came their way, a petite young Asian with spiky hair. The doctor who had operated on Gianna. She looked exhausted but not as if she were about to deliver a death notice. She stood directly in front of Mimi. "Okay if I talk in front of everybody?" she asked.

"Yes, of course," Mimi said.

"The short version: She's going to be fine." The group exhale was audible. Mimi started to thank her, but the doctor raised a hand to stop her. "But it's going to take a while. She lost a lot of blood, Ms. Patterson. A lot. Almost too much, especially after what she just went through. A body can only take so much, even a strong, healthy body."

Mimi heard the words and the meaning behind them: Gianna had almost died, and she swayed. Freddie's strong arms encircled and held her and she leaned into him. "Is she conscious? Can I see her?"

"No and yes. She's going to be out of it for a while. Repair of the artery was tricky. Whoever tied that belt and packed the wound saved her leg—and her life."

"My neighbors," Mimi whispered. "A retired nurse and a retired Marine."

"You owe 'em," the doctor said, "big time. You can come with me; the rest of you can't, I'm sorry."

Mimi started to follow the doctor, stopped and turned to face her friends. "I just want to see her, and then I'll be back, OK?"

Tears filled Beverly's eyes and she reached for Mimi. "More than okay." Then she was smothered in a group hug as they all piled on.

"We'll wait right here," Sylvia said, holding Bev tightly.

Mimi had to trot to catch the doctor, who moved really fast for such a small woman, she thought, then remembered the tiny young physician was also one hell of a trauma surgeon. She'd operated on Mimi when she'd been attacked by a lesbian-hating nutcase in the lobby of the newspaper; she'd operated on Cassie when she'd been assassinated by a Muslim-hating nutcase; and now she'd operated on Gianna, who'd taken the bullet that was meant for Mimi herself. Could one consider an ER trauma surgeon one's primary care physician?

The ICU suite was busy, with lots of people moving around doing life-saving things with fast efficiency, none of those whose lives were being saved aware of the purposeful activity on their behalf. Gianna lay in one of the glass-enclosed spaces surrounded by beeping, data-gathering-and-reporting machinery. Blood dripped into one arm, clear fluid into the other. Her left leg was heavily bandaged and slightly elevated. A cap of some kind covered her beautiful hair, and her beautiful eyes were closed. She was chalk-white. Mimi looked at the doctor. "Are you sure she's—"

"She's had a tough time but she's going to be fine."

"She looks—"

"Like she's had a tough time," the doctor said. "And she's going to sleep for a while."

"I need to tell my friends—" she waved her hand at Gianna, "then I'll be back," Mimi said. Then, "I can come back, right?"

The doctor nodded. "You're the next of kin. You can stay all night if you like."

Mimi had a small smile working when she left the ICU suite. It faded when she saw that her editor—her former editor—was with her friends. She wasn't thrilled to see him, but it helped that he carried her purse and satchel. Now she had a laptop and a cell phone and their chargers and her keys. But not her car. *Damn.* "Tyler," she said by way of greeting.

"How's Gianna?" he asked, and she was able to tell all of them how Gianna looked, if not exactly how she was. She wasn't going to die. That's what she had to hold onto at the moment. But she'd had a tough time, the second tough time in a week.

"Do you want us to stay with you or get out of your hair?" Cedric asked, and Mimi hugged him.

"Well, there's your answer," Freddie said, and he hugged her, too. "You know we're just a phone call away if you need us."

"I know, and thank you," Mimi said. "All of you. I don't know what I'd do without you, and that's the truth."

They all hugged her and took their leave, Beverly last. "Please, Mimi, let's talk?"

"I don't have any words right now, Bev, but when I find some, I'll need to talk to you." And Bev walked away, having heard more honesty from Mimi Patterson in that one sentence than she'd heard in fifteen years of friendship. And it frightened her.

That left Tyler. "The Weasel is gone—fired or quit, not really sure which. The lawyer is gone—fired. Ian is gone—fired. And I'm promoted. I'm the new Weasel, though I hope you won't call me that."

"Congratulations, Tyler. You deserve it. But I won't be calling you anything because I won't be there. I quit, remember?"

"We can talk about that later—"

"Nothing to talk about. Really. I mean that. And thanks for bringing my things," she said, reaching for her bags.

"Your job is waiting for you, Mimi. Come back when you're

ready," Tyler said, and walked away. She followed him, but only so she could go outside and use the phone. She called the Chief first and said she'd call again when Gianna woke up. Then she called Eric and told him the same thing, only with more detail. Then she called Tommi and repeated what she'd told Eric. Then she did something she didn't remember ever having done before: She turned off the phone. Off—not on vibrate or in airplane mode. *Off.* And she went back inside the hospital, back to the ICU suite, back to Gianna who was still alive, no thanks to Mimi.

"I've never seen her like this, Chief. I think she means it. She's done with the newspaper." Tyler was a pitiful-looking mixture of fear and sadness.

The Chief paced a few steps away from the editor and the reporter, deliberately not making eye contact with either of them, and it wasn't a power play on his part. At least not totally. The real reason was that he didn't want them to see how rattled he was at Tyler Carson's proclamation that Mimi Patterson probably would not be returning to the paper. "So that means I'm supposed to trust Zemekis here on your say-so?"

"He's done a lot of good work lately, much of it while working closely with Mimi—"

"Who spent a lot of years earning her position of trust with me," the Chief said, finally looking at Tyler and Joe. "So I'm supposed to automatically transfer that trust to Mr. Zemekis here? I don't think so. Let him earn the right to my trust."

"I think I've earned your trust over the years, Chief," Tyler said.

The Chief nodded. "Yes, you have. You were a good reporter and you're a good editor, and I believe you earned your promotion. Congratulations, by the way. But so what?"

"Look, Chief. Every good politician needs a reporter he can trust—"

"I'm not a fuckin' politician!" the Chief thundered, and he had to work not to laugh at the expressions on the faces of Tyler and

Joe. Of course he was a politician—one of the best Tyler had ever seen. The man would be unstoppable if ever he ran for office, which he never would. He hated the elected version as much as he hated perps and dirty cops. Speaking of which . . .

"We've gotta do a story on Davis and Diaz and their sergeant, what's his name, Joe?"

"Berry," Joe Zemekis answered. "Mike Berry."

"We're going to do the story, Chief, on the dirty cops—and on the clean one: Lieutenant Maglione, who risked her own life cleaning up behind the dirty ones. And it'll be a much better story with your input than without it."

"How the hell can you do it without me?" the Chief growled.

"I haven't forgotten how to be a reporter any more than you've forgotten how to be a cop," Tyler said, and watched with satisfaction and relief as he saw that he'd won the man's cooperation.

"I'm only agreeing to talk to you because Maglione deserves it," he said.

Tyler didn't care why, as long as he cooperated. Joe was wondering how to get Mimi to cooperate and talk to him since Lt. Gianna Maglione couldn't.

"Here's a fact I'll start you off with: It's Captain Maglione now."

Gianna woke up the first time, saw Mimi, smiled, and returned immediately to sleep. She awoke the second time and remained awake long enough to hold Mimi's hand and eat a few ice chips before drifting off again. The third time indeed was the charm. She was still groggy but she really was awake. And hungry. Mimi left the room when the doctor entered to examine her patient, and she returned to hear the news that Gianna was being moved to a private room. That meant the doctor really and truly believed she was out of danger. Mimi believed it, too, until Gianna gasped and moaned when she was transferred to the bed in her new room. Her face went that chalk white color and she closed her eyes for a long moment. Mimi stood over her, watching and waiting and wondering why the nurses didn't seem concerned. Gianna was in pain, dammit! But they were all cheerful efficiency.

One of them frowned slightly when she checked the dressing on Gianna's leg but said nothing, so when they all left the room, Mimi lifted the sheet and looked at Gianna's leg and saw spots of blood on the dressing.

"What are you looking at, Dr. Patterson?" Gianna asked lightly.

"Just making sure everything is as it should be, Captain Maglione," Mimi replied, trying for light and almost stumbling over the "captain" part, which she wasn't used to yet.

"You're here with me so everything is as it should be," Gianna said.

"Is it all right if I move in with you?" Mimi asked, and had to laugh at the look on Gianna's face.

"Only if you'll marry me," she said, recovering.

"I can do that," Mimi said, bending low to kiss her.

"No wonder she's making such a speedy recovery," they heard from the doorway, and a smiling nurse entered carrying a small tray.

"What's that?" Gianna asked, with a suspicious look at the tray and the syringe it held.

"Antibiotic," the nurse answered. Then, "I understand you're hungry? What do you want to eat? Your diet is not restricted. You may have whatever you like."

"Chinese food!" Gianna exclaimed. "Whole crispy fish, sesame noodles, sautéed string beans with bamboo shoots—"

The nurse cut her off with a laugh and a look at Mimi. "You're making a Chinatown run, I take it? Sweet and sour soup for me. I'm easy." Then she lifted the sheet and looked at Gianna's leg. "I need to change that dressing, clean the wound, make sure nothing is amiss."

"What would be amiss?" Mimi asked.

"Nothing should be," the nurse responded, "which is why I need to check." Mimi knew when she was being dismissed so she grabbed her purse and headed out. She'd call the Chief and Eric and the Yangtze River, their favorite Chinatown restaurant.

When she returned with the food, including the nurse's sweet and sour soup, the Chief was there and Gianna was looking like she wished he wasn't. "I'll be really upset with you if you're upsetting her," Mimi said, entering the room.

He gave her a look. "Unlike you, Maglione hasn't quit her job."

"Give her time," Mimi shot back, and took pleasure at the look of astonishment on his face.

"Enough, both of you," Gianna said, trying out a captain's voice. Her Chief saluted her and left. Mimi rolled the tray to the bed, fixed her food, and went to take the nurse her soup. When she returned Gianna was eating as if she'd been deprived of food for a month. "This is so good!" she said, her mouth full. "Thank you, darling."

"You're welcome," Mimi said, preparing to make a similar attack on her mushu vegetables and sautéed broccoli and snow peas, when Gianna's sergeants arrived.

"Boss!" Eric Ashby enthused as he hurried over to her bed and grabbed her hand. "A crispy fish doesn't stand a chance in your presence!"

Sgt. Thomasina Bell held back but grinned widely. "Hey, Boss. I can't tell you how glad I am to see you puttin' a hurtin' on that poor fish!"

Gianna laughed and extended a hand to Tommi who eagerly came forward and took it. Then she watched happily as Mimi hugged both sergeants. "Thanks for keeping us in the loop, Mimi," Eric said. "We'd have gone crazy without your updates."

"I could use an update if you don't mind," Gianna said, and she listened without speaking while Eric and Tommi filled her in, sparing no detail. Four of the men who ran the sex-trafficking ring in the warehouse were in custody, the fifth was still being sought, three of the girls had died from a combination of malnutrition and drug overdoses, two others still were hospitalized, and interpreters were still working to identify the girls and get them home—if they had homes to go back to.

The Metro GALCO bombers belonged to an Idaho-based religious group violently opposed to same-sex anything. They considered themselves soldiers in an army charged with wiping transgender and same-sex people off the earth. In addition to the five who had been arrested the night of the bombing, three more were apprehended in the rented suburban Virginia townhouse where police recovered enough bomb-making material to level several entire blocks which, according to materials found inside the house, was the plan. Neighborhoods where gay bars existed were their targets, as were the homes of nationally known gay, lesbian, and transgender figures prominent in the D.C. area.

Sunset View residents struggled to regain the place once considered normal but they were finding it difficult, especially their relationship with the police. Despite the best efforts of Gianna, Alice, Linda, and Bobby, the memories of Dexter Davis, Phil Diaz, and Mike Berry remained potent and ugly. Add the fact that it was a drunk Pittsburgh city cop who had caused the turnpike crash that killed the Sunset View men, and that some of the state guys were covering for him . . . add the fact that Gianna had shot and killed Alfreda Tompkins's son . . . Sunset View residents did not have the warm fuzzies for cops.

"What about the fact that Alfreda Tompkins's son was on my property trying to kill me?" Mimi asked. "They choose to dump their anger on Gianna rather than on Dexter Davis? What about the fact that Alfreda Tompkins let Dexter Davis take her children? And she's mad at Gianna? She's lucky she hasn't been charged with reckless endangerment." The rage that had been building inside Mimi toward Alfreda Tompkins finally erupted and she had to leave the room.

"Can't say I blame her," Eric said, watching Gianna closely.

"No," his Boss replied, watching the empty space where Mimi had been.

"Will she be all right?" Tommi asked.

"I don't know," Gianna said, "but I need to go find out," and she started to get up, to get out of the bed. The pain made her cry out, which made Eric run for the nurse, which made Mimi run back to Gianna's room. She'd heard her cry out and saw Eric and the nurse, running.

"What happened?" She ran into the room, to Gianna. "Are you all right?"

"I would be if I could get out of this damn bed!" Gianna snapped. "How long is this going to last?" she demanded of the nurse. "Where's the doctor? Get her in here!"

"It's not a her; it's a him." The nurse hastened to explain that the ER trauma surgeon's job was done when Gianna safely transferred out of ICU, and that she was now under the care of a vascular surgeon who specialized in the repair and treatment of the artery that had been damaged in her leg.

"Will he let me get out of this bed and out of this hospital?"

"Maybe," said a voice from the doorway, who introduced himself, asked everyone but the nurse to leave the room, bristled when Mimi said she had no intention of leaving, and then ignored her as he examined Gianna's leg and explained in great detail all the options available to her.

"I'll take the walking cast, the session with the physical therapist, the pain management drugs, and immediate discharge," Gianna told him, and they all laughed—Mimi, Gianna, and the nurse—when he wrote the orders on the chart and hurried out of the room as if he feared they might harm him in some way. But he was as good as his word, and Mimi had Gianna home and comfortably settled on the sofa within twenty-four hours.

She had expected to need a period of adjustment to calling Gianna's condo home, but it was as easy and natural as planning the three-couple wedding, for Beverly and Sylvia and Freddie and Cedric all agreed that it was time they, too, took the next step. The adjustment Mimi needed to make was to the change in Gianna's rank: She was now a captain. The Chief had insisted that she take all the necessary tests and she had, naturally, passed them all. But neither of them wanted to talk much about their work. Or in Mimi's case, the lack thereof. They still had very raw places left by the events of the past three months, beginning with Cassie Ali's murder and culminated with the shooting of Will Tompkins in Mimi's front yard. Gianna had agreed to see the department shrink when she returned to work, and Mimi had agreed to see Beverly. She had not, so far, agreed to return to work, though she was seriously considering it since she no longer had to apologize to a Weasel.

The six of them were spending July Fourth with Freddie and Cedric, the highlight of the day being the fireworks display they'd watch from the patio of Freddie's penthouse apartment along the Potomac River. But first Gianna had a surprise for Mimi, someplace they had to visit before they got to Freddie's. Gianna had insisted on driving (it was her left leg that was injured, not her right one), and Mimi didn't argue. She didn't even wonder why Gianna had the garage door opener to the underground parking of a beautiful old building on St. George Drive. They had the opener to Freddie's building; people who lived in secure buildings in densely populated areas often saved guests the hassle of having to look for a parking space. However, when she saw Gianna had the key to Apartment 607, Mimi's curiosity was piqued.

"Whose place is this?" she asked when they entered the spacious, beautiful—and empty—living room. The high ceilings and arched windows spoke to the elegance of another time.

"Ours," Gianna said, smiling. "If you like it, that is."

Mimi was open-mouthed and wide-eyed. "If I like it! It's gorgeous!" and she ran through the apartment with the excitement of a little kid on Christmas morning. Three bedrooms—a working fireplace in the master bedroom! Three bathrooms—a Jacuzzi in the master bath! A gourmet kitchen! A library! A balcony! "We can't afford this, Gianna!"

Gianna gave her a sheaf of papers which she read through with increasing amazement: the sale price of her house, the sale price of Gianna's condo, the sale price of the place they were standing in. "As you can see, we can easily afford it."

"But I don't have a job!"

"You don't need one. I'm a captain, remember? They make more than lieutenants. Besides, you'll have a job eventually. When you decide you want one."

Mimi turned around in circles. "How did you manage this?"

"Freddie's real estate guy did all the work. We just have to sign the papers that sell the places we own and that make this ours."

Mimi kept walking around in circles while rereading the contracts. "I feel like I've died and gone to heaven," she said.

"Nobody gets out alive," Gianna said.

Ain't that the truth, Cassie said.

About the author

Penny Mickelbury has always been a writer and storyteller, but it became her profession when she began working as a newspaper, radio and television reporter in Washington, DC. After 20 years as a journalist, though, she took the leap—or the plunge—and moved to New York to launch her novel and playwriting career—and she's still at it. Penny is the author of 11 published novels—10 of them mysteries spread across three different series. The Mimi Patterson/Gianna Maglione novels were Penny's first mystery series, and *Death's Echoes* is it's fifth title. Black Lesbian Feminist Press will publish Penny's short story collection in Fall 2018, and she's already at work on the sixth Mimi Patterson/Gianna Maglione mystery, and an historical fiction novel, both for Bywater Books. A native of Atlanta, Penny lives in Los Angeles with her partner of 18 years.

Acknowledgments

Writing a novel is a solitary pursuit, one that is made so much more comfortable, however, when the writer can feel the support at her back. I write knowing that the women of Bywater Books have my back. Thank you Salem West, Marianne K. Martin, Ann McMan, Kelly Smith, Nancy Squires, and Elizabeth Andersen for your constant presence.

Bywater
BOOKS

At Bywater Books we love good books about lesbians just like you do, and we're committed to bringing the best of contemporary lesbian writing to our avid readers. Our editorial team is dedicated to finding and developing outstanding writers who create books you won't want to put down.

We sponsor the Bywater Prize for Fiction to help with this quest. Each prize winner receives $1,000 and publication of their novel. We have already discovered amazing writers like Jill Malone, Sally Bellerose, and Hilary Sloin through the Bywater Prize. Which exciting new writer will we find next?

For more information about Bywater Books and the annual Bywater Prize for Fiction, please visit our website.

www.bywaterbooks.com

CPSIA information can be obtained
at www.ICGtesting.com
Printed in the USA
LVOW03s2048250318
570951LV00005B/9/P